Dear Mystery Lover,

If you're like me, you have a list somewhere with all of the things you want to try when you have some free time on your hands. Well, the top activity on my list is fly-fishing. All of the fishing fanatics I know rave about how soothing and worry-free casting a fly rod is and how you just haven't lived until you've caught and released a trout.

One day while riffling through my calendar in an effort to block out some prime fly-fishing time, a manuscript landed on my desk that snared me hook, line, and sinker. *Casting in Dead Water* by David Leitz is a wonderful debut mystery featuring fly-fishing guide and Vermont lodge owner Max Addams. Max is the perfect companion for all armchair fishermen and lovers of regional mysteries. He gives you a guided tour of his favorite fishing spots and tons of tips about one of our nation's most beloved sports. And, on top of that, David's depiction of a fictional small town in Vermont and his mystery plotting are superb. When you finish *Casting in Dead Water,* you'll get the real flavor of the sport and will come to know a cast full of engaging characters.

I've yet to block out the time to learn how to fly-fish, but I know I'm well prepared for that fateful day. With Max Addams introducing me to the sport and with some of his wisdom under my belt, I'm itching to get in the water. But, then again, maybe I'll wait to read the next Max Addams adventure and see what else he has stuck in his waders.

Yours in crime,

Shawn Coyne
Senior Editor
St. Martin's DEAD LETTER Paperback Mysteries

Other titles from St. Martin's Dead Letter Mysteries

I floored the Jeep down the mile of bumps and muddy ruts. Showers of sparks and smoke as thick as fog covered the road. I could feel the intense heat before I even rounded the corner and I slammed on my brakes, jumped out, and ran into the yard. John was right behind me. The entire lodge was engulfed in flames. Half of the roof had geysers of it shooting fifty feet in the air. Part of the porch was burning on Stephanie's car. It had obviously blown up and thick, oily black smoke rose from where the trunk had been, mixing with the white from the logs. Something else exploded inside. More windows shattered. I could smell my beard singeing. I threw my good arm over my face and backed away from the heat. I bumped into the blackened trunk on a birch, slid to my butt, and stared, horrified and sick, as the giant tongues of flame ate my dream.

CASTING IN DEAD WATER

A Max Addams Fly-Fishing Mystery

 **DAVID LEITZ**

St. Martin's Paperbacks

FOR FRAN AGAIN
. . . and all the loyal friends of Max, Stormy,
Rayleen and Whitefork Lodge.

CASTING IN DEAD WATER

Copyright © 1996 by David E. Leitz.

ISBN: 0-312-95779-3

Printed in the United States of America

St. Martin's Paperbacks edition/April 1996

10 9 8 7 6 5 4 3 2 1

CHAPTER ONE

Every year, up here in northern Vermont where I have my fly-fishing lodge, a local microbrewery puts out what it calls, "The *Loon Lager* Total Vermont Calendar." Obviously designed to give jingoistic beer drinkers as many occasions to quaff pints of amber brew as possible, every month has days marked, not with ordinary holidays, but with events unique to our state. In that Vermont was the last state to join the original thirteen, that day, March 4, is marked. The day Jemima Toot was captured in Brattleboro by the Indians is marked, as is the day she returned after slaying her captors somewhere in Canada and walking all the way home. Of course, Ethan Allen's birthday is noted, as is the day his Green Mountain Boys captured Fort Ticonderoga. You can drink to the battle of Bennington, the day MacDonough defeated the British on Lake Champlain, and the day the blue law was repealed. Hunting season is indicated as beginning on the second Saturday in November and fishing season, on the first Saturday in April. The date we all laugh about is March 5. It says simply, MUD SEASON BEGINS.

The funny thing is, give or take a day, it usually does.

According to a friend of mine who is with the U.S.

Geological Service, what causes and dictates Mud Season's debut and duration is the permafrost. The sun and warm air of spring thaw the ground above the permafrost and then it just sits there like soupy unbaked chocolate cake batter waiting until the frozen layer below it melts. Vermont's charming unpaved, country roads become nightmares of almost unnavigable, axle-deep, sucking goo. Schools close, loggers play cards all day, and the Whitefork River, already deep and treacherous with snowmelt, turns the color of café au lait.

It's a perilous time for the river's trout. Too much spring rain and the usually crystal clear Whitefork can choke with the suffocating mud. The gravel beds needed for spawning and egg laying can silt over and, worse, the fragile aquatic insects upon which the fish feed risk dying.

I've learned to live with it. I cross my fingers, leave my front hubs locked in four-wheel drive and my mud-heavy boots outside on the porch because, just as suddenly as the mud arrives, one morning I wake up and find it gone. The permafrost finally thaws and the water that created the mud simply disappears.

This year, because of an extremely cold, tenacious winter that wouldn't go away, Mud Season didn't even start until the thirty-first of March. Since that's only a short week from the beginning of fly-fishing season, I was obliged to telephone my six incoming fly-fishing guests, warn them about the mud and the Whitefork's turbid water, and suggest rescheduling later in the season. The Reynolds, a retired couple from Florida, were easy. They changed to the following week. The two architects from Albany said they'd wait until the weekend. If the mud hadn't gone by then, they might consider a week later in the season. Only the honeymooners said they were coming anyway. It made sense. They had other things to occupy their time if the fishing turned out to be bad.

As it worked out, not only did the mud stay and the fishing turn bad, but the trout in the Whitefork started dying by the basketful. When I attempted to rectify the problem, violence erupted. And by the time the permafrost relinquished its hold on the land, two close friends were dead and my dream had been reduced to ashes.

It all began with Stephanie Wilcox. Unlike the mud, however, she wasn't late. She was one week early.

It was Tuesday and fly-fishing season, as it was, barely had begun. The young couple from New Orleans on their fly-fishing honeymoon had arrived right after lunch and, like all first-time guests, hadn't even unpacked. They were out on Sweet Lake in our sixteen-foot Old Town. My assistant, Red Crosley, was guiding them from the twelve-footer, showing them where to cast around the sunken trees.

I was at my fly-tying table in the reading room at the back of the lodge, experimenting with a new version of the reliable Prince nymph. I'd replaced the usual dubbing under the white wings with three small brass beads. I liked the way it looked and felt in my hand. The beads would give it the kind of quick-sinking weight and trout-attracting sparkle needed in the Whitefork's fast, still slightly muddy spring water. I had just finished cementing the head threads of a number 12 when I heard Stephanie calling my name.

"In here," I yelled back. Spotter, my half English Setter, half Labrador Retriever, raised his black and white head from his place under the table and gave me a puzzled look. He's old now and almost deaf.

Stephanie poked her head around the door jamb and smiled. "Busy?" She crossed the room and kissed me on the beard. She's a tall, strikingly attractive blond with a child's big brown eyes and legs like a Rockette's. She's the first to admit that it's those looks, coupled with her uncanny ability to close a sale, that has turned the small Boston-based company she inherited into what *Northeast Business* magazine lauds as one of the area's one hundred fastest growing businesses. The company is called Tear-Pruf and it markets a line of innovative outdoor and work clothing for men made from a tightly-woven, all-cotton fabric so tough it resists tearing even on barbed wire. While I find most of the garments she gives me as presents to be too stiff for my purposes, farmers, construction workers, and loggers love the stuff. Of the ten or so customers she has in my area, the largest by far is the big Collari International paper pulp mill in the nearby town of Loon.

"I'm taking advantage of a lull in the action," I said, taking off my magnifier half glasses and putting my arm around her small waist. "As usual, the new guests wanted to fish as soon as they got here." Stephanie wore a short navy skirt and a tan man's workshirt. Like everyone who came into the lodge during Mud Season, she had left her boots on the porch and was in her stocking feet. The French twist in her hair was decomposing gracefully and loose ringlets hung around her face.

"Is the mud worse this year," she said, snuffing out the cigarette I had smoldering in the ashtray, "or is it my imagination?"

"Mostly, it's just late," I said.

Stephanie is the only guest who stays at the lodge with no intention of ever casting a fly over one of my famous brook trout. Like her father did before her, she uses Whitefork Lodge as an office and base of operations while she calls on customers.

"I saw Red out on the lake on the way in." She stooped and scratched Spotter behind the ears. He groaned in ecstasy and his tail flopped back and forth against the table leg. "Where's Stormy?" she asked, referring to my housekeeper and cook, Stormy Bryant.

"Stormy's in town buying vegetables and brown rice," I said. "We just found out the new girl out on the lake's a vegetarian."

"Poor Stormy," Stephanie said, picking up one of the new flies I'd just tied and turning it in her fingers. "What's this thing called?"

"I think I'm going to call it the Dead Princess," I said. I thought it looked more feminine than the ordinary Prince.

"Dead?" She wrinkled her nose and put it back on the table. "I thought you didn't kill fish up here."

"The 'dead' is for the way it'll be fished," I said. "Dead drift."

"Still, why don't you give it a nice name?" she said, going to the couch. "It's too pretty to be a dead something." She sat and crossed her legs in one movement.

I lit another cigarette and watched Spotter get up and join her on the couch. He laid his head on a bare knee. He was a leg man too. "A name like what?" I said.

"I don't know." She smiled. "You could name it after me."

Stephanie had been only thirty and just had earned her MBA when we first met. She was traveling with her ailing father, meeting customers and learning the ropes. When he died five years ago and she began coming to the lodge alone, our relationship changed and, for about six months, she no longer had stayed in the room her father had used on the second floor. She stayed in mine.

Our affair began as things like that do sometimes with a few drinks, a nice dinner, and mutual curiosity. It was intense while it lasted and although we finally stopped sleeping together, our affection for each other never really ended. Stephanie and I simply grew and the affair moved to another plateau of feeling. Where statistics show sexual familiarity destroying friendship, the metamorphosis we experienced simply seemed to strengthen our compatibility. We gained rather than lost, and the memory of sexual intimacy that remains has become a comfortable foundation to our unique friendship.

Stephanie never has been especially interested in my outdoor lifestyle and, I think, tolerates my rough edges. To her credit she has never indicated a wish to change me. At least, I don't think so. I do know, however, that she loves Whitefork Lodge in many of the same ways I do, never tiring of studying the dim, dark oil paintings and stuffed trout, deer, and bear heads mounted on the walls; the wide-board floors scattered with faded oriental rugs and all the bedrooms with high, old-fashioned beds with heavy, ornately carved headboards and matching, stately armoires.

"I thought you weren't coming until next week," I said.

"Me, too. But Collari's purchasing department called the office and said they had a big order that was too complex to give over the phone." She smiled. "So, here I am." She uncrossed her legs and recrossed them the other way.

"How big an order?" I said.

She shrugged. "I don't know, but it could be the one I've needed to put me over the top. I've decided it's time to sell Tear-Pruf, Max."

"Sell?"

She nodded and stroked Spotter's head. "I've been thinking about it for some time now and I've had a couple feelers in the last few weeks. The Tear-Pruf line would make an attractive addition for one of the big manufacturers." She smiled. "I received a letter from an attorney for Woolrich Mills yesterday."

"But sell? What would you do?"

"Not much, I hope," she laughed. "I still own seventy percent of the stock. My accountant says I could make two or three million."

I whistled through my teeth.

"I've got other things I'm thinking about, Max." She brushed a coil of silky hair from her eyes. "There's a lot more to life than business."

Red Crosley appeared at the doorway. "Excuse me," he said, looking from Stephanie to me. "Max? Don't mean to bother you, but I wanted to . . ."

"Come in, Red." Like many people in Loon these days, Red worked two jobs. When they needed him, he was a cat skinner and skid driver for Collari. He guided for me most afternoons, evenings, and every weekend.

He took off his cap, ducked his head under the door frame and stepped awkwardly into the room. "Hello, Miss Wilcox," he said. Although Red is only thirty-five, weather, hard work, and years of living just above the poverty line has made him look twenty years older. His once bright orange hair is dull as sand and what remains of his freckles are lost in worry lines and crevasses that look like they were put there with a wood-burning tool. Only his sparkling, pale blue eyes betray his youth. He'd taken his waders off at the front door but still wore his fishing vest. A Dead Princess hung from the wool drying patch.

"How'd the Princess work?" I asked. He had taken my first attempts out on the lake with him to try with the honeymooners.

"Dunno," he said. "Never got a chance to use it. We had a little caddis hatch out there, so I had 'em usin' number eighteen light cahills instead." His big hands nervously fingered the brim of the cap.

"They catch anything?"

"Young girl can't cast too well yet," he said. "But, yeah, they caught a few."

"Anything big?"

He nodded. "That young fella, Chad, had a brown on. Big one. Mighta been Jack, but I dunno. Broke off 'fore we could get him close enough to see." Jack was "One-eyed Jack," a four-pound brown who five years ago had lost an eye to a hook. He was not only very selective and leader shy, but you had to get your fly in the feeding lane on his good side. Usually, catching him was an accident.

"Did you leave them on the lake?"

"Yeah. Told 'em I hadta go, but they wanted to fish 'til supper." He shrugged. "Suggested they try out by the beaver dam." Red knew the Whitefork River and Sweet Lake as well as I did. Even with the discoloration, the deep water by the dam was like trout soup this time of year.

"You leaving now?" I asked him.

"Yeah. But wanted to tell you I ain't gonna be able to work at all the next couple days," he said. "Hope you don't mind."

"Not problems at home, I hope." Red and his wife Wilba had two boys, five and eleven. The oldest, Samuel, was diabetic.

"Nah." He shook his head. "Collari's been doin' some loggin' off and on up on Morning Mountain all winter. Stopped when the mud come but I guess now it ain't as bad as they thought it would be." He smiled. "Up there in the woods, anyways."

"Up here behind us?" Morning Mountain was directly above and behind the lodge. "You've been logging up there?"

"Not me, Max," he said. "Up 'til now I was runnin' a skidder for 'em down at the mill. But they been up there, since, hell, maybe early in February."

"No wonder I don't know about it," I said to Stephanie. "I was in Key West all of February."

"Key West?" She looked surprised.

"My annual saltwater fly-fishing trip with my friend, John." Every year, John Purcell and I escape the tedious grip of winter and head for a warmer climate. Most years we go to Belize for our Tarpon and Permit. This year, John had wangled a condo in Key Largo right on the Gulf.

"John?" she asked. "Is this John, the geologist from Colorado?"

I nodded and looked back at Red. "I'm happy for you, Red," I said. "I know how you hate working in town."

"Yeah," he nodded. "Nice to be back in the woods. Might last a while too. There's already quite a gang workin' up there. Big job, I guess. Overtime even, once it gets started again."

"You'll still be able to be here this weekend, I hope," I said. "Stein's coming Friday and asked for you specifically." Many of my customers, like architect Bill Stein, booked through the weekend just to be with Red.

"Sure, like always." He winked. "Tips is still better than cat skinnin' wages." He smiled at Stephanie. "Nice seein' you again, Miss Wilcox," he said, backing toward the door.

"Nice to see you, Red." Stephanie smiled back. "Say hello to your family for me."

"I'll do that." He ducked back under the door frame. "You want me to drop the garbage at the dump, Max? Stormy's got two bags by the back door."

"If you wouldn't mind."

"Nope." He shook his head. "It's on the way."

We listened to his footsteps fade and then the front door slam. "Maybe that's it, Max," Stephanie said. "Maybe this logging is what my big order's all about."

"Maybe. When's your appointment at the mill?" I asked.

"Tomorrow at ten. You think Stormy will mind another guest for dinner?"

There was the sound of a horn honk and I stepped into the reading room doorway and peered through the dining room out to the front of the lodge. "You can ask her yourself," I said. "She's back with the groceries."

Stephanie and I went to the porch to help Stormy carry in the grocery bags. Spotter, normally almost comatose around people, bounded by us and jumped enthusiastically at Stormy as she climbed unceremoniously from the cab of the lodge's Jeep pickup. "Get down, you old fart," she laughed, the Camel in the corner of her mouth bobbing as she talked. "I ain't got nothin' in here for you." She saw us standing on the porch. "Ain't you a week early?" she said to Stephanie as she stood on tip-toe reaching for the grocery bags in the truck's bed.

Stephanie nodded as we came down off the porch. "I hope it doesn't inconvenience you," she said, holding out her hands and taking two bags.

Stormy shook her head. "I can use the help in the kitchen, to be honest." She frowned at me. "Just found out I gotta make two dinners tonight." She handed me three bags.

Stormy was built like a beer keg and not a lot taller. Her 1099 had said she was sixty-four and, except for her hair, she looked it. Where most women her age had their hair short, permed curly, and blued, Stormy's hung down her back in a long, heavy braid like a fraying steel cable. Her bright green eyes sparkled when she talked and her cheeks were permanently flushed pink, like she'd just come in from a lap around the lodge. I'd never seen her in anything but exotic print caftans and loosely laced sixteen-inch Bean boots. She was a chain smoker, seldom without at least one going in an ashtray somewhere nearby as well as one dangling from her mouth. She was also a recovering alcoholic and in her own words, "Damn proud of it!" I couldn't have run the lodge without her.

Stormy grabbed the remaining bag and Stephanie and I followed Spotter who followed Stormy down the hall into the lodge kitchen. "Passed Red as I was comin' in," she said through the smoke over her shoulder. "Leavin' a little early, ain't he?"

We put the bags on the big chopping-block island counter. "He's starting some new logging job with Collari," I said. "Won't be here the rest of the week."

"New job, huh?" she said as she began to unload the bags. "In town, all's I hear is everybody bitchin' 'bout how slow it is at the mill. Folks is afraid there's gonna be layoffs." She took three large bunches of carrots and put them in the refrigerator. "Red say where they're cuttin'?"

I handed two large bags of rice to Stephanie who handed them to Stormy. "Up behind us on Morning Mountain," I said.

She took the rice and carried it into the pantry. When she came out she said, "Up here? Right behind the lodge?" She took a five-pound bag of frozen shrimp from another bag and tossed it in the sink. "Hope they get it over with quick," she said. "I sure as hell hate listenin' to them damn chainsaws whinin' all day." She looked at Stephanie. "So what got you up here so early?"

Stephanie told her about Collari Purchasing's phone call and how the new logging might be the reason.

Stormy shook her head slowly and ground out her cigarette in the ashtray on the counter. "Wouldn't count on this loggin' to be the reason for your order," she said, tossing a bag of onions in a deep drawer. "They've taken a few trees before. It don't amount to much. Collari's got an agreement with the town to only do . . . ," she looked at me for help, ". . . what do they call it, Max?"

"Selective cutting," I said and looked at Stephanie. "It means they only take a few of one species."

"Yeah." Stormy nodded. "They agreed when they first come in here that the logs pulped in the mill would only come from their land up in Canada." She laughed and lit another cigarette. "Hell, good thing too. What that damn mill eats up in a week would take every tree we got up there on Morning Mountain."

CHAPTER ✒ TWO

W hile she helped Stormy in the kitchen, I wrestled Stephanie's suitcases from her car and lugged them upstairs to the little room she liked with the view of Morning Mountain. After opening the window, I went out onto the dock and helped the newlyweds, Chad and Tonya Harper, tie up the canoe and unload their gear. They wore identical baggy, khaki shorts and Topsiders. In my opinion it was a little early for shorts and now that it was cooling off, they had identical goose bumps, too.

"Any luck?" I directed my question to Chad who, when they had initially made their reservation last winter, had indicated he was the fly fisherman and Tonya was just learning.

He shrugged. "Some small brookies. Eight, ten inches." He was a big, good-looking kid, maybe twenty-five, with a big smile, square jaw, blue eyes, and dark hair that hung like cupped crow wings on both sides of his forehead. His pale blue tee shirt said MTV UN-PLUGGED on the front. "I had something big on there for a minute, though. Red said it might have been a fish called One-eyed Jack?"

"Could have been," I said, stooping and tying the

stern of the canoe to a cleat on the dock. "You try at the beaver dam like Red suggested?" I said, pointing out toward the far end of the lake. "Usually you'll find the bigger brookies holding in the deep water there."

"See," Tonya said. "I told you we should've listened to him, Chad." Tonya looked like she'd stepped off the cover of a California surfing magazine: sunglasses pushed up in long, sun-streaked blond hair, a long neck, long fingers, long tan legs and a long, bare midriff below a dark blue halter top. She was sexy in a little girl sort of way. I liked her. Any woman who'd consent to a fly-fishing honeymoon was all right in my book.

"How did you like using a fly rod?" I asked her as the three of us walked up through the lawn toward the lodge. The ground was spongy under our feet.

"Oh," she said as she shrugged and pulled on a wool shirt, "I caught a couple fish by accident. But I must be doing something wrong. The line keeps dumping in a tangle right in front of me."

"I think you should teach her, Mister Addams," Chad said. "Maybe she'll listen to you."

Tonya gave him a dirty look. "I can't listen when you're yelling," she hissed.

"I wasn't yelling."

"I'd be glad to give you some lessons, Tonya," I said quickly. "And," I looked around her at Chad, "call me Max, please."

"Sure, Max."

"It's hard learning to cast in a canoe," I said to her. "I can start you on the dock and then, as you get more proficient, we'll move to the river."

"When?" Chad wanted to know.

"Whenever Tonya wants to start."

Tonya made no comment and instead looked up at the lodge. "Those logs are amazing," she said to me. "Did you build it?"

"God, no," I said. "It was built by a relative of Daniel Webster's back in the early nineteen hundreds."

"Daniel Webster?" Chad said. "You mean, *the* Daniel Webster?"

I nodded. "The man with the devil himself."

Whitefork Lodge was built in 1908 by Daniel Webster's great-grandson, a Boston shipping tycoon named Thornton Randolph Webster. His intention was to create a comfortable, low-maintenance retreat for his family and friends and he succeeded. Designed by the famous Adirondack architect, Wellesly Hinton, it is indicative of that period, sitting on the highest ground on the point where the Whitefork River joins Sweet Lake. It is a massive rectangle, two stories of authentic log structure with a porch that runs along the front facing the west over the lake. It has giant shuttered windows, two walk-in fieldstone fireplaces, and wide, rough-sawn board floors. Webster spared no expense in its construction and the three-foot diameter native spruce logs are chinked with river clay and sit firmly on a rip-rap of cut and intricately-fitted massive granite boulders brought in by mules from a quarry five miles away. According to records, two workmen died when the south wall of the foundation buckled and tons of stone blocks caved inward and crushed them. It took two weeks to remove the mangled bodies. Some mornings in the kitchen, when she's making breakfast and a breeze is blowing just right, Stormy says it sounds like men moaning under the floor.

At the porch, we leaned their rods against the wall and Chad said, "Well, Max, I think we'll go up to our room, unpack, and get some warmer clothes on."

"I'll have a fire in the dining room," I said. "Come on down whenever you want. We've got beer and wine and a few other things in the bar in there." I held the screen door open. "Or, just listen for Stormy's bell. That means dinner's on the table."

"I hope my being a vegetarian hasn't loused her up," Tonya said. "We should have told you earlier."

I smiled. "Stormy likes a challenge every now and then." I followed them into the lodge. Stormy and Stephanie's voices and the aroma of garlic being sautéed in olive oil drifted up the hallway from the kitchen. "Besides," I said, "does that smell like she's having a problem?"

They laughed and I watched them trot up the wide staircase. They were going to have good-looking children.

The first floor of the lodge is cut into four basic living areas. The hallway I now stood in runs the depth of the building down the middle. At the back, a swinging door on the left leads to the kitchen, pantry, and laundry room. On the right, a doorway leads to the reading room and a small storage room. Another door, just forward of that on the same wall, opens onto the stairs to the cellar. The stairs to the second floor are in front of that. My apartment and its bathroom look out over the porch and lake on the left front. The dining room does the same on the right.

I went into the dining room. A long plank table the size of a barn door sits along the front windows under two large hanging chimney lamps. There are four captain's chairs on a side and one at each end. The fireplace is built into the logs on the back wall. You could rig a fly rod inside. An original watercolor by Milton Weiler of two guys casting from a canoe hangs above the rough-hewn log mantel. Red had filled the kindling box and a nice stack of split yellow birch logs stood to the left of the hearth.

I got the kindling snapping, set two logs on top, and put the screen in front. Our small bar is in the sideboard beside the fireplace and I poured myself a scotch. I took a big sip and then, like I'd done hundreds of evenings before, got twelve cups of coffee dripping in the Bunn, took out the plates, glasses, coffee cups, and utensils, and set the table. I took the small crock of dried asters from the mantel and set it out as a centerpiece. Then I lit a cigarette, picked up the scotch, and went out onto the porch to watch the river and wait for Stormy's bell.

The Whitefork River begins in a series of small beaver ponds about twenty miles across the Vermont border in Canada. It is a gin-clear, twisting ribbon that snakes west through some of the most beautiful, rolling, forest country in New England. Once it crosses into the state of Vermont it threads together fifty or so mere dots of towns with names like Moosenose, Birch, Whitetail, and Graniteville. Just southwest of the town of Loon it curves by my fly-fishing lodge. Eventually it dumps into Lake Champlain.

Lumber, dairy cattle, and tourism are the area's primary sources of income. In season, however, the loggers, farmers, and their families open their homes as hotels and offer their services as guides to out-of-state hunters and fishermen in search of trophy deer, moose, bear, landlocked salmon, and native brook trout.

I had been one of those fishermen for twenty years, spending two weeks of my four-week vacation from a New York City advertising agency fly-fishing the Whitefork and its spring creek tributaries for native squaretails and, occasionally, stocked rainbows and browns.

Then, suddenly at forty-three, like a lot of men my age and income bracket, I found myself divorced and, as the result of a major company cutback, unemployed. Free of everything that held me to the New York metropolitan area, I decided to turn avocation into vocation and, with another fly fisherman I knew, purchased

seventy-five plus acres on seventeen miles of the Whitefork River and the log Riverbend Hunting and Fishing
Lodge on Sweet Pond. We renamed the lodge Whitefork and opened for business with what was, at that
time, a new concept of catering only to fly fishermen
like ourselves.

Hard as we tried, business was terrible and by the end
of the first year my partner threw up his hands in frustration, sold me his share, and returned to civilization.
He left his dog, Spotter, with me, promising to send for
him when he got settled elsewhere.

He never sent for his dog and Spotter and I hung on,
resorting to a part-time job at an advertising agency in
Montpelier and commuting the sixty-eight miles each
way three days a week in order to cover child support
for my teenage daughter and make ends meet at the
lodge.

Ironically, it was the advertising business that finally
aided me in filling the guest beds at Whitefork and the
profit columns on my ledgers.

When the agency's largest account, the Vermont
Dairy Farmers' Association, decided it needed a short
film highlighting the many uses of butter in cooking, I,
as the writer on the project, was only too eager to volunteer Whitefork's classic country kitchen as a location for
the filming. If nothing else, the dairy and other food
products left behind would save me on groceries. When
the film was finished, it toured that year's trade shows
and conventions, finally being picked up as a short special on PBS at Christmas time. The results were phe-
nomenal. Not only did Vermont-branded butter enjoy a
hefty increase in sales, but Whitefork began receiving
phone calls and reservations from fly fishermen as far
away as Florida. After a year, business got good enough
to allow me to leave the agency business for the second
time. My dream was actually coming true.

The second year after the film's release, however, I discovered the downside to Whitefork's popularity. The number of trout being taken by my guests was depleting my part of the river and Sweet Pond. Their size was disappointing and total catch numbers were down.

The third year was even worse and, after the season, I consulted the Vermont Fish and Game Department for a solution. Elmer Ernwright, a fisheries biologist working for the department, came up to the lodge to take a look.

"You tried catch and release?" Elmer had asked over the lunch I provided after our morning of wading and shocking the river.

I confessed that I hadn't. I told him that my customers were looking for trophies and meat. "We have a smoker out back. A lot of the sports like to have the brookies they catch smoked and shipped to them."

"You're gonna have to start smoking ham, Max," Elmer had said. "Another couple years of the kind of pressure you been puttin' on this part of the Whitefork, there won't be any trout to catch, much less smoke."

So, with a considerable amount of apprehension, I made the decision to make Whitefork a catch-and-release fishing lodge and over the winter wrote letters to all of my regular customers explaining the change. To my amazement I lost very little of my original business and picked up more than enough new customers to cover it.

The brook trout population responded well, too, and, after two more years, a state-supervised shock test showed my piece of the Whitefork with more than two hundred trout over one pound per hundred yards of water. Today, I can provide my guests with some of the largest wild brookies in the east.

* * *

Wednesday morning I awoke to the smell of coffee. Two mugs steamed on the bedside table and Stephanie, her robe clutched tightly in her hand at her neck, smiled down at me. "I made the coffee," she said.

I yawned and smiled. "Seeing you in that robe like this reminds me of the old days."

"I know." She smiled and sat on the edge of the bed.

"What time is it?" I couldn't see the clock behind the coffee mugs.

"Almost six."

"Stormy here?"

"Not yet."

"So?" I yawned. "What's with the room service?"

She fingered the hem of the robe. "Have you ever thought of getting married again, Max?"

I laughed. "You're kidding."

"No, I'm serious." Water reflections from the lake danced on the ceiling behind the golden silk of her hair. "Have you?"

"No. Why?"

She shrugged. "I want to get married again."

As far as I knew Stephanie had never been married. "When were you married?"

"A long time ago. Just after college. It only lasted a year."

"What brought this up?" I sat up.

"Those kids at dinner last night." She sighed. "And while I was waiting for the coffee to finish, I was looking at the pictures of your daughter out there on the wall." She gestured toward the hall where I had a rogue's gallery of sorts of pictures of my daughter from infancy to the most recent, taken in her wedding dress. "I want to have a child, Max. Before it's too late," she said.

"I thought that was out of the question since your operation." Stephanie had lost her left breast to cancer a couple years before I met her. She'd beat the cancer but the chemotherapy she'd endured to do so had sup-posedly left her unable to have children.

"I want to adopt," she said. "I have a better chance if I'm married."

"That sounds a bit prejudiced to me," I said. "I thought single women today could . . ."

"They know about the cancer, Max." She shrugged. "And that makes me a risk." She forced a smile. "They're only thinking of the child. They don't want to put an orphan into a situation where it might become an orphan again."

"I thought you'd been cured."

She shook her head. "The word is *remission,* Max. My cancer could be in remission the rest of my life, but it's never cured."

We looked at each other. The old clock in the hall slowly bonged six times. "You're not suggesting what I think you are?" I said.

"Why not?" She turned and the robe fell open. "We're a lot alike. We talk about things. We make each other laugh. We enjoy a lot of the same things." She smiled and ran a long finger down my chest. "We were really good together in bed, remember."

"I remember," I said. "But that's over, Steph. We put that fire out a long time ago. Together."

"The spark is still there and you know it, Max Ad-dams." She smiled softly. "It wouldn't take much to get it going again."

"I like things the way they are. I like us the way we are."

She smiled. "I'll even promise to learn to fly-fish."

"Boy, you really want this badly." I laughed.

She looked at her hands in her lap but didn't say anything.

I put one of mine on her shoulder. "C'mon, Steph," I said, "I'm too old for that kind of crap. You know that."

I flopped back down on my back. "A baby? Good God, I'd be in my late sixties before it was out of high school." I took my cigarette pack from the other bedside table, pulled one out, lit it, and laid my head back on the pillow. "Why me?" I said, exhaling a cloud toward the beamed ceiling. "You must know hundreds of men who'd jump at the chance."

She shrugged. "I trust you."

"I'm flattered," I said, "but deep down you know I'm not your guy."

"What I know is," she said, lying down on her back on top of the covers beside me and yanking the robe tight over her, "I'll be thirty-seven this October, Max." She turned her head and looked at me. "It's a cliché and not exactly appropriate in my case, but my clock is ticking." I could smell her hair. "I've done the business thing. I've proven myself. Now I want to do what I was created for." She crossed her arms over her chest. "I want to be a real woman. A mother. I want to have a child."

I pushed myself up on one elbow and looked down at her. "Then this is a proposal?"

She frowned. "In a way, yes."

"No." I shook my head.

She ran her fingers over the beard on my jaw. "I could be a very rich woman, Max," she said with a smile. "And very soon."

I laughed. "With the kind of money you told me about, you could buy an adoption agency."

She laughed also, sat up, and propped a pillow behind her. "Maybe I'll do just that," she said, handing me my coffee.

We sipped on the coffees and listened to a family of blue jays squabbling in a spruce out in front of the lodge. Finally she said, "Would you mind if I used your shower this morning, Max?"

"No." I shrugged. "Why?"

"I don't want to wake the honeymooners."

The two upstairs bathrooms were the only problem at the lodge. They had been added in the forties and were shoe-horned in between the larger rooms. The walls were thin and poorly insulated and as a result, once one guest was up in the morning, so was everyone else. I had added the bathroom in my room a few years ago and not only was it private, my shower had three luxurious shower heads.

Stephanie put her coffee mug on the table and slid off the bed. "I'll go get my makeup case," she said and I listened to her bare feet go up the stairs.

While she was gone, I used the bathroom and replaced the cracked sliver of soap in the shower with a new bar. Then I pulled on my jeans and went out into the dining room, poured another cup of coffee, and started the morning fire. When I got back to my room, Stephanie was just hanging her robe on a peg on the bathroom door. She had tan lines from a low-backed one-piece bathing suit that had been cut very high in the legs. "Nice tan," I said, sitting on the end of the bed.

"This year's convention was in Las Vegas," she said, reaching into the shower stall and turning on the water. "We all got fried."

"You play the tables?"

She shook her head. "Only the slot machines." She stepped into the spray and closed the glass door which instantly fogged and framed her like an impressionistic watercolor. "New soap," she said. "Thanks."

I watched her for a minute and then began making my bed.

"If this Collari order is really as big as I think it is," I heard her say, "I'll probably stay in Loon for a few days."

I walked to the bathroom door. "You want to just stay here?"

"No." She leaned and soaped her feet. "I'll want to be closer to the mill." She straightened and let the shower spray hit her in the face. "Besides I'll want to take Al to dinner. That sort of thing."

"Al?" Alphonse Collari was the founder and head of Collari International.

"Yes, Al. I've known him for years. His daughter, Andrea, and I were roommates senior year in college. We're still best friends." She stood on tiptoe and peeked over the top of the door. "I thought you knew."

"No." I shook my head. "But that's convenient, isn't it?"

"It doesn't hurt," she said. "And he's helped me a lot. But, I don't think he's very involved in the day-to-day anymore. He's in his late sixties, Max. I think he spends most of his time down in the Boston offices. Actually—" she peered over the top of the door again "—I happen to know Al's hot for my body."

"Can't blame him for that," I said. "Is he married?" I put the lid down on the toilet and sat on it.

"No. His wife died years ago," she said. "But, Max— Al thinks I'm still all in one piece."

"Take it from a male chauvinist," I said. "You've got all the pieces you need."

"You're a sexist pig," she said, turning off the water. "But I like it."

I grabbed her a towel, opened the shower door, and handed it to her. "So, are you staying at the hotel?" I asked.

"No." She shook her head and buried her face in the thick, navy blue terrycloth. "That new place. The River Edge Inn. I don't like the bar at the hotel. The men in there are all on the make." She stepped out onto the sheepskin I used as a bathroom rug. "I just want you to know I'm going to be around a lot, off and on, in the next few days," she said, wiping the haze from the medicine chest mirror. "So, if you change your mind about marrying me, all you have to do is make a local call."

I laughed. "Don't hold your breath."

By the time Stephanie was dressed and ready to go, she was more nervous than I'd ever seen her.

"Wish me luck, Max," she said, kissing me on the beard. "This could be my big day. I look all right?" Her hair was up and she wore a tan tweed pants suit with a collarless, ivory silk blouse under the jacket. A single strand of small pearls swung from her neck as she stooped and scratched Spotter between the ears.

"You look great," I said. "Relax."

"I've been thinking about what you said earlier." She picked up her briefcase. "About the adoption agency?"

"What? The thing about buying one? I was only kidding. . . ."

"I know, but in a way, you were right. As crude as it sounds, my financial statement could make a big difference."

"What I should've said is, with that kind of money," I said, laughing, "you could buy a husband."

She smiled tolerantly and opened the door. "With that kind of money, Max, I don't think I need a husband."

Stephanie hadn't been gone fifteen minutes when Stormy pulled up in front of the lodge in her brother's old International pickup. Spotter might not have been able to hear the truck, but somehow he knew she was there. He stood, nose to the door, his tail swinging back and forth so hard his hips moved.

Even though she worked for me seven days a week from the first week in April to the end of October, Stormy preferred to live in the town of Loon and, during the season, usually was driven to the lodge every morning at six by her older brother, Rayleen, on his way to work at the mill. Unless he'd had a beer too many after work, he joined us for dinner and then took her home around nine.

"Sorry I'm late, Max," she said, blasting by me, and, with her braid swinging, clumped down the hall to the kitchen. "Newlyweds up?" She was carrying a medium-sized white paper bag.

I followed her. "Nope."

She dumped the small paper bag on the counter. "That figures." She smiled, took her apron from its peg by the back door and put it on. "Bought some pastries in town," she said, emptying the contents of the bag onto a large platter. There were enough elephant ears, cinnamon sticky buns, and apple fritters for twenty people. "Who made the coffee?"

"Stephanie made a pot at six. I just made another one."

"She comin' back tonight?"

"No. She's staying in town." I took an apple fritter. It was still warm.

She nodded and opened the refrigerator. "We'll have breakfast in an hour," she said, taking out a half dozen eggs and two packages of sausage links.

"Where's Rayleen?" I asked.

"Told me things was slow at the mill." She lit a cigarette. "He was goin' in late. Figured he could walk. He'll get a ride out to the Starlight tonight with one of the boys. I'll pick him up there." The Starlight was a popular road house on Route 16 about ten minutes west of the lodge. Stormy began cracking eggs into a big yellow bowl. "Stephanie told me 'bout wantin' a kid," she said. "Last night while we was fixin' dinner."

"Yeah, she told me too. This morning."

"What'd you tell her?"

"I wished her luck."

"Told her you wouldn't want no part of it." She

chuckled. "That's one determined woman, though, Max."

"That's why she's so successful," I said. "She doesn't let much get in her way if she wants something badly enough."

"Well, she sure wants to be a momma."

"She'll get it." I finished the fritter and wiped my hands on Stormy's apron. "This big order from Collari is all she needs and then she'll find a buyer for Tear-Pruf. I told her she'll have a financial statement that'll satisfy even the pickiest adoption agency."

"So, she really is gonna sell, huh? I thought she was just talkin'."

"No, like I said, when Stephanie wants something, there's not much she won't do to get it."

CHAPTER ✦ THREE

I grabbed another fritter from the platter and, with the sound of the electric can-opener whining on a can of dog food for Spotter, went out the back door to the workshop. I figured that, as long as I had a little time, I'd try the Dead Princess myself.

The sun was warm on my face as I cut across the yard. The air was crisp and the smell of the combined aromas of the balsams and the woodsmoke from my morning fire was like incense. A small flock of canvasbacks, their short wings whistling, streaked across the treetops and out over the lake. They cupped their wings, lost altitude, and, with a series of splashes, landed in the center. A chorus of quacking from the ducks already there broke the silence for a minute while each of them fluffed their feathers, wiggled their tails, and jockeyed for position. I stood and watched them for a second. A flash of white in a dark spruce on the right side of the lake turned out to be one of the two osprey who nest all summer in the top of the big dead oak by the beaver dam. Spring was definitely here. The tiny new leaves and swelling buds on the maples, oaks, beech, and birch made the once monochromatic mountains in the distance appear dusted in a soft pastel patchwork of chartreuse and pink.

. The back door to the kitchen opened and I turned to see Spotter lumber down the steps and begin his nose-to-the-ground, morning search for the perfect toilet. The spell broken, I turned and continued on to the workshop.

It stands about ten yards up and behind the main lodge. Made of logs also, it originally had been a stable and boathouse. The left two-thirds now garaged the lodge's old work-horse Subaru station wagon, the Jeep pickup, and the pieces of the '89 Harley Davidson Sportster I'd bought the year before that Rayleen was rebuilding for me in his spare time. The actual work-shop area was a ten-by-twenty-eight-foot room entered through a door beside the Harley. It had been used for tack and hay storage, but now, along with a workbench, paint cans, extra fishing gear, and all the tools necessary to perform emergency maintenance at Whitefork, it contained a kerosene space heater, a stuffed chair, and a twin bed, which made it an adequate extra guest room in a pinch.

I clicked on the light. My six pairs of waders hung like half cadavers from a beam on the far side of the main room. The river would be cold this morning so I picked a pair made of heavy neoprene with built-in wading boots and struggled into them. As far as I am concerned, donning waders is the only facet of the gentle sport of fly-fishing that is violent. No matter how I approach the task of putting them on or removing them, it is a fight I never really win.

I grabbed my net and vest and rigged my three-piece, eight-and-a-half-foot, five-weight Winston with floating line.

When I emerged from the workshop, Spotter fell into step beside me. I scanned the yard for today's toilet, saw it, and imprinted the spot in my mind so I could return later and scoop it up before someone stepped in it.

As Spotter and I crossed the lawn in front of the lodge, Chad Harper, a Saints baseball cap backwards on his head, stepped off the porch and intercepted us. He had his chest waders and vest on. His rod was in his hand. "Mind if I join you, Max?"

"Not a bit," I said, as he fell into step beside me. "Your wife still asleep?"

He nodded. "Tonya's not a morning person," he said, taking a deep breath. "I keep telling her she misses a lot."

"She'll miss a lot of fish. This is a great time of day around here."

"Yeah." He took another deep breath. "I want to get us out of the city as soon as I can. Someplace like this."

"You both work right in New Orleans?"

He nodded. "My job's all right. Nine to five, you know? But Tonya, she's an assistant editor at a film company. Her hours are all screwed up. Sometimes she doesn't get home until after midnight." He shook his head. "They have ten muggings a day, at least, in our part of town. I don't like it that she's out at those hours."

"My daughter lives in New York City," I said. "She took a karate self-defense course."

"I wish Tonya would do that," he said. "Meanwhile, until we can find something outside the city, she carries a little can of mace in her purse."

"You looking for a place?"

"Yeah. My dad said he'll front us if we can find a small house. Going to start looking as soon as we get back." He smiled and followed me through the trees to a section of the river I'd named the Cobble. The size and density of the rocks on the bottom reminded me of the cobblestone streets on Nantucket.

Once Mud Season's over the Cobble is classic, calf-deep, fast-moving, crystal-clear riffle water. Right now it looked to be over our knees and was slightly cloudy.

Chad and I stood in a cluster of white birch at the edge of the river. I could feel the cold radiating from it. Spotter had gone to the water's edge and sat looking intently at a spot near the far bank.

"What's with Spotter?" Chad asked.

"He's watching the trout," I said.

"He sees them?" Chad tipped his sunglasses forward and peered at the water. "Really?"

"Really." There are coon and fox hounds, rat terriers, and bird dogs, but, as far as I know, until Spotter, there's never been a fish dog. He can locate trout from the bank of a fast-moving river that I can't see from midstream wearing expensive Polarized sunglasses. His trick is, he remembers.

In the winter, trout crowd themselves caudal fin to caudal fin in the deepest spring holes where the water temperature is dependably the highest. As soon as the snow melts and the river begins getting sunshine, they tend to return to the same holding areas they use year after year. The brookies scatter through the riffles and into the eddies and pocket water behind boulders. Some move into the lake and return to their favorite spots under fallen logs or rock formations on the bottom. The few brown trout we have in the Whitefork hunker beneath the mossy overhangs along the banks and at the bottom of some of the deeper plunge pools. Since I insist on catch and release, once Spotter knows where the trout are, they're always there. He is infallible. In fact, there are times Spotter is embarrassing. More than once I've positioned a sport in the Whitefork only to look over at the bank and see Spotter sitting on his haunches watching us. I am positive that if he doesn't like the place I've picked, he slowly shakes his head "no" and then points with his nose to the spot in the river where he knows the fish really are. All of this from a dog who can barely hear and abhors getting more than the bottoms of his paws wet.

I took out a box of flies and gave Chad a number 12 Dead Princess.

"What's this?" He turned it over in his fingers.

"Something I made the other day for water like this," I said. "You can be one of the first to try it."

"Cool."

I suggested to Chad that he replace the nine feet of 6X tippet he had on his leader with four feet of 4X and while he was working on the knots, I waded in. At midstream, the water was at my crotch. The current was strong and the cobbles slippery. Several squabbling chickadees fluttered over our heads and into the low hemlock branches on the other bank. Chad waded in after me and positioned himself a little upstream and to the left. He began false casting immediately.

"Spotter says over there near the far bank," I said, pointing at the other side of the river about thirty feet up. "You see that seam that separates the fast from the slower water?"

Chad nodded.

"Put your fly above it and drift down into it. Give your line an upstream mend, if you can."

He nodded again and his fly line whistled in the damp air. He had a nice, graceful cast. Tight loops, the rod doing the work. When he had enough line out, he shot the Dead Princess, reached across his body with a perfect upstream mend, and the fly plopped into the water about a foot short of where he'd intended. It instantly sunk out of sight. Spotter whined and we all watched Chad's orange line dead drift down the far side of the river. I couldn't see it, but I could picture the Princess rolling and bouncing along the freestone bottom hopefully imitating the toothsome nymphal stage of some helpless aquatic insect the current had torn from an upstream rock. When the line was below him, Chad stripped it partway back, expertly rolled it out of the water, turned and, this time, placed the Princess perfectly, right in the seam. He bent at the waist and, keeping tension on the line, watched intently where it entered the water. Again, it drifted back toward him.

I saw the line tightened with the strike and Chad quickly lifted his rod tip. It arched, quivering. "Hey, Max," he yelled, "this is a big one."

It was a large trout and it took off upstream. I watched Chad let the running trout take the line slack from the water at his knees and, when it was on his reel, lift the bent rod over his head and wade a few yards after the retreating fish. The reel buzzed loudly.

"Get your rod tip down to the water," I yelled. "Make him drag your line."

He lowered the rod and, twenty yards upstream, the big fish turned and headed back toward us. Chad reeled in fast but the fish was faster and he streaked by the bank just below Spotter on his way downstream. It was a big brown.

A downed beech tree lay halfway across the river twenty yards downstream. "He's going for the tree," I yelled. If the brown got into the branches he'd break off.

Chad palmed the reel and, just this side of the blowdown, the trout turned and jumped, clearing the water by a foot and shaking his head like a bass.

"Whoa!" Chad hooted, as the big fish splashed back into the river. "Never seen a brown jump like that!"

Neither had Spotter, who was on his feet, barking and racing along the bank keeping track of the fish. The big brown made another couple short runs but the fight was over and by the time Chad scooped him into his net, the fish was so exhausted it rolled onto its back. It weighed at least three pounds and took a couple minutes of Chad pulling it back and forth in the current to revive it. When it was fighting mad again, Chad let it slide from his hands and we watched it fin away. Its ego bruised, it would sulk in some dark hole for the rest of the day.

Spotter was already pointing at the seam again and three casts later Chad had a brookie on. It fought harder than the brown and when he finally got it to his net, unhooked the Princess from its jaw, and let it go, I stepped up to take a turn. I caught a big brown and two robust, thick-bodied, fourteen- and sixteen-inch brookies in as many casts. The Dead Princess wasn't just a good fly, it was a great fly. It got down quick and not only could the trout see it, it looked appetizing.

"This is a great fly, Max," Chad said, casting downstream this time and immediately stripping the Princess back toward us in fast, wake-producing jerks. Now it looked like a small, terrified bait fish trying to escape and a big brookie charged out from under the bank. He hit the Princess like an alligator chomps a gazelle and Chad's line went limp. Chad smiled sheepishly and reeled the severed line in. "Damn," he said. "It was a great fly."

I gave him another.

It went on like this for over an hour. We stood almost side by side, casting the Dead Princess wherever Spotter pointed and catching trout after trout, each one more angry about being fooled and more beautiful than the last. When we heard the clanging of Stormy's bell at ten-thirty, neither of us wanted to leave.

Even though I know cooking is Stormy's thing, I'm continually amazed at her repertoire. I don't think she serves the same breakfast twice all season long. This morning we had three-grain pancakes made with corn meal, oats, and buckwheat, topped with yogurt, warm maple syrup, and blueberries she'd frozen last summer. There were big, fat, link sausages for those of us who ate meat, fresh squeezed orange juice, coffee, and, of course, the pastries from town.

Tonya was sitting at the table, her hair still damp and her face scrubbed and shining, when Chad and I entered the dining room.

Unlike other lodges where the owners and help take their meals in the kitchen, Stormy and I always eat with the guests and, as usual, it wasn't more than a couple minutes before she was holding court from her place at the end of the table opposite me. I listened as she talked to the Harpers about their wedding, gave them advice on buying a house, and discussed the pros and cons of children right away. When she finally paused to eat her pancakes, I changed the subject to the day's fishing.

Tonya wanted to try the lake again in the canoe. "Only this time," Chad said with a smile, "over at the beaver dam."

I suggested that after they fished there a while they might like to beach the canoe and hike down the Whitefork below the lake. "We own about eight miles of it down there," I said. "Not only is it beautiful but there are a couple good-size waterfalls with deep plunge pools that hold big trout."

"If you're gonna do that," Stormy said to them, "I'll pack you a lunch."

"Can we take Spotter with us, Max?" Chad asked.

"If you can get him in the canoe, sure." Spotter liked the canoe once he was inside and confident he wasn't going to get wet.

Chad went on to tell Tonya how Spotter pointed at fish. "Also," he said to me, "would you pick out some flies for us? And a couple of those Dead Princesses too. I'll bet that Princess would work great fished deep in the lake."

"Right after we eat." I had various sizes of flies I'd tied for sale in the Shelf Shop, which was the name Red had given the long shelf in the reading room where we carried a variety of leader sizes, fly floatant, tippet spools, split shot, sinking tips, postcards, and embroidered Whitefork Lodge patches.

The telephone began ringing. "I'll get it," Stormy said, wiping her mouth on her apron, pushing her chair back, and standing. "Might be Rayleen with a change in plans." She went out into the hallway and answered it. "Max?" she shouted. "It's Red. For you."

"I hope he's not calling to say he won't be here this weekend," I said, getting up from my chair. I went into the hall and took the phone from Stormy.

"We need a portable, Max," she whispered and then returned to the dining room.

"Hello, Red," I said. "What's up?"

"Max?" There was a lot of static. "I'm callin' from Ben Frey's car phone. The one in his pickup? I'm up on Mornin' Mountain. We're on coffee break up here, so I can't talk long."

"What's going on?"

"Max, I think you're gonna wanta look at this up here."

"At what?"

"At what Collari's doin' up here."

"What are they doing?"

"They're clear-cuttin', Max. Every damn tree."

"What?"

"Yeah. Gonna play hell with the Whitefork."

Red was right. Natural Mud Season run-off was bad enough. But erosion of upstream topsoil caused by clear-cut logging was another entirely. It was probably the worst thing that could happen to trout water. Not only did it literally pave over the river bottom, it created a chain reaction that caused the water temperatures to go up. Algae bloomed and the fish either died or went somewhere else, usually the former. "Are you sure about this?" I said.

"Max, I know clear-cuttin' when I see it."

"How do I get up there?"

"No," he said. "You better not come up now."

"Why?"

"I don't want no trouble, Max."

"What kind of trouble would there be if I just came up and took a look?"

"They'd know I told."

I sighed.

"I'm serious, Max. Just wait until after quittin' time. Most everybody should be gone then. I'll meet you at the Starlight around four-thirty. We can go up together."

"All right," I said.

"And Max?"

"Yeah?"

"Don't say nothin'," he said. "Not even to Stormy yet."

"Why?"

"There's some new boys from Canada runnin' this job, Max. And they're pushin' pretty hard to get it done fast. I don't think they'd like to know I called. . . ." He lowered his voice. "Gotta go," he whispered. "See you at the Starlight." He hung up.

I went back into the dining room and tried not to look concerned.

"What'd he want?" Stormy asked.

"Guy stuff," I said. "Just some guy stuff."

She narrowed her eyes but didn't say anything. I knew she didn't believe me and as soon as we were alone she was going to get the truth.

* * *

At four-fifteen I took the Jeep and left for the Starlight.

Stormy had cornered me in the kitchen as I was on my way out and demanded to know what Red had wanted on the phone and what was going on.

I told her.

"Jesus, Max! Clear-cuttin'? Collari ain't supposed to be really loggin', much less clear-cuttin'."

"I know."

"Who said they could clear-cut?"

"We don't even know for sure," I said. "You know how Red is."

"Red Crosley knows loggin', Max," she said. "He says they're clear-cuttin', then they're clear-cuttin'."

"I still want to see it myself," I said. "Then we'll decide what to do about it."

She nodded and we both stared at the roasting chicken she was preparing to stuff. "You mind pickin' up Rayleen?" she finally said. "Long as you're goin' to the Starlight?"

"I'll do better than that," I said. "I'll leave the Jeep for him and Red can bring me back here after we've been up on the mountain."

"Don't know whether that's such a good idea, Max," she snorted, putting her hand in the stuffing. "Knowin' he don't hafta wait for me, that old buzzard Rayleen could sit at that bar drinkin' Loon Lager and jawin' all night."

"So, I'll tell him I need my Jeep back by supper."

Her face reddened. "Better do more than that, Max," she said, jamming a fistful of stuffing into the chicken. "Tell him I'll break his neck if he ain't here at five-thirty."

The Starlight is a rectangular, one-story building that sits perpendicular to the highway just out of the trees at the back of a large, unpaved parking lot. In the fifties, it had housed an auto body shop. In the sixties and seventies, the Vermont Department of Highways had used the building for snowplows and the parking lot for a couple small mountains of sand and road salt. Skip Willits and his Vietnamese wife, Lo Ming, had bought and turned it into a bar and restaurant in the eighties. Through good, honest food, free pouring, and fair prices, they'd become the home away from home for just about every pickup owner in the area. In fact, on any Friday and Saturday night, no matter what the weather, the parking lot overflowed and trucks crowded the shoulders of both sides of Route 16 for a mile in each direction.

This afternoon, the lot was a sea of mud and only about half full. I parked the Jeep in some soupy tire ruts in an empty slot ten feet from the door.

I could see the Starlight's circular sign standing high on a pole out by the road. It stayed lit day and night and read STARLIGHT CAFE in neon script. The *R* in Starlight had been missing as long as I could remember, making it read just as it was pronounced by the locals.

A horn honked and I looked in my rearview mirror. It was Red in his jacked-up silver Ford pickup. I threw the keys under the seat and climbed out of the Jeep. "We'll take my truck," he said from his window.

I signaled for him to wait one minute and, jumping over the worst spots, crossed the mud to the Starlight's only door. I wanted to tell Rayleen the Jeep was outside and where I'd left the keys.

As usual, it took a few seconds for my eyes to become accustomed to the comparative darkness inside the windowless Starlight. Johnny Cash's "A Boy Named Sue" blared from the dark and I was hit with the thick aroma of stale beer, men's bodies, cigarette smoke, and fried food. "Eau d'Loon," Stormy called it, claiming that by Sunday morning, every redneck in town smelled like it.

The Starlight is basically one long, deep room. The ceiling beams are exposed and hung with years of customer memorabilia, ties, business cards, photographs, two giant copperhead skins, and literally hundreds of caps. I saw our sheriff, Darren Foley, in one of the booths which are built into the long wall to the right. We waved at each other. I couldn't tell who the men with him were and they didn't turn around.

The juke box was now playing "Moon River." It sat beside the raised stage Skip used for Friday and Saturday night's live music. A twenty-by-twenty, wood-grained, linoleum dance floor spread out in front of it and a haphazard arrangement of tables and chairs filled the rest of the floor space up to the bar which runs almost the full length of the wall on the left. The kitchen is behind this wall and a door and pass-thru window are built into it halfway down.

There were about twenty-five men at the bar and most of them had the Tear-Pruf inverted triangle logo patch on their work clothes. I nodded or said hello to the ones I knew. Our mailman, Ed Garvey, and little Whitey Laycock had their heads together over a couple hi-balls. "Have a drink, Max," Ed said with a definite slur. Others I only knew by nicknames; Dub, Ranger, Big Bill, Whiffle, Roady, and Switch. They were all loggers and nodded at my reflection in the mirror behind the bar.

I saw Rayleen hunched over a half empty bottle of Loon Lager about midway down. Like a lot of Vermonters these days, Rayleen is a born-again Christian and typical of many of them, he doesn't hesitate to attempt on-the-spot conversions. He'd given up on me years ago, but it was obvious from the empty stools on either side of him that he'd been working the bar.

I walked up behind him and tried to catch his attention in the mirror. Wrinkled from years out in the weather, Rayleen is essentially a dehydrated version of Stormy in overalls and a red plaid shirt. His greasy John Deere cap was lying on the wet bar by his beer and two Dagwood tufts of thin gray hair stood out like the Z-lon wings on a Baetis spinner.

He saw me and his face lit up with a big grin. He didn't have his teeth in. "Max," he said, turning awkwardly on the stool. "What're you doin' here? Have a beer, boy." He signaled to Skip, who was drying pint glasses by the sink.

I shook my head at Skip. "No, I can't," I said to Rayleen. "I just wanted to tell you the Jeep's outside. Keys are under the seat. You take it back to the lodge for me, huh?"

"Where you goin'?"

"Red and I have a couple errands to run," I lied. "He'll take me back to the lodge when we're through."

"What's with that boy, anyways?" He lifted his beer and sipped it.

"Who? Red?"

"Yeah." He gestured down the bar. "Here we all was celebratin' the good Lord's blessin' that things is gonna pick up at the mill, and Red, he come in here, had hisself a beer and didn't so much as say hello to nobody. Leastwise me." He turned back and faced me in the mirror.

"Things are going to pick up at the mill?"

"Yep. God come through." He nodded and drained the beer. "Heard today. A big shipment of logs is comin' in." He scratched his head. "Hell, Red oughta be thankful like the rest of us."

"I don't know about Red." I patted him on the shoulder. "But Stormy told me to tell you she'll be thankful if you don't show up later than five-thirty."

"Did she now?" He held up his empty bottle and

signaled Skip for another. "Her face have any color when she said it?"

I tapped a red square on his plaid shirt. "About like that," I said.

"Well, then—" he looked at me in the mirror and smiled "—guess I better keep my eye on the time."

CHAPTER FOUR

About a quarter mile beyond the Starlight, Red turned right onto Hooker Hill Road. It's a dirt road that cuts up over the west side of Morning Mountain and comes into the town of Loon from the north by the pulp mill. A week ago the road had been so muddy it was barely passable. Although still wet now, it had been packed rock hard. Except for an occasional washboard of bumps in the low areas, it felt and looked like it was paved. I mentioned it to Red.

"Yeah," he said. "We've brought a lot of equipment up here. A lot of trucks."

A half mile up, Red slowed and shifted into four-wheel drive.

"The track to the site's right here, Max," he said, turning right again, this time directly into the trees. "I can drive 'bout three miles in and then we'll hafta walk."

For a second all I could see were pine branches hitting the windshield as we bounced violently into the woods, then the area ahead of us cleared and I could see we were on a narrow, deeply-rutted, newly-cut, logging road.

"Just smoothed this baby myself this mornin'," he

said, gripping the wheel as the left front of the truck lurched high over a boulder. "Shoulda seen it before I did."

We banged down hard and bounced and I grabbed the hand grip on the dash as we fishtailed up through the churned mud, leaves, and downed saplings. My sense of direction is pretty good and I guessed we were running parallel to Route 16, just above the Starlight, heading back in the direction of the Whitefork River. It seemed like the long way around for a logging road.

"Why didn't they just run this road straight up from sixteen?" I asked.

"I know. Outta the way, ain't it?" He shrugged as we hit another big bump. "Prob'ly don't wanta draw attention to all the logs startin' to come outta here."

He was right. If Collari was trying to hide what they were doing, this would do it. By taking the logs around Hooker Hill Road instead of Route 16, it would appear they were coming in from the north as always.

After another mile of gut-shaking bumps we topped a rise and, ahead of us, I saw several muddy pickups with the ubiquitous gun racks in the back window parked in the trees. We stopped just behind them. "I thought we were going to be alone up here," I said.

"Me too." Red looked at his watch. "Some of the boys must be gettin' in a little overtime," he said. "Hope they don't see us."

The mountain fell gradually away to our right. I estimated we were now not much more than a mile directly above Whitefork Lodge. Red nodded and said, "Mile an' a half exactly, Max. Roll down your window. You can even hear the river." He pointed. "Comes down through the big gorge right over there."

I rolled the window down and could distinctly hear the roar of the Whitefork in front of us through the thick trees. I could also hear the whine of chainsaws and, faintly, the clanking of a bulldozer coming from somewhere above us.

I've always known Collari's land abutted mine but never really worried about them logging it. Initially I was concerned Collari might put in some sort of yuppie ski chalet development because of the popularity of nearby Thunder Mountain Ski Area.

My fears appeared ill-founded. The years went by and, except for some occasional selective cutting, Collari International seemed more content to sit on the land abutting mine than develop it. Quite frankly, I forgot all about them. The business was good at Whitefork Lodge and I was having fun doing what I loved to do.

Even when Collari announced five years ago they were building a six-million-square-foot pulping mill on the north side of Loon, it didn't bother me. Like just about everyone else in the area, I attended the big Loon City Council meeting where Alphonse Collari himself and several of his executives had made their presentation and answered questions. They'd come all the way up from their Boston headquarters to talk about environmental impact, traffic, noise, and where the trees would be coming from. We were assured the trees to be used were going to be brought in from logging operations Collari had in Canada. They would be using state-of-the-art water reclamation techniques and would not use town streets for their trucks. I believed him and like everyone else in Loon was looking forward to the positive effect the plant promised for the economy; hundreds of jobs would be created and the taxes could be plowed into repairing our pockmarked streets, expanding the emergency room facilities at Loon Memorial Hospital, and replacing the ancient Loon Regional High School.

A couple more years went by and Collari was true to their promises; Loon hummed with a new school and a new prosperity as big, dark green, diesel-belching trucks rumbled into the plant almost every hour of every day from Quebec. They were piled so high with logs that Northern Vermont Electric had to raise the power lines that crossed County 18. At any given time we could see thousands of logs piled five and six stories high in the mill's muddy yards waiting to be fed into the whining pulping machines. As Rayleen described it after his first few days of driving a forklift at the mill, "I never seen so many trees, Max," he said. "They got whole damn forests layin' in there waitin' to be gobbled up by them grinders."

Red climbed out of the truck. "We walk from here, Max," he said. "It ain't far."

I climbed out, ducked under a broken branch and we started up into the old growth maple, spruce, oak, beech, and birch trees. Other than massive bleeding white scars on some of the larger birches and oaks made when the track was cut, the woods looked intact to me. The chainsaws and clanking got louder and a faint aroma of diesel exhaust and woodsmoke rode the light breeze coming down the mountain.

It was tough walking. The dozers not only had packed the mud and leaves in spots to an icelike slime, they had crushed just about everything in their path and I tripped several times on the clawing branches of flattened saplings.

About a half mile up the winding track, the trees suddenly disappeared.

I stopped and stared at the scene in front of me. Red hadn't exaggerated about the devastation. I was outraged at the atrocity. The forest from here on up the mountain was almost gone. Collari loggers had stripped virtually everything off the landscape from just about the top of Morning Mountain down to where I stood. Every place where there once had been a tree, now a three-foot-high stump stood oozing sap. It made no difference how big, young, old, or what species it had been, it was gone. In the ten or so acres I could see, there was nothing left but stumps and massive, tangled piles of burning trimmings. The smoke made it look like a battlefield. Opportunistic chickadees, nuthatches, and titmice, oblivious to the carnage around them, nervously flitted through the debris helping themselves to seeds and exposed insect larvae. Raucous blue jays swooped across the open area scolding anything and everything. Halfway up the clear-cut on the right, freshly-cut logs lay on top of each other in piles as big as houses. High on the hill to my left a crew of a half dozen or so men in green Collari hard hats were trimming the limbs from felled trees. A yellow bulldozer idled blue exhaust just below them. Farther up the mountain, chainsaws screamed and, as I watched, a one-hundred-year-old beech with wrinkled gray bark like an elephant's skin crashed to the ground in an explosion of broken limbs.

"Told ya," Red said. "This is where all the logs is comin' from that everybody's celebratin' about."

I didn't say anything. I couldn't. I waded through the logging debris and around four fifty-five-gallon drums with DIESEL stenciled on their sides to the river. Either the loggers hadn't gotten to them yet or didn't intend to, but the trees closest to its banks had been spared, making the meandering little valley containing the river look like a crooked mohawk haircut on the shaved hillside. I walked into the thin screen of trees and looked at the water. From where I stood I could see that one of the big Caterpillars had crisscrossed it several times, turning over boulders and grinding muddy tracks up the banks. Red joined me, looking over his shoulder at the men high on the cut and then back at me. "It ain't right," he said. "Cuttin' this way."

"The river's still okay."

"For now," he said.

"They're not going to put in hay bales?"

"Nobody's said nothin' about 'em." He shook his head. "I think if we was, we'd be puttin' 'em in right now, wouldn't we?"

I nodded. Hay bales were used to hold back erosion. They were usually strung along the uphill side of rivers and watersheds end-to-end and staked down. They acted like strainers, holding back most of the mud and letting the cleaner water through until the natural vegetation grows back. I stood and walked back out of the trees into the clearcut. "Don't they realize—" I gestured to the men up the hill "—how bad this is?" No one seemed to have noticed us yet.

Red eyed them nervously. "Some of 'em do. Only nobody'll admit it. Too afraid to lose their paychecks." He took me by the sleeve and started us back toward the cover of the logging road and his pickup. "C'mon, Max." He still had his eyes on the men on the hill. "We better go now. I'm pushin' my luck here with you as it is."

When we were back in the trees, I said, "Are you the only one who cares enough to say anything?"

"I grew up in these woods, Max. Hunted and fished here with my daddy and now with my two sons." He shook his head slowly. "You know I ain't one of them environmental types, but I care about stuff. And I know when things ain't bein' done right. I ain't afraid to say if I think they oughta be different."

At the truck I said, "What happened to all the logs that were supposed to come down from the land in Canada?"

"Played out, I hear." He gestured back toward the clear-cut. "Cut it all off just like that, I bet." He opened the door and climbed in.

"What do you think we can do?" I climbed in my side and he started the engine.

"I done all I can, Max," he said. "Maybe more'n I shoulda." He glanced nervously through the windshield as we backed up. "You're the one's gotta do somethin'. You know 'bout stuff like this. I mean, you're real smart about carin' for the woods and river. Havin' catch 'n release and like that." He put the truck in first, the wheels spun for a second and then we began the bumpy descent back down the logging road. "Seems to me," he said finally, "you oughta know who to talk to to get this stopped. Comin' from New York City like you did and all."

"Have you said anything about the way you feel to anyone else?"

"Hell no." He laughed ruefully. "Just you. I have a family. We gotta eat. My Whitefork paycheck's nice but I need this one too."

"How many more trees are they supposed to take up there?"

He shrugged. "Nobody's said. But, if these are feedin' the mill then we ain't stoppin' 'til we've cut 'em all." We churned through the mud over a small rise. Coming up the other side was a dark green Range Rover, its two roof antennas whipping violently back and forth. Red hit the brakes. "Oh, Jesus. It's Bull."

"Bull?"

"Bull Turlock," Red said, grinding the gears as he jammed them into reverse. "Collari's foreman. Runs this job up here." The truck's engine whined as he backed up to a wider place in the road and pulled off onto the narrow shoulder.

The Range Rover growled up beside us and stopped an inch from Red's outside mirror. The tinted side window slid down. There were two men in the front seat and someone in the back, who, because of the dark windows, was only a shadow. I knew the silver-haired man on the passenger side. It was Claremont Taylor, Loon's former mayor. The driver, a broad shouldered man with a thick, black beard, black hair, and small dark eyes, leaned out the window and looked at Red.

"Hi, Bull," Red said, touching his cap brim.

"Didn't know you were working this shift," Bull said.

"I ain't."

Bull looked around Red at me. "Then what're you doing up here? Running sight-seeing tours?"

"I . . . ah, I was just . . ."

"My name's Max Addams," I said quickly. "I own the fishing lodge down below here. Red works for me part-time. Don't blame him. It's my fault. I've been hearing the chainsaws. I asked Red if he'd show me around." I looked at Claremont. "How are you, Claremont?"

Taylor smiled and nodded politely. "Howdy, Max." With his silver hair, tie, and pale gray rumpled suit he looked enough like Colonel Sanders to be his twin. Claremont looked at Red. "You know better than to bring someone up here, Red," he said. "It can be dangerous. Our insurance doesn't cover outsiders."

"Sorry." Red's leg was jiggling on the brake pedal. "We never went up on the cut, Mr. Taylor," Red said. "Stayed right in the woods. We was only there a minute."

Bull's eyes narrowed. "This is private property, Red. You know that."

Red nodded sheepishly.

Claremont put a bony hand on Bull's shoulder. "No harm's been done, Bull," he said, looking back at Red. "You git now, hear?"

"Yessir. That's what we was doin'."

Claremont looked at me. "Nice seein' you, Max."

I smiled.

The Range Rover's window slid silently closed and

they pulled away and up the track. I tried to see who it was in the back seat but there still was only a shadowy shape.

Red pulled out and we continued down the hill. "Oh, Jesus," he said. "Oh, baby Jesus. I'm in trouble now."

"Why?"

"Anything happens, they're gonna know it was 'cause of this."

"Maybe not," I said. "I'll talk to a few people. See if there's a quiet way to fix this."

"That's the trouble, Max. You can't fix somethin' like this," he said. "You gotta stop it."

The sun was low over the lake as Red and I pulled up in front of the lodge. "You sure you won't come in for a beer?" I said, looking at my Jeep parked in front of us. "Rayleen's here. I know he'd like to see you."

"No thanks, Max," he said, shaking his head. "I'm not up to his Sunday school lessons. Besides, I gotta get home. Wilba has her book club at the Y tonight. I gotta feed the boys. Give 'em baths. All that stuff."

I opened the door. "Thanks for showing me the clear-cut, Red."

He shook his head. "It was stupid to go up there."

"Don't worry about it. I'm sure they believed it was my doing, not yours."

"Maybe Bull," he said. "But not Claremont Taylor. That man can be trouble, Max."

"Call me tomorrow," I said. "I'll let you know if I've been able to do anything." I slammed the door, went up on the porch, and watched him turn around and drive back up the access road.

Red was right about Claremont. He could be trouble. Last November, after twelve years as mayor, the *Loon Sentinel* exposed Claremont's ten-year affair with his secretary and the misappropriation of funds in her behalf. As a result, he not only lost his bid for reelection to thirty-five-year-old Ruth Pearlman, but his wife of thirty years committed suicide. The carefully typewritten note she left said, she couldn't continue living with the embarrassment and shame. Claremont, it seemed, could, and not only did he return to his private practice, but a couple months later secured a position very high on the board of Collari International.

I kicked off my muddy boots and went inside. I could hear the newlyweds laughing with Rayleen in the dining room and Stormy clanking pans in the kitchen. Ordinarily, I would have called my lawyer, Bill Dorrance, but he was a partner in the law firm Taylor and Dorrance, the Taylor being Claremont Taylor. I doubted if Bill would be able or even want to give me objective advice.

I didn't know what to do, so I went to the kitchen to talk to Stormy.

She was squatting like a baseball catcher in front of the open refrigerator, half of its contents on the floor around her. Spotter sat on his haunches beside her. He looked hopeful. A cigarette smoldered in an ashtray on the island. "Well?" she asked, opening a carton of half and half and sniffing it. "Is it as bad up there as Red says?"

"It's bad," I said. "What are you doing?"

"Somethin' smells in this refridge," she said, setting the carton back inside.

"I was going to call Bill Dorrance. See what he thinks I should do," I said. "But Claremont was up at the clearcut."

"Claremont?" She opened a plastic tub, looked at the contents, and set it on the floor before Spotter. He instantly stuck his muzzle inside and began slurping. "What was that windbag doin' up there?"

"I don't know," I said, taking a drag from her cigarette and replacing it. "He is on Collari's board, you know."

She shook her head in disgust. "That man should be in jail, you ask me," she said. "Still can't buy that suicide bull. I knew Martha Taylor and I don't care what the sheriff says he found that day." Claremont's wife had been found in her big Cadillac in their garage, the doors shut and sealed with wet bedsheets.

Stormy unwrapped a large rectangular shape of aluminum foil. She sniffed and instantly pulled her head away. "Pee-hew!" she said. "Found it." She handed it up to me. It was about a pound of sticky-looking, partially decomposed pork spareribs black with decay. "When did you put them in there?" she said.

I smiled sheepishly. "February," I said, and threw them in the garbage while she replaced the food from the floor back into the refrigerator.

"Well, I can sure see why you might not wanna talk to Bill Dorrance," she said, slowly standing. Her knees cracked. "Who are you gonna call?"

"I don't know who to talk to now."

"What about your fishing friend? The geologist."

"He's down in Mexico, I think."

"Then, how about Ruth?" She stuck the cigarette in her mouth. "She'd know what to do. Or, at least, be able to tell you who to talk to."

"I don't know, Stormy," I said. I had to be careful what I said about Loon's first woman mayor. Stormy had been very active in Ruth Pearlman's campaign, carrying signs, telephoning constituents, and distributing literature. "She's probably just learning who to talk to herself." Ruth had been mayor only sixteen months.

"Max. Before this, Ruth was a lawyer. A damn good one too." She looked up at me through the smoke. "If you ain't forgotten."

I hadn't forgotten. I'd met Ruth Pearlman while she

was still practicing law. I was trying to keep the lodge afloat working for the ad agency in Montpelier. She was with a firm across the street from where I worked and we started commuting from Loon together. Dating just naturally followed. Stormy told me that everyone in town thought we were made for each other. Not only were we both recently divorced, but her love for the outdoors and finesse with a fly rod surpassed mine. We had fun together but the relationship never had much of a chance to get serious. Ruth added college night courses to her already busy legal schedule and was seldom in Loon anymore and I was busy coping with the new popularity of Whitefork Lodge. The only sexual relationship we had was one afternoon when Spotter jumped her husky, Betsy, who, I was told, had five weird-looking puppies. Once Ruth returned to Loon we had dinner a couple of times during her run for mayor and tried to rekindle the flame, but other than a quick peck on the cheek at the door of her small house, the electricity we'd once had seemed gone. She'd become a politician and, to me, local politics seemed pretty silly. One mayor was going to be pretty much the same as the next. Whoever got the office still had to deal with that imbecilic quagmire called the Loon City Council. I'd supported Ruth, of course. But more for Stormy's sake than because of what Ruth and I once were.

"I don't feel comfortable just calling Ruth out of the blue," I said.

"Why not? Think she'll think you're tryin' to hit on her again?"

"She might."

"Men." She gave me an exasperated look. "She's the mayor, for God's sakes, Max. Collari's breakin' his promise not to log 'round here. And he's doin' it big time. Call her. You don't and I will."

I pointed to the clock on the wall. "It's a quarter of six," I said. "She won't be there."

"I happen to know that woman's in her office 'til nine or ten every night, except when she's jogging. Call her!"

I sighed and went back into the hallway. I looked up the Loon town offices' number in the phone book, dialed, and asked the man who answered to speak to the mayor. Ruth Pearlman answered on the second buzz.

"Ruth Pearlman," she said. I always liked her voice. It had that husky, Lauren Bacall quality.

"Ruth, it's Max."

"Max?" I heard a chair squeak and she said, "Hold on, I just got back from a run. Let me close the door." There was silence and then I heard a door click shut and then more silence until she picked up the receiver again. "Max. It's so good to hear your voice," she said. "How's Stormy? How are things out at the lodge?" She was pleasant and seemed genuinely interested. "How are you?"

"That's why I'm calling," I said. "I've got an ecological problem out here that I need some advice on."

"An ecological problem?"

"Well, maybe. Collari is logging the mountain above the lodge."

"They're taking trees on Morning Mountain?"

"More than that. They're clear-cutting."

"You've seen this?"

"About half an hour ago," I said.

She was silent for a second. When she finally spoke, her rich voice was all business. "I wasn't aware of any logging being done in Loon. I was under the impression that Collari's raw materials were coming from Canada."

"It might look like they are," I said, "but they're not. Not today anyway. Or from now on. They're bringing them around Hooker Hill Road."

"You're sure?"

"Positive."

"What do you think I can do, Max?" she asked.

"Look, Ruth. I didn't know who to call. Stormy suggested you. She thought maybe you could tell me what to do. I want it stopped before it gets any worse. Hell, they haven't even taken the simplest steps to prevent the topsoil from eroding if it rains."

"That's interesting."

"It's more than interesting. If my part of the Whitefork fills up with mud, I'm out of business."

She was silent for a few seconds more. "Max," she finally said, "perhaps you and I should talk face to face. Would tomorrow morning be alright? Say, at eleven?"

I tried not to think of how many more trees would be cut by eleven. "I guess," I said.

"Why I'm suggesting seeing you then instead of first thing is I'd like talk to a few people who understand the legality here. Also, I know someone from Montpelier who knows a little about the ecological implications of things like this. He'll need some time to get here. Besides, if I can squeeze it in, it might not hurt for me to go up to Morning Mountain and take a look myself."

"All right," I said. "Eleven's fine. See you then." I thanked her and she thanked me and we said goodbye. I didn't feel any sparks.

Stormy stepped out of the kitchen doorway lighting a cigarette. She'd been listening. "There," she said with a smile, "was that so hard?"

I shook my head. "She seemed surprised they were logging, that's for sure."

"She going to help stop it?"

"I don't know yet," I said. "We're meeting tomorrow. At eleven."

"Good. What the hell could happen overnight?"

CHAPTER ✦ FIVE

After we all cleared the dinner dishes from the dining room to the kitchen, Tonya stayed with Stormy to help load the dishwasher. Chad went into the reading room to look at a couple of my Gary Borger "Anatomy Of A Trout Stream" videos and Rayleen and I took Spotter and our brandies and went out onto the porch. Spotter went down the steps and disappeared into the dark yard.

"Gonna rain tonight," Rayleen said, settling back in the rocker.

I looked out at the billions of stars reflected in the still, black lake. "How do you know?" I asked, sipping the brandy.

"Listen to them peepers," he said.

"I hear them." Of all the sounds in the world, I think a spring peeper chorus is my favorite.

"Hear how rushed them peeps is, Max? How they overlap each other?"

I listened. He was right. Instead of each peeper's voice being separate and distinct, they did seem to engulf each other. "Yeah," I said. "They do sound a little speeded up tonight."

"They are," he laughed. "They're hurryin'. Tryin' to locate a mate 'fore the rain comes."

I put my feet up on the porch rail. Spotter climbed back up onto the porch and, after several turns, flopped with a groan under my legs.

"Stormy told me 'bout the clear-cut," he said. "How you're gonna talk to the mayor. What you thinkin' of doin' 'bout it?"

"I want it stopped."

"Why? The mill needs them logs."

His comment surprised me. "Not that way," I said, trying to see his face in the shadow.

"Max." He leaned forward in the rocker. "Lot of this forest up here was once clear-cut off." He pointed out at the lake. "When I was a boy, that woods out there was nothin' but fields of 'taters. Not a tree for fifty miles. Old man Garvey and his sons cleared it. Piled all them stone fences you still find down in there today. Good Lord brought all them trees back."

"It's different today, Rayleen."

"Not up here, Max. We've always used what we needed. And it's always been here to use again." He laughed. "Hell, sometimes we've used it two, three times."

I sighed.

"Lotta folks up here still look to the good book as the guide, Max," he said, "God said hisself, right in Genesis, chapter one, verse twenty-six, things was put on this here Earth for us to use."

"He also said something about replenishing the Earth," I said. "If I remember right."

"Collari'll replant, Max. Hell, that mountain'll be good as new 'fore you know it."

"With what? A tree farm? And what happens to the Whitefork River and the trout in the meantime?" I looked at him. "You ever see what happens to trout water after clear-cutting?"

He shook his head. "No. But I know what happens when you take away a man's income. God meant for a man to work, Max."

"I'm not trying to take away anyone's job. I just want to stop the clear-cutting."

"Right now, Max, clear-cuttin' is the jobs."

I heard the phone ringing and then Tonya's voice say, "Good evening, Whitefork Lodge." There was a pause and she stuck her head out the screened door.

"It's for you, Max," she whispered.

I got up and stepped over Spotter. "You need one of them portable phones, Max," Rayleen said as I went into the hall and picked up the phone.

"Hello?"

"Max?" It was Stephanie. "Guess what?"

"The order as good as you hoped?"

"Good? Max, that's what I'm calling about. It's great. They've contracted for over half our entire year's production. Almost every item we make."

"Wow. You find out what's going on that's so big?"

"Nobody's said anything specific."

"How about your buddy, Al?"

"I haven't seen him yet, Max. He's been out of the office all day." She paused and I heard ice clinking in a glass and a swallow.

"Celebrating?"

"A little sherry on the rocks is all," she said. "This order is everything I hoped it would be."

"When should I start calling you mommy?"

"Oh, Max. I love the sound of that."

"I know," I said. "I'm really happy for you."

"I'm going to stay in town for another couple days," she said. "Just to make sure every detail is covered. I don't want anything screwing this up for me."

"Makes sense."

"Then I'd like to move back into the lodge, if that's okay. Kick back and relax. I'll bring some big steaks and champagne. You and Stormy can help me celebrate."

"Sure. When?"

"Maybe day after tomorrow. How's that?"

"Perfect." I decided not to tell her about the clear-cutting.

"Well, I have to go, Max. I'm having dinner with Al in twenty minutes and I'm still sitting here with just a towel wrapped around me."

I looked at my watch. "Kind of late for dinner, isn't it?"

"Not among the 'nouveau riche,' " she giggled.

I laughed and as we said goodbye and hung up, Stormy and Tonya came out of the kitchen. They were rubbing cream into their hands.

"Where's Rayleen?" Stormy asked.

"He's on the porch," I said and looked at Tonya. "Chad's in the reading room looking at fishing videos."

Tonya smiled and headed for the reading room and Stormy and I went out onto the porch. "Let's go, old man," she said, rubbing the small of her back. "I'm beat."

Rayleen got slowly to his feet. "You tell Max we was gonna be a little late tomorrow?"

She looked at me. "We both get our yearly physicals tomorrow at the hospital, Max," she said. "Shouldn't take long, but don't expect me 'til 'bout nine." She smiled. "You can sleep in like them kids."

"Bet they ain't sleepin'," Rayleen said, with a wink.

"What would you know?" Stormy grabbed him by the sleeve and pulled him down the steps toward his truck. "You old goat."

* * *

The peepers were right.

I awoke at four Thursday morning with the distinct sound of rain drumming on the roof. It was pouring.

I pulled on my jeans, hooded green sweatshirt, and the old Wellingtons I keep by the front door, grabbed a flashlight, and slogged out through the mud in the yard to the river. I shined the flashlight at the water speeding by near my feet. As best I could see, it was off-color, but nothing unusual for Mud Season. So far, so good, I thought. The clear-cut wasn't affecting the river.

I went back to my bedroom and stripped off my clothes. Spotter looked up from his place on the small Oriental by the door and gave me the same blank look he'd given me when I went out.

It seemed like I'd just shut my eyes when someone's fist began pounding on my door. "Max! Max?" It was Chad. "Max? You better get out here!"

I squinted at the alarm. It was seven-thirty. "I'm coming," I mumbled. "I'm coming." I pulled on the damp clothes I'd just taken off and went out into the hall. Chad, with a long poncho over his vest and waders, stood by the front door. He was soaked. "What the hell's going on?" I growled.

"I'm sorry, Max," he said. "I was going to fish the lake, but, but . . . but I was sure you'd want to know."

"Know what?" I peered around him at the rain sheeting across the porch floorboards.

"The lake's full of dead trout."

"What!?" I pushed by him, through the door, down the porch steps and across the lawn through the rain to the lake. I was barefoot and rain beat at my face, soaking my clothes by the time I was to the dock. Then I noticed Spotter. He'd run ahead of me and now stood at the dock's edge, his tail straight out behind him, staring at the water with his all-too familiar "I-see-a-trout" look. I didn't get more than two steps farther when I saw what he was looking at. Floating everywhere were the white bellies of dead trout.

I jumped off the dock into the shallow water and waded a few yards out into the lake. There were a dozen dead trout within a fifty-foot radius of where I stood. More were visible in small clumps to the left and right down the shoreline. As I stood there, my hair matted to my head, my beard running like a waterfall onto my chest, the odor of diesel fuel filled my nostrils and I could see its greasy, rainbow stain dancing in the raindrops on the water's surface. Almost in shock, I backed out of the lake, the oily slick from the water gilding my blue jeans black.

With Spotter galloping behind me, I ran by Chad across the yard to the river and, without stopping, slogged in. Staggering against the current and over the slippery boulders, I waded out into the center through frothy suds of diesel fuel and stood waist deep as half a dozen dead brook trout swirled between my legs and around my jeans. I turned and watched the bloated white bodies as they bounced through the riffle water below me, spun into an eddy behind a boulder and then disappeared around the bend.

Spotter whined. I looked back upstream. Two more pale, puffy trout floated toward me. One was a big sixteen-inch male. I gently scooped his limp body into my hands. He was still dying. His gills pulsed slowly. His mouth opened and closed. I stooped and cracked his head hard on a rock at my feet. The soft, cold body quivered and blood leaked from his gills, washed over my hands, and turned the pale brown water at my feet a dark sepia. As the once beautiful trout's eyes glassed over, I stood in the cold, cloudy water, tears of frustration running into my beard. I lifted the carcass above my head, shook it and screamed upstream, "Collari! You son of a bitch! You're killing my river!"

*   *   *

The town of Loon is twenty minutes down Route 16 from the Whitefork Lodge and separated from us by the Sunrise Mountain Range of which Morning Mountain is the most prominent. A series of tight switchbacks that follow Gracey Gorge lead down to the town affording spectacular, almost cliché calendar views of the valley and mountains, the town with its white church steeples, the glistening Whitefork River, and, in the distance, the neat sprawl and three dark green smokestacks of Collari International's pulp mill.

It isn't until you get down onto the crosshatch of streets that you notice the subtle signs of poverty; the occasional empty storefront and decaying, paint-peeling houses; the block of three-story, redbrick buildings along the river that once housed prosperous shoe manufacturers, printing plants, and furniture building companies, now empty with broken windows, graffiti, and knee-high weeds.

Loon has a permanent population of about 12,300. Hardly enough, I'd always thought, to qualify for the complexities of a mayor and city council. But Loon is better off than most Vermont towns. From the beginning, it had always had the river. And now we had Collari International.

The rain had stopped by the time I parked my Jeep on Main Street in front of the shell of what had once been our movie theater and walked the two blocks to the town offices. I was still wearing my wet clothes and didn't care. I had waded directly out of the river, pulled on my Wellingtons, climbed into the Jeep, and driven to town. I was mad.

It wasn't even nine and no businesses were open except Freddie's Lunch. Freddie opened at four A.M. and, depending upon which shift you worked at Collari, was packed with people eating either supper or breakfast behind the steamed windows. I passed the high, darkened windows of the Triangle bar, Loon Lanes bowling alley, Woolworth's, Ace Hardware, and the Loon Hotel. Although I couldn't see anyone inside, a sweet smell of fabric softener came from the laundromat. On the corner, the big display windows of Sam's Sporting Goods were dark, as were those in the offices of the *Loon Sentinel* directly above it.

I crossed the street and stormed into the town offices. The office of the tax collector and the woman who issued hunting licenses was on the left. The mayor's was right across the hall. The door was closed. I didn't knock.

The outer office was as large as Whitefork's dining room and all six heads in the room turned as I barged through the door. "Can I help . . . ?" a woman said, extending her hand. I ignored her and went through the door with Ruth's name on it. She was on the far side of the room behind a large desk and was dictating into a handheld recorder. She clicked it off as I slogged up to the desk.

"Max," she said, standing quickly. "Our meeting isn't until eleven . . ."

"Collari's killing my trout!" I said, trying to remain calm. "Look at my jeans." I ran a finger over the slick surface and held it out to her. "That's diesel."

The office door was still open and now the three staff members were stacked in the opening watching us. A trail of greasy water led from where I stood across the floor and back out beneath their feet.

"I can smell the diesel, Max," Ruth said. "Why don't you sit down?" She went to the door and spoke to one of the people outside. "See if Wally Murray would mind coming over a little early," she said. "He's staying at the River Edge Inn. And get Jake in Maintenance to mop this up before someone slips and breaks something."

Then she closed the door, recrossed the room, and sat back down behind her desk. The chair squeaked. "Please. Sit down, Max." She pointed at a wooden chair against the wall. "Drag that one over. It might be better, considering your trousers."

I put the wooden chair beside the two upholstered chairs in front of her desk and sat. I wanted a cigarette.

Ruth leaned back in the chair and folded her arms over her breasts. The heavy black sweater looked handmade. She studied my face. "When did you grow the beard?" she said. "I sort of like it."

"Forget the beard," I said. "The Whitefork is full of dead trout."

She frowned. "What do you mean, dead trout?"

"Just what it sounds like," I said and told her what I'd just seen and about how I'd noticed drums of diesel fuel near the river up at the clear-cut. She listened calmly, occasionally leaning forward and writing something on the yellow legal pad on her otherwise empty desk. I'd almost forgotten what an attractive woman she was. I had seen her smiling face on dozens of election posters last year, but they did nothing to project the magnetism she radiated in person. She still wore her chestnut hair short with a feathery fringe of bangs to just above her big, green eyes. She had a small nose, startlingly white skin, and deep dimples that showed themselves whether she smiled or frowned.

When I finished talking, she wrote a few more things on the yellow pad and said, "You want some coffee, Max?"

I shook my head. There was a light knock on the door and it opened. She looked up and I turned. "Wally," she said, "come in." She motioned the bespectacled man in the doorway to the seat beside me, making introductions as he crossed the room. Wallace Murray and I shook hands and he sat. He set his large briefcase on the floor between our chairs and eyed my wet clothes. He was a thin, balding, fortyish man who had deluded himself into believing the hair above his right ear could be pulled up over his head to disguise his baldness. His skin was sick-room pale and not at all helped by the bank of fluorescents above Ruth's desk. Responding to some nervous tic he no longer was aware of, his bushy eyebrows never stopped moving up and down above the rims of his glasses.

"Wally and I used to be partners in that law firm in Montpelier," Ruth said to me. "I think he might be able to give you some options, Max. Especially in light of these recent developments." She fidgeted in her chair. "But before you tell him what you just told me, I want to tell you both something." She cleared her throat and looked at Wally. "I'm almost embarrassed by how much I didn't know about our town's largest employer until Max called me last night." She drummed her pencil on the pad. "I checked into some things and, evidently, Alphonse Collari has very little to do with the day-to-day operation in Loon anymore. As chairman of the board of directors, Claremont Taylor makes most of the decisions these days."

"Claremont?" Wally said. "I thought he was just counsel."

"He's that too."

"What's the difference who's running it," I said. "I thought they made a guarantee to the town that logs for the mill would come only from Canada."

"That's the other assumption I made also, Max," Ruth said and looked at Wally. "Did you bring copies of the land use documents?"

Wally nodded, unsnapped and opened his briefcase. He took out a sheaf of papers and looked at me. "When Ruth called me, Mr. Addams, I had the same questions you do." He shrugged. "But," he licked his index finger and leafed through the top several pages, "I found out different." He stopped leafing. "It seems that a couple years ago, while Claremont Taylor was still mayor, he authorized a rider to—" his finger trailed down the page and stopped "—paragraph sixteen that, in essence, gives Collari the option to temporarily log their properties within Loon . . ."

"Temporarily log?" I said. "What's temporarily?"

"Let me finish, Mr. Addams." He returned to reading. "It says they can log if the quantity of raw materials from other sources fall below the number of board feet needed to keep the mill operating at a minimum of sixty percent capacity."

"You mean, what they're doing is legal?"

"Well," his eyebrows bounced, "yes. Even though there seem to be a few discrepancies to the titles on some portions of the Morning Mountain property," he shrugged, "from my point of view what Collari is doing is legal."

"It was, Wally," Ruth said. "Give him a brief rundown of what you've just described to me, Max."

Eyebrows dancing, Wally listened attentively while I told him about the diesel in the clearcut, the lack of hay bales, and my dead trout. When I'd finished, he nodded and smiled. "You're lucky," he said.

"Lucky?" It seemed a poor time for jokes. "Diesel fuel killing my trout?"

"Yes," he said, looking at Ruth. "The diesel spill creates an ecological problem we can prove right now."

"Then, we can stop them?" I asked. "When?"

"As soon as I get the T.R.O. paperwork done." He shrugged. "And we get Judge Emery to sign off on it."

"T.R.O.?" I looked at Ruth.

"Temporary restraining order," she said. "It'll stop them until they clean up the source of the diesel."

"Yes," Wally said, "there will have to be a waiting

period to see that the problem doesn't recur. And they'll have to have the area inspected." He ran his hand gently over his thin hair. "I would imagine they'll be out of business for a week. Maybe ten days."

"That's not good enough," I said. "I want to stop the clear-cutting permanently."

Ruth sat forward. "You want to what?" She looked stunned.

Wally looked at her and then back at me. "That changes things quite a bit, Mr. Addams."

"How?"

"It's not that easy. You'd need evidence to prove they should be stopped permanently."

"Like what?"

"Well," Wally glanced at Ruth again, "you'd have to produce proof in court that what Collari is doing on Morning Mountain seriously affects the environment long-term. Then you would be able to serve them with a permanent injunction." The eyebrows were going up and down like crazy. "That would stop what they're doing. For good."

"When would I go to court?"

"Depends on Judge Emery," he said. "There are a lot of things on the docket this time of year." He looked at the mayor. "What do you estimate, Ruth? A month?"

She nodded. "No more than that. Probably a lot less. Every day Collari's not logging because of the T.R.O. is going to cost them plenty and as soon as Claremont gets wind of a possible injunction, he'll do everything he can to reduce the time Max needs to gather evidence. He'll get it in court as quick as possible. You know that he has the clout to push them to the front of the line."

"I appreciate how important your business is to you, Mr. Addams," Wally said, "but, if it's a permanent injunction you want, you're going to have to be able to prove more than just a few dead trout. The case you'd need to build," he pulled Ruth's legal pad to his side of the desk, thumb-clicked a pen, and began to write, "would have to have human implications. You'll have to prove that potentially serious long-term environmental damage has been and is being done. It's not easy and the court seldom smiles fondly on those who cry wolf." He tore off the page and handed it to me. "I've made a list of some things you would need to do as soon as possible after we get the T.R.O. and the court order."

I looked at the list. He'd printed three items in the center of the page. "I've been testing the water in the river for years," I said. "But how am I supposed to sample the aquifer? And the soil?"

"You'd need a registered U.S. geologist for that," he said. "Someone with not only the equipment and expertise to take core samples, but a professional who's testimony will be admissible in court." He made a note on the yellow pad. "I'll be happy to contact a couple we have here in the state."

"I know one," I said. "He's from Colorado, however."

"As long as he's a registered U.S. geologist," Wally snapped his briefcase shut, "and you have the court order with which he can operate, he's legal." He smiled. "Coming from another state isn't a bad idea, actually. Once Claremont knows what you're up to, he'll probably attempt to make sure all the local geologists are busy until well after any trial date you can get."

"Max," Ruth said, "are you sure you really . . . ?"

I ignored her. "How do I get this court order?" I said to Wally.

"You'd have to file for the court order after you get the T.R.O." His eyebrows jumped. "It's not as easy as it sounds. You'd have to prove to Judge Emery just cause."

"Will you represent me?"

"If it's all right with Ruth." He looked at her.

She shrugged. "You're already involved, Wally."

"Okay," he said, pulling a business card from his breast pocket and handing it to me, his demeanor shifting abruptly from matter-of-fact to enthusiastic. "The T.R.O. is the easy part. The key will be to get the court order and begin accumulating evidence as soon as possible, before Collari has a chance to really clean things up or, more likely, block access to the site. With the court order we'll have a legal right to gather evidence anywhere on their land."

"What do you mean, block access to the site?"

He shrugged and his eyebrows danced. "Once it becomes common knowledge we intend to go for an injunction, Claremont's not going to sit still while we gather evidence on their land against them. There are several ways they could legally deny you access," he said. "Court order or no court order. As an example, it would only take a small accident up there to make it possible for Claremont to declare the clear-cut area temporarily unsafe and therefore closed."

I was a bit overwhelmed, but I nodded anyway.

"And don't worry about that diesel in your water, Mr. Addams," Wally said. "I'll stipulate immediate removal of all equipment and fuel supplies in the T.R.O. It'll be gone by the end of the day." He stood. "Can I call you Max?"

I nodded.

"Good." He smiled and his eyebrows slowed. "I'll need you to take me out to your lodge, Max. I want to get some Polaroids of the dead trout and the clear-cut. I'll also need a vial of tainted river water to show to Judge Emery."

I stood also. "I assume," I said to him, "that you aren't free. What's all this going to cost me?"

He told me his standard rate and this time my eyebrows jumped. "But let's wait until the data's accumulated," he said. "And the injunction is filed. Perhaps then we can sue for damages." He picked up his brief-case. "That way Collari will pay me."

"What damages? The dead trout?"

"That's one thing. They are your livelihood, Mr. Addams," he said. "Also, I assume you're going to lose some business. It won't take long for a fish kill on the Whitefork River to make it into the newspapers."

"Wally?" Ruth said. "Could you wait outside for a second? I want to say a few things to Max."

Wally's eyebrows bounced and he nodded.

When the door closed behind him, she said, "I hadn't planned on you seeking a permanent injunction, Max." She stood and looked out the window behind her desk. "Collari International has been quite good for the economy of this town. Many of our citizens' and businesses' livelihoods depend almost exclusively on the plant." It was the first time since entering the room that I'd even looked at her figure. It was all still there and as nice as I remembered. She turned and faced me. "If you succeed in stopping the logging for good and shut them down, Max, there's bound to be trouble. For all of us. Claremont's already indicated he intends to run against me next election. So as you can imagine, this will probably put me in a tight spot politically." She sighed. "As Wally said, there will no doubt be a great deal of publicity. Add to that, you and I and our . . . ah, our personal history and, well," she leaned on the desk, "I'm going to need your cooperation, Max. For the record, this meeting never happened. Publicly, you're on your own on this."

"I understand," I said.

"Privately, however," she smiled, "you, of all people, should know how I feel about things like clear-cutting. And you must know I'll do everything, behind the scenes, that I can to help you." She scribbled something on a sheet of paper, tore it off and handed it across the desk to me. "I moved. This is my new home phone number. Keep me informed." She crossed the room to the door and put her hand on the knob.

I watched her, then folded the paper and stuck it in my back pocket. "Thanks," I said, joining her at the door. "And sorry about barging in here like I did."

"That's all right," she said. "You never were very predictable." She smiled and opened the door. "I always kind of liked that."

CHAPTER SIX

"Max. Come out here quick." Stormy stood in the middle of the front yard, her hands cupped around her ears, the breeze blowing the skirt of her caftan around the tops of her Bean boots. "Come here."

I stepped out the screened door onto the porch. Spotter shot by me down the steps to Stormy.

"Listen to that," she said, pointing up over the lodge toward Morning Mountain. "Listen."

"I don't hear anything."

"Exactly." She beamed and scratched Spotter's ears. "Them goddamn chainsaws have stopped."

I looked at my watch. It was four o'clock. "It must be the restraining order," I said. "Wally told me the sheriff would serve it between three and four."

"You get the mail yet?"

"I'll get it as soon as I talk to John," I said and went back inside to the phone where I'd been when Stormy began yelling. I redialed John Purcell's office number in Boulder, Colorado. He was a geologist, specializing in plate tectonics, and worked for the U.S. Geological Service. We had met one year on Montana's Madison River as we huddled with several other anglers under a cut in the bank waiting out a severe electrical storm. We'd fished the rest of the week together and had been friends ever since.

The woman who answered at John's office said he'd just come back from Mexico, but was now out of the office at a meeting.

I left a message for him to call me when he returned. "Write the word *important* on it," I said to her. "And underline it."

Then with Spotter wandering, sniffing, and peeing as we went, I walked up our mile-long access road to get the mail. I tried to keep him on the shoulder and out of the mud but the numerous deer tracks punched into the soft earth had to be investigated and he went diligently from one to the next, sticking his muddy snout into each hole and inhaling deeply. I smiled. For Spotter, every road was an information highway. Halfway up the hill, the access road cuts close to the river and I walked over to see if the fish had stopped dying. I could see Chad and Tonya down through the trees waist deep in a run I call "the Billiard." They were casting into a big pocket of holding water behind one of the six massive granite boulders dumped there years ago by the road-building crew. Tonya saw me and waved. Although she looked like a young Joan Wulff in her hat, vest, and waders, Tonya still couldn't cast to save her life.

"How are the trout?" I yelled.

"Big and hungry," Chad yelled back.

"Any more dead ones?"

"A couple."

I waved and Spotter and I continued on up to the mailbox.

At the top of the access road, I saw it. Spotter did too and began barking. My brand new, four-foot-by-four-foot, carved Whitefork Lodge sign with the jumping brook trout in the middle lay on its side, the post that held it cut cleanly through three feet from the ground, obviously the victim of an enraged logger's chainsaw. My mailbox hadn't fared much better. It hung askew on its post, a large dent in its side. The mail was scattered in the mud and Spotter sniffed each piece as I picked it up. It was only junk and bills and I stuffed them in the pocket of my jacket. I could hear the scolding caw of crows up on the mountain across Route 16.

Strangely, I wasn't angry about the sign. Red and I could put in a new post in less than an hour and with three screws fix the mailbox. No, I wasn't angry. I understood why the loggers had done it. I'd stopped the logging. I was the enemy. In their anger, they couldn't know that the real enemies were the people who presumed the Earth to be theirs for the taking. The farmers, developers, miners, and lumbermen like Collari hid behind the facade of public progress and raped ecosystems for personal financial gain. The loggers who cut down my sign couldn't see it yet, but the same thing happening to the world's rainforests was happening on Morning Mountain.

Spotter was barking again, this time from the other side of Route 16, where I could see him wagging his tail just inside the trees.

At night, Whitetail deer use the lodge's access road to get to the lake and it isn't uncommon to be sitting on the porch, watching the last streaks of a sunset, when suddenly a dozen nervous does materialize in the front yard. They come down from the thick hemlock groves high on Collari's land using a faint deer trail that, once you know it's there, you can see directly across from my mailbox.

That's where Spotter was now and since I was curious to see how many more trees Collari had cut before the sheriff had served the T.R.O., I decided to follow the dog and take a look. I also wanted to make sure the loggers had taken everything with them, especially the drums of diesel.

I whistled for Spotter to wait, crossed 16 and we began picking our way up the narrow trail. Nose to the ground and ears flapping, he wormed his way ahead of me, seeming to shed a year with every hundred or so feet of elevation we ascended until, with the clear-cut finally visible through the trees, he was romping like a puppy.

I could hear the sound of metal striking metal from above me and I stopped just inside the treeline. I peered up into the clear-cut. Not only were another five or six acres of trees gone, but the dark green Range Rover was back. And it wasn't alone. A red, extended cab pickup loaded with hay bales sat beside it.

My eyes followed the clanging sound. To the right, I could see two men wrestling hay bales into a zig-zag line along the river while a third pounded metal stakes through them. Fifty yards further up, near a still-smoldering pile of trimmings, stood Alphonse Collari and Bull. Collari was talking on a small cellular phone, his gold watch glinting in the sun.

Spotter barked and bounded playfully toward the men at the hay bales. Before I could get him back, Bull saw us and said something to Collari who slowly turned his head and glowered down at me. "Addams!" he yelled as he folded the phone. "Addams! I want to talk to you." He stuffed the phone in his shirt pocket and, pointing his big finger at me, lumbered down the hill. "Hold on there, Addams!" Bull followed at a respectful distance.

The men working around the hay bales stopped and watched. I held Spotter's collar and wished I'd left well enough alone and just taken the mail down to the lodge.

Collari was almost as mountainous as Bull with a snow cap of white hair, bushy black eyebrows, a flat nose, and a permanent tan. He was a handsome man, looking closer to forty than sixty. The sleeves of his trademark khaki shirt were rolled to the biceps, his khaki trousers creased and tucked into high-laced, well-oiled Gokey boots.

The two of them stopped at a peeling yellow birch ten feet away and glared at me. Bull reached out and bent a branch down and away from Collari's head. It splintered. Spotter growled.

"Do you realize what you've done, Addams?" Collari said.

"You're the one who's done it," I said. "I'm just protecting what's mine."

"This isn't yours up here," Bull said.

"Yes, I know this land up here isn't mine." I pointed to the hay bales. "Maybe now, some of it will stay up here."

"If you had a problem with what we were doing," Collari said, "why didn't you contact me?"

"I might have if my trout hadn't started dying," I said. "Then it was too late for conversations."

"This restraining order of yours is costing me a great deal of money."

"You should have thought of that before you began clear-cutting."

"You better watch it, Addams." Bull took a couple steps toward me. "There are worse things that can happen down there at that lodge of yours than trout dying."

"Is that a threat?"

"No one's making any threats, Addams," Collari said and he pulled Bull back and said something to him I couldn't hear. Bull gave me a dark look and reluctantly went over to the men working on the hay bales. Collari watched him go and then looked back at me. "Bull is angry, Addams," he said. "As are most of the men who were working up here. But I've told them"—he pointed to the hay bales—"that diesel was a stupid mistake. Precautions should have been taken. It should not have been allowed to leak into the river." He looked at me as if he expected a comment. When I said nothing, he said, "But it's fixed now." He smiled, "And as soon as the inspection verifies that fact, I hope we can resume our roles as good neighbors."

I shook my head and gestured to the naked mountainside. "Not if you're going to keep cutting like this."

He sighed. "This is the way it's done, Addams. To get at the trees we need, a few others have to be sacrificed. You obviously don't understand modern logging."

"I guess not," I said. "But then, I don't understand strip-mining either."

"There's no law against cutting like this."

"That doesn't make it right."

"I want to remind you, Addams," he said, "now that the accident has been rectified, the terms in your restraining order have been satisfied." He shrugged. "It's really no business of yours any longer what I intend to do."

"I think it is," I said, but I didn't think it prudent to mention the court order or the permanent injunction I had in mind.

He looked at his watch. "I've wasted enough time here." He turned and waved Bull back. Then he looked at me again. "Mark my words, Addams, I'm not going to put up with any more of this kind of inconvenience. I've spent the better part of my life building this company. The mill in Loon is important and I'm not about to let you, or anyone like you, threaten it." He took two steps toward me. "If you think you're going to take this any farther than a restraining order, you'd better be well prepared. Because if you fail, I'm not just going to sue you. I'm going to squash you—" he slapped his big palm on the birch "—just like that." Then he smiled. "You understand?"

There wasn't much I could say so I didn't say anything. I just shook my head, turned, and, dragging Spotter by the collar, walked away. As I picked my way back down the deer trail, I heard him call after me, "Don't let this thing get any bigger, Addams."

It wasn't until Spotter and I were back at the mailbox that I noticed my hands were shaking. And by the time I got back down to the lodge and into the hallway, I'd thought of a dozen pithy things I should have said to Collari instead of just walking away, and when the phone rang, I reached for it, ready to kick ass.

"No, Max." Stormy came running from the kitchen carrying an empty saucepan in one hand and a big steel ladle in the other. "Let me get that, Max. I'm ready for 'em now." She rapped the spoon on the pan with an almost deafening clang.

I stepped between her and the ringing phone. "What's going on?"

"Obscene phone calls," she said. "Been gettin' 'em almost since you left." She banged the pot again. "A shot of this in the ear'll fix the bastards. Pick it up and hold it over here."

I held up my hand. "Wait a minute, huh? It could be John calling back." I picked up the receiver. "Whitefork Lodge," I said.

It was Stephanie. She was mad. "Dammit, Max," she said. "What the hell are you trying to do to me?"

"You?"

"Yes, me. Collari Purchasing just canceled my order. And you know why? Because of you and your damn restraining order is why."

I sighed. "I'm sorry, Steph," I said. "I didn't have any choice. They were killing my fish."

"Your fish? Jesus!"

"Steph, c'mon, I . . ."

"You could have waited!" She almost sounded like she was crying. "Or, at least told me, dammit!"

"I said I'm sorry. I didn't know I was going to do it until this morning." I suddenly felt like shit. "There'll be other orders."

"No! I want this one, Max."

"Is it canceled for good?"

She was silent for a couple seconds.

"Steph?"

She sighed. "I don't know," she said. "They say that if this thing is resolved soon enough, the order will stand."

"What do they mean by that?"

"I said, I don't know," she snapped. "I guess if you're happy with the way they clean things up and rescind the restraining order then they can go back to work and . . ."

"I'm not going to rescind anything, Steph."

"You're not? What? Why, for chrissakes?"

"Because they're clear-cutting is why. They're taking every tree off the mountain."

"They're loggers, Max. Damn you! That's what loggers do. They cut trees. If . . ." She started to say something and then was quiet.

I waited. I could hear her breathing. Finally I said, "You all right, Steph?"

"No, I'm not all right! How would you be?" Another long pause. "I want this order. I want that child, Max."

"You'll get it," I said, but the line was already dead. She had hung up.

The phone rang again immediately. "Now, it's my turn," Stormy said, grabbing the receiver, dropping it in the pot, and beating on the pot several times with the spoon.

I snatched the spoon from her hand and dug the receiver out of the pot. "Hello?" I said.

"Good God, Max," the voice said.

"It's Red," I said, glaring at Stormy.

"Oops." She smiled sheepishly.

"What was that noise, Max?" he said. " 'Bout damn near broke my eardrum. Over."

I frowned at Stormy. "Stormy's had some obscene phone calls this afternoon and . . . what did you say?"

"I said 'over.' I'm on one of Collari's two-way radios. Phone company patched me through. Over."

"Where are you?"

"Up on Hooker Hill Road. Max, I gotta talk to you. Over."

"So, talk."

"Not on this thing. Over."

"Then when?"

"I'm comin' down to the lodge, Max. Wait 'til you hear what I just found out. You're never gonna believe who's got a big piece of the action up here. Over."

"The clear-cutting?"

"Yeah. And all the land we been doin' it on too." There was a crackle of static. "I gotta drop off some tools at the mill first. See you in about an hour. Ten-four."

The line went dead and a woman's voice came on. "Is your radio call concluded, sir?" I said yes and hung up.

"What was that all about?" Stormy asked.

"Your guess is as good as mine." I shrugged. "Something about the clear-cut. Someone else involved. I don't know. He wouldn't tell me. He was on one of the two-way radios. He's coming down here in about an hour."

"What's the difference who's involved?" she said. "Long as they've stopped cuttin'?"

The phone rang again. "What is this?" I said. We don't usually get two phone calls a week.

"Give it to me, Max," she said, reaching for the

phone. "I know this is one of them dirty calls. This time I'll . . ."

Once again I beat her to the receiver but this time wished I'd let her have it. "Max," the nasal voice said, "this is Gordon Miller at the *Sentinel.*"

I mouthed "Gordon Miller" to Stormy and she rolled her eyes. "Hello, Gordon," I said to him.

"We're running a story, Max, about your fight with Collari and I'd like to check a couple things."

"My what?"

"Your fight. This thing with Collari. Is it true you don't intend to rescind the restraining order even if they clean up the site and guarantee you won't experience another diesel spill?"

"Where did you hear that?" I'd only told Stephanie a few minutes earlier.

"You know I can't divulge my sources, Max. Is it true?"

"Gordon," I was trying hard to be polite and not just hang up on him, "I really don't have anything to tell you at this time."

"How many trout died, Max?"

"I haven't counted them."

"Gonna hurt your business?"

"It hasn't yet."

"So, your business is good while the pulp mill prepares to close down? Hmm, doesn't seem fair, Max. It's going to close if they can't get to those trees and a lot of people are going to be laid off. How do you feel about that, Max?"

"It's not my fault."

"Are you saying that if the mill closes, it's Collari's fault?"

"I'm not saying anything. Goodbye, Gordon." I hung up.

"God, I hate that kid," Stormy said.

Gordon Miller Junior had been in his last year of journalism school when his father was killed in a hunting accident and left him the bi-weekly *Loon Sentinel* newspaper. That was two years ago and since then, twenty-two-year-old Gordon had managed to aggravate just about everyone in Loon township with his sensational tabloid style of reporting. Under his father's tutelage, the *Sentinel* had been a responsible community newspaper with a down-home brand of news that was actually enjoyable reading. Its community-oriented features like "Main Street Profiles," "School Sports," "Backcountry Hunter & Fisherman," and the ever-popular, "Loon Police Blotter" were looked forward to every Monday and Thursday. Gordon Junior's *Sentinel* was completely redesigned and looked to me like a cross between *Mad* magazine and the *National Enquirer.* Its biggest feature each week was a libelous thing called "Upcountry Insider." Little Gordon authored all four pages of its borderline slanderous gossip. For Gordon, having Whitefork Lodge and Collari International in a pissing contest that was likely to cost the latter hundreds of thousands of dollars a week in downtime was a dream come true.

By six-thirty, the Harpers were back from the river with excited stories of seeing a bull moose in velvet, all the beautiful brook trout Chad had caught, and the brown Tonya had hooked accidentally. I was only listening half-heartedly. It had been well over an hour since Red's call, and he still hadn't shown up. I excused myself and went to the kitchen.

"Call down to the Starlight, Max," Stormy said when I asked her what she thought. "Prob'ly stopped for a beer and forgot the time."

Stormy followed me out to the phone and I called the bar and Skip yelled into the phone over the background noise that he hadn't seen Red since lunch. "But, hell, that was hours ago. Want me to give 'im a message when he comes in?"

"No. Thanks, Skip." I hung up and looked at Stormy.

"Maybe he forgot," Stormy said. "Call Wilba. Bet he's there."

I did. He wasn't. "I was just going to call you, Max," Wilba said. "I was hoping he was at the lodge. He should have been home by now. He called me from up on Hooker Hill Road too. Said he was taking something to the mill then going to the lodge for a few minutes. He said he'd be here in plenty of time for supper."

"Did you call the mill?" I said.

"Yes. They never saw him."

"I don't want to alarm you, Wilba," I said. "But maybe you should call the sheriff."

"I'm going to. It wouldn't be the first time he's been stuck in that mud up there."

"Let me know, will you?"

She said she'd call me as soon as she found him and we hung up. I looked at Stormy and shook my head. "She thinks he's hung up in the mud somewhere."

"That don't make sense," she said. "He's got that two-way. He was in trouble, all he'd hafta do is start broadcasting. Even the sheriff would hear him sooner or later."

"I know," I said. "This isn't like Red at all."

CHAPTER SEVEN

Rayleen and Stormy came rattling down the access road first thing Friday morning. I took my coffee cup and went out onto the porch to meet them. The old International idled thin, blue exhaust while Stormy climbed down from the cab. She looked like she hadn't gotten any more sleep than I had.

By ten last night, I had talked to Wilba Crosley four times, Sheriff Darren Foley twice, and Stormy once after each. The bottom line was, by midnight, still no Red and not even a hint as to where he might have gone. I went to bed at one A.M. worrying about where he might be and frustrated with the feeling that there was nothing I could do about it.

Stormy clumped slowly up onto the porch, looked at me hopefully. "Nothin' yet, huh?" she said. "This just ain't like him."

"You talk to Wilba this morning?"

She nodded. "Poor woman. And them little boys keep askin' where's their daddy."

Rayleen leaned out the truck window. "Run into the sheriff down at Freddie's," he said, sipping at the lid of a takeout coffee.

"You talk to him?"

He shook his head. "Was gettin' my coffee. Stormy talked to him, though."

"Get this, Max," Stormy laughed ruefully. "He said they're thinkin' maybe Red was depressed."

"Depressed? About what?"

"About how the mill most likely will be closin'," Rayleen said.

"Can you believe it, Max?" Stormy shook her head at the absurdity of it. "They're startin' to say maybe he mighta gone off on a toot."

"Well," Rayleen said, "stranger things have happened. And yesterday was payday."

"Dammit, Rayleen!" Stormy stomped her foot. "Red didn't go off on no toot. Red don't toot. He hardly drinks and you know it." We heard a door slam upstairs. "Well," she said, "I got me a couple guests who'll be wantin' some breakfast 'fore long. We ain't helpin' nobody standin' here jawin'."

Rayleen nodded and ground the truck into gear and then, trailing a morse code of exhaust, rattled back up the access road and out of sight.

Stormy walked by me into the lodge.

"Don't worry. Red will turn up," I said after her. "And he'll have a good reason for being gone too."

At breakfast Chad asked if he could help me clear the dead trout from the lake. "If we each take a canoe," he said, "it'll go faster."

Stormy smiled and poured him a cup of coffee. We both liked guests who pitched in without being told. She sat down and Tonya passed her the scrambled eggs just as the phone rang. "Might be news of Red," she said. "Want me to get it?"

"I'll get it." I took a sip of coffee and stood. "If it's not Red, it could be John calling me back."

"Red?" Tonya's eyes widened. "What's happened to Red?"

I left Stormy explaining Red's disappearance to Chad and Tonya and went out to the phone.

"Hey." It was John. "What could possibly be going on out there that's so, quote unquote, important?" He laughed. "With an underline, no less. What's up, Max?"

"I need your help."

"Help?"

"Yeah." And I told him what had been happening.

When I'd finished he said, "Christ! Even I've heard of Collari. Boston, right? I think they've got land out here. Up near Loveland." Then he laughed again. "And you've got a restraining order? And they actually stopped logging?"

"For now," I said. "That's why I need you. I want them to stay stopped. I'm going for a permanent injunction. I need cores taken of the aquifer. See if there's anything in the ground that I can use in court."

"Jesus, Max. When?"

"As soon as you can get here."

I heard him sigh. "I don't know, Max. I'm committed. I'm the featured speaker at a conference on mountain building the first of next week."

"Where?"

"In Boston."

"So come here first. We're on the way."

"On the way?" He laughed.

"It's your chance to finally fish the Whitefork." In all the years we'd been friends and fished together, John had never been to Whitefork Lodge. "I only have two guests right now," I said. "When was the last time you fished for big, wild, hungry brookies with only two other rods on the water?"

"Now, that's a dirty trick, Max."

I knew it was and I laughed. John had once told me

that the main reason he was a geologist was because of the field work. It took him near so much great trout water.

"All right," he said, "you got me. What do you need exactly?"

"According to my lawyer," I said, "I need some cores taken, as well as soil and water samples. You bring what's necessary."

"We've got a portable unit I've been wanting to try," he said. "Fits in a thing the size of a golf bag."

"Good. How soon can you get here?"

"Tomorrow night okay? I gotta go to San Francisco first and look at a crack in the field at Candlestick Park."

"A crack?"

"Yeah. A fissure's been opening on the third base line since the last big quake. They keep filling it with dirt and the dirt keeps disappearing. Eats ground balls too."

We laughed.

"I'll come directly to Vermont from there," he said. "Where do you want me to fly in to?"

"Burlington would be best. It's about an hour and a half from the lodge. I'll pick you up."

"Just remember, Max. I can take the cores, but there's no guarantee they'll show anything. It might be too early yet. It can take a long time for stuff to seep down into the aquifer. Especially when it has to go through all that Triassic sill you've got in those mountains of yours."

"I have to try."

We talked a few more minutes. He said he'd call back with his flight numbers and I said I'd reimburse him for my part of the fare. He didn't argue. After we said goodbye, I returned to the dining room.

"It was John," I said.

"He gonna take those core things you need?" Stormy asked.

I nodded and sat down. My eggs were cold.

"When's he comin'?"

"Tomorrow night."

"Well, well," she smiled, "I'm finally gonna meet the famous fly-fishin' Cyrano." She looked at Chad. "I hear tell, there are a lot of men who wish when they die that John Purcell's life would flash before their eyes."

A columnist for *Fly, Rod & Reel* magazine, in an article about fly fishing in Vermont, gave the Whitefork Lodge his highest rating, describing our portion of the White-fork River as being "brook trout cold and brook trout clean." I've always liked that description. In fact, I like it so much that it's been on the cover of our brochure for the last three years.

Unfortunately, "brook trout clean" can become "brook trout dirty" real fast because the more fragile brookies are the first of the three species we have up here to suffer the effects of pollution. So it didn't come as a surprise when, of the 181 dead trout Chad and I collected from the lake, 177 were brookies.

We used our nets and it took us almost four hours to criss-cross the lake, scooping the dead fish from the water into the bottoms of our canoes. It was sickening. Most of them were well over a foot long, had bloated in the sun, and were beginning to smell, and every time we'd think we had them all, one of us would spot another clump of white bellies floating somewhere else.

Once we had them all, we dragged them up behind the lodge and buried them deep in Stormy's vegetable garden. Then we washed out the canoes and went to take showers, although I was positive it would be a long time before I forgot the smell.

Stormy was just putting out the lunch buffet when I

got out of the shower. Tonya and Chad were setting the table.

"You just missed Stephanie," she said. "Came and brought her bags."

"Was she mad?"

She shrugged. "A little. Said she'll be back for dinner. You can ask her then."

We heard the rattle of Rayleen's truck and Stormy peered out the window. "What's he doin' here?"

Rayleen parked in front of the porch, climbed out of the truck, and slammed the door. There was raw egg splattered on his windshield.

Stormy wiped her hands on her apron and we all went to the screen door. "What's goin' on?" she said.

"They fired me." He pushed his cap back on his head. "Got to the mill and that damn Bull come over and says to go collect my severance. 'You're through here,' he tells me. You believe it?"

"Bastards," Stormy said, stepping out onto the porch. "It's startin', ain't it?" The Harpers and I followed her.

"What did they fire you for?" I asked.

"Didn't say. But hell, didn't need to ask. You know as well as I do, Max."

I looked at Stormy.

"Max, you thick?" she said. "Rayleen's my brother. I work for you. It's simple as that."

"Is that egg on your truck?" Tonya asked him.

"It was that damn picket line up at the end of the driveway. They throwed 'em." He pointed back up the access road. "Almost weren't gonna let me through."

"What?" I said. "There's a picket line?"

"You bet," he snorted. "Least a dozen women. Carryin' signs, the whole nine yards. Mad as hornets too."

I sighed and sat on the steps. Stormy was right. It was starting.

"Max?" Stormy put her hand on my shoulder. "I

might know some of 'em. Want me to go up there and see what's on their minds?"

"Don't take no genius to see what's on them girls' minds," Rayleen said. "Most every sign they're carryin' says the same thing about lettin' Collari back at them trees on Mornin' Mountain." He looked at Stormy. "You'll see."

"No," I said. "Everybody stay here. I don't want any of us dodging rotten eggs or getting into shouting matches." I stood. "I'm going to call the sheriff. Let him break it up."

Stormy sighed, stuck a Camel in the corner of her mouth, and sat in my place on the step. She looked up at the Harpers. "Welcome to Beirut, kids," she said, cupping a match and lighting the cigarette. "Hope you ain't in no hurry to go nowhere."

Loon County Sheriff Darren Foley was a tall, gaunt man about my age with a narrow, hawkish face, hook nose, and arching eyebrows. He dyed his hair and, in the sunlight streaming in the spotless dining room windows, it looked more purple than the dark brown I was sure he'd intended. He was the only elected official in the county who wore a sport coat, tie, and white shirt every day, and, except for the jeans, today was no different.

Stormy, Rayleen, and I were sitting at the table in the dining room. Spotter was out on the porch and occasionally I could hear his paw thump the screen door telling me he wanted in. Chad and Tonya were out on the lake. Darren stood at the end of the table, his foot up on the seat of a chair. Window light glinted from the handle of the revolver in the holster under his arm.

"Okay," he said. "Them picketers are gone." He looked at me. "They come back, Max, you call me. I told them all, what they was doin' is illegal. If there's a next time, I'll take a few to jail."

"Thanks, Darren," I said. "And thanks for helping us clean up the garbage." The picketers had tossed two large plastic bags of garbage into the Whitefork from the Route 16 bridge as they exited. One had broken open in the river and it had taken all of us an hour to fish out the plastic wrappers, cans, and food that had clogged about two hundred yards of water.

"I don't think you've heard the last of this, Max," he said. "Them folks are pretty mad. Can't say I really blame 'em." He looked at Rayleen. "Heard you was laid off today."

Rayleen nodded.

"You ain't gonna be the last. Soon as them logs in the millyard run out everybody'll be gone." Darren looked back at me. "Max, you really opened a can, didn't you?"

"I didn't have any choice."

"That ain't the word in town," he said.

"I don't care what the damn word in town is." I was getting mad again. "And people better get used to it too. I intend to make sure that bastard stops clear-cutting, period. If it means he closes the mill down for good, tough."

"That's not good, Max," he said.

"I'm sorry," I said. "That's the way it is. You know what clear-cutting does, Darren. Jesus. Yesterday, I had dead trout coming down the river by the bushelful."

"I know, Max," he said, putting down his foot and straightening his jacket. "But a lot of folks don't see it that way. Fish to them ain't the same as they are to you. Far as they can see, it's fish against people. A lot of us think people should come first."

"You're on their side?"

He shrugged. "Don't make no difference whose side I'm on, Max. I enforce the law. Your restrainin' order's a legal document. I served it and I'll make sure it's respected. And them folks picketin' up there on 16? That ain't legal. They was obstructing a state by-way, trespassin' on your property, and intimidating innocent people." He smiled at Rayleen. "It's my job to stop that. What I think about it all ain't relevant." He stooped and peered out the window at the squad car parked in front. A uniformed young man in a Smokey hat leaned against the front fender. "I gotta go," he said, "before Deputy Richards out there falls asleep standin' up."

"Any news on Red?" Stormy asked.

Darren shrugged. "We've had a couple calls on the hotline we set up. None of 'em panned out though. This mornin' I sent Richards all the way to Burlington to look at a John Doe they fished outta Lake Champlain. Wasn't Red, of course." He walked to the dining room door. "So far, there's nothin'. Not a sign of him or his truck."

"You talk to Bull yet, like I told you this mornin'?"

He rolled his eyes. "Stormy," he said, "like I told *you,* this here's still a routine missin'-person thing. I ain't gonna start gettin' folks riled up by makin' them think it's anything more than that." Darren looked at me. "Max, you gotta help me here." He sighed. "This woman thinks she's some sort of Sherlock Holmes. Will you tell her to leave the investigatin' to the people who know what they're doin'?"

I looked at Stormy.

Stormy ignored me and ground her cigarette out in the ashtray. "You got deputies runnin' all the way to Lake Champlain looking at dead bodies, when you ain't even talked to the most obvious folks right here. That's knowin' what you're doin'?" She shoved her chair back and clomped to the doorway, where she stood with hands on her hips and her nose an inch from his tie. "They fired Rayleen 'cause of Max. Maybe they done somethin' to Red for the same reason." She pushed him aside and disappeared down the hall.

We listened to the rubber squeak of her boots fade toward the back of the lodge and then I said, "Sorry, Darren. Red is a good friend."

"I know." He shrugged. "Goes with the territory, Max. You're never doin' enough when it comes to family and friends." He started for the door. "Just tell Stormy to knock this detective stuff off, huh? No sense adding insult to injury. Folks are mad enough already."

Rayleen and I stood and then I accompanied Foley to his squad car. Mark Richards, his pimply-faced deputy, was leaning against the fender scratching his crotch. He stood quickly and clicked his heels together when he saw us coming down the porch steps.

"I told you, Mark," Darren said, opening the passenger door, "cut that heel-clickin' shit out. Makes you look like a Nazi. It's embarrassin'." He climbed in.

"Sorry, sir," Mark said, closing his boss's door and running around to the driver's side, climbing in and starting the engine. He gunned the big V-8 a couple times.

"And cut that out too," Darren said to him and looked up at me through the open window. "Kid watches too many cop shows," he said.

I nodded. "Thanks for your help, Darren."

"I don't begrudge you doin' what you gotta do, Max," he said. "Only do it quick, huh? Before somebody really gets hurt." And then, with a spray of muddy gravel, the big Ford roared away up the access road. I distinctly heard Darren yell just as they rounded the curve, "Dammit, Richards! We ain't in pursuit! Slow down!"

I turned and watched Stormy and Rayleen come out onto the porch. Stormy continued down the steps. "Sorry, Max," she said. "I didn't mean to get so riled in there."

"That's all right. You made your point." I looked up

at Rayleen. "How would you like to start working on the Harley full-time?"

His face brightened. "You mean it, Max? When?"

"How about now?"

"Yessir!" He practically danced down the steps. "Bet I can have that V-twin hummin' by May." He slapped me on the shoulder and, rolling up his sleeves, limped toward the workshop.

"You didn't hafta do that," Stormy said as we started back into the lodge.

"I know. But it's my fault he lost the job at the mill." I smiled. "Besides, I would like to ride that thing one of these days." I held the door for her.

"What would you think if me and Rayleen just stayed here 'til this whole mess ironed itself out? I don't like leavin' you while this is goin' on."

"We've got the room."

"Good. I'll take one them empty rooms upstairs. Rayleen can stay out in the workshop. He'd like that, bein' close to the bike 'n 'all." She squinted out toward the lake. "Think maybe you oughta spend some time with them honeymooners," she said. "They been awful patient through all this."

I turned and looked. Chad and Tonya were at the dock and just tying off the canoe. "You're right," I said. "I promised to give her some casting lessons and still haven't done it."

"Whyn't you take 'em both out on the river? It'll take your mind off Red. I hear anythin', I'll come a-runnin'."

I went down to the dock. "How about that casting lesson now?" I said to Tonya.

She blushed and looked at Chad.

"Can we take a raincheck until tomorrow morning, Max?" he said. "We've been talking and thought we'd do a little sight-seeing this afternoon."

Tonya nodded. "Things seem pretty busy here right

now, so we thought maybe we'd get out of the way for a while."

"You're not in the way," I said. "But I understand. I guess this isn't exactly the vacation you had in mind."

"We don't mind, Max," Chad said. "As long as you don't mind waiting until morning for the lesson."

"No," I said. "But I do apologize for all the aggravation."

"Aggravation?" Tonya laughed. "I think it's exciting."

CHAPTER ✒ EIGHT

I gave the Harpers directions to a few of our local tourist traps including the tasting room at the microbrewery in town that made Loon Lager, then I went to the workshop. I thought I would go see if Rayleen needed anything.

He was already working. The Harley had been winched off the floor and it still swung slightly from the chains attached to its front and rear forks. Dressed in dirty coveralls, he was spreading newspapers beneath it. "Thanks again, Max," he said, unfolding a section of the *Loon Sentinel* and laying it on the floor. "Rather do this any day than work at the mill. Reminds me of when I useta tinker on my own bikes. Hell, we'd go sometimes twenty hours if we had a race comin' up." Rayleen had raced motorcycles in the thirties and was the main reason I'd bought the used Sportster in the first place. Although I had yet to hear a noise from it, he had promised me it was fixable.

"You can work on it night and day if you want," I said. "Stormy and I just agreed that the two of you'll be staying at the lodge for a while instead of town." I gestured to the side room that had the twin bed. "She said you'd like living in there."

He smiled and shuffled to the workbench. "Gonna hafta order a few things from that Harley dealer down to Montpelier," he said, picking up a greasy Harley Davidson parts catalog and thumbing it. "You're gonna want plenty a chrome, I imagine."

"I don't know."

"It's a Harley, Max," he said, walking back to the suspended motorcycle. "Chrome's their middle name."

"You decide." I smiled. "Take what you need from petty cash and give Stormy the receipts. Just get it running, huh?"

"That's easy, Max." He put his dirty hand on the front wheel and gave it a spin. "What I wish is, I knew howta help fix this other mess for you. Collari ain't got but about one or two days worth of logs left at the mill." He gripped the wheel and stopped it. "When them grinders shut down, lotta folks is gonna get laid off real quick and all hell's gonna break loose." He picked at something in the tire tread with his index finger. "That picket line today was mostly women. Them boys down at the mill and up doin' the loggin', now, they're somethin' else again, Max. They ain't gonna be carryin' signs once they lose them paychecks."

"Then they'd better go find logs somewhere else."

"That ain't likely," he said, squatting under the bike and poking a finger in around the mufflers. "Not now anyways. What you and Collari's got here's a pissin' contest, Max. And Collari ain't even doin' the pissin'." He stood and looked at his finger in the light. Then he said, "It's that Claremont who's got the reins now and I'm bettin' he don't care 'bout paychecks any more 'n he cares 'bout fish dyin'." He shook his head. "Nope, that old boy's got his eyes on bein' mayor again and he knows the worse this thing gets, the worse it's gonna make your friend Ruth look. My money says he ain't gonna let Collari back down."

"There's nothing I can do about it, Rayleen."

"I know, Max." He wiped his hands on his coveralls. "I was just sayin' I wish I knew of somethin' that'd help."

"I wish you knew how to find Red."

He sighed. "I ain't said nothin' to Stormy, Max," he said, picking up a socket wrench, "but, I'm thinkin', we ever find that young man, he ain't gonna be breathin'."

"Don't say that, Rayleen."

"Well, somethin's not right about this whole thing, Max. I can feel it. Think the sheriff knows it too. Hell, I've known Red a long time. Knowed his daddy too. Family men, both of 'em. They wasn't the kind to run and hide from nothin'."

The sound of a big car's engine vibrated into the workshop and, thinking it might be Stephanie or someone with news of Red, I stepped outside into the bright sunshine just in time to see Collari's dark green Range Rover pull up in front of the lodge. It was covered with mud. Rayleen stepped out beside me, pulled his cap low and squinted. "Lord, Max. It's Bull and Collari," he said, stepping back into the shadow of the doorway. "What'd'ya s'pose they want?"

"I'm going to find out," I said and walked across the yard toward the Rover.

"Them fellas don't look very happy," Rayleen said from behind me as Alphonse Collari climbed out of the passenger side and Bull Turlock got out from behind the wheel. As I closed the distance, I could see Claremont Taylor was in the back seat. He didn't seem interested in getting out.

I met them at the porch steps.

Collari's hands were in his pockets. He put a boot up on the lowest step. "Nice place you've got here, Addams," he said, looking up at the lodge. "You don't find spruce logs like those anywhere but out West these days."

"What can I do for you, Collari?" I climbed the steps and stood above them.

Bull crossed his forearms over the tan front of his Tear-Pruf jacket. "You can stop this restraining order bullshit, is what you can do," he growled. I couldn't see his mouth move in the thick black beard.

"I can't stop what's been done."

"Hell, you can't," he said, and drew a deep breath as though he was going to say something else. He didn't.

Instead, Collari said, "Look, Addams. I've come out here because I don't think you understand what's at stake." He gestured toward the mountain behind us. "I need that timber."

"You didn't hear me very well yesterday, did you?" I said.

"Oh, I heard you, Addams," he said. "I was just hoping perhaps you'd had the time to see things my way." He glanced at the Rover. "You must know I'm going to have to close down the mill if I don't get logs."

"So I've been told." I shook my head. "But as I told you, get your logs from someplace else."

"I can tell you," he said, "the people in town aren't going to like that." I could see the muscles in his jaw working.

"They already don't," I said. "We've had threatening phone calls and they've been out here picketing." I looked down at Bull. "Not to mention my sign cut down and sacks of garbage in the river."

"Listen, Addams, you pussy." Bull came around Collari and up one step. He was just below me. Only a couple feet away. I could smell alcohol on his breath. "You ain't seen nothin' yet."

"Bull!" Claremont Taylor opened the car door and slowly climbed out. "Bull," he said, "back off, boy."

Claremont walked toward the porch. Static electricity had stuck the cuffs of his wrinkled gray suit pants high on his calf-length socks. He pushed Bull out of the way and stepped up in front of me. "We ain't here to threaten, Max." He smiled, brushing a loose lock of silver hair from his forehead. "We just come by for a friendly little chat." He winked. "And, to make you an offer. If you're willing to listen."

Bull glared at me. I didn't say anything.

Claremont continued, "Mr. Collari here is prepared to reimburse you, handsomely, I might add, for any inconvenience the little accident up on Morning Mountain might have caused you. In return"—he slipped his hand into the inside pocket of his crumpled suit jacket and produced a folded sheet of paper—"I've taken the liberty of drawing up a document that, well, lets you end this foolishness once and for all."

"I'm listening," I said.

He unfolded the paper and held it out to me.

I shook my head. "Just give me a summary," I said.

He sighed and took a pair of gold-rimmed half glasses from his breast pocket. When he had them on, he tipped his head back and looked at the paper. "Basically," he said, "Collari International will pay Whitefork Lodge fifty thousand dollars for inconveniences, aggravations, and business lost as a result of the diesel fuel leak on Morning Mountain. In return"—he looked at me over the glasses—"Whitefork Lodge agrees to rescind the temporary restrainin' order and not pursue a permanent injunction"—he glanced at me over the glasses again—"or any other foolishness designed to keep Mr. Collari here from his trees."

"In other words," I said, looking at Collari, "you get to go back to clear-cutting. Right?"

"Well, yes," Claremont answered for him. "Logging would resume as before." He handed the paper to me, took off the glasses, and smiled. "Of course, we would guarantee that special care would be taken with fuel and other materials to prevent another accident."

I refolded the paper. "You guys don't get it, do you?" Their faces darkened as if a cloud had just passed over. "The diesel spill isn't what this is about. This is about the way you cut trees. The clear-cutting. Stripping every damn tree from that mountain." I stuffed the paper back into Claremont's hands. "I don't care about the diesel. It's the long-term I'm worried about. You take all those trees and more than likely I kiss all this goodbye."

"You're gonna kiss a lot more than that goodbye," Bull sneered.

"Screw you, Bull," I said and then looked at Collari. "And screw this bribe too."

"I told you before, Addams," Collari said. "And I'm telling you again. You're making a very big mistake." He had amazing control.

"We know you're mullin' over seekin' a permanent injunction, Max," Claremont said. "Certainly would hate to see it come to that."

"You know how to avoid it," I said.

Claremont smiled. "It'll take a lot more than a few dead trout to convince someone like my friend Judge Emery. Your attorney advise you of that, Max?"

"My attorney advised me of everything."

"He tell you, that's private property up there on Morning Mountain? You come on Mr. Collari's land without proper cause and that's trespassin'. Punishable by fine or jail, or both?"

"Or you could get your ass shot off," Bull chuckled.

I ignored Bull and continued to look at the old lawyer. "And did this attorney of yours tell you, Max," he said, "that Collari employees have to be present on the site should you ever get that far?"

I nodded. It was quickly becoming obvious that they

didn't know about John coming to take cores or the fact that we were already seeking a court order.

All three of them just stood there and looked at me. Finally, Claremont said to Collari, "C'mon, Al. There are other ways to handle this."

Bull stepped back up on the porch and put his face in mine. "He's right, Addams," he hissed. "There are plenty more ways to handle this."

"Come, Bull," Collari said, pulling him back off the step. "I think Mr. Addams gets the point." He looked at me. "I'll give you until tomorrow at noon to change your mind. Think about it, Addams. Fifty thousand dollars is a lot more money than you would have made here this summer." He shook his finger at me. "You don't need the kind of trouble I can give you. Not for a few acres of trees. Not for a river. Not for anything."

"I'd think twice about comin' up to that clear-cut, I was you," Bull said over his shoulder. "Unless you've got the U.S. Army with you." He laughed, climbed in the Range Rover behind the steering wheel, and started the engine.

I watched Claremont and Collari get in and then it backed up, turned, and, in a spray of mud, disappeared around the corner into the thick spruce that lined the access road. I lit a cigarette and sat on the porch railing. My heart was thumping hard in my chest. Stormy immediately came out onto the porch. She had been listening from behind the door.

"Phew," she said. "Fifty thousand dollars, huh? That man really wants you off his back."

I nodded.

"Maybe you shoulda talked to me 'fore you said no."

"Now what?"

"The architects called and canceled while you was out in the workshop with Rayleen. Said someone called them about Red bein' gone and the fish kill."

"Goddammit!" I side-armed my cigarette out into the yard. "Who called them?"

"Dunno." She shook her head. "But whoever it was, they got to them folks from Florida too."

"The Florida couple called and canceled?"

"Yep. No more 'n ten minutes after the architects. Same thing."

"How the hell did someone get the names of our guests?"

"Question ain't how, Max, it's who."

There was not a word about Red all afternoon and what Rayleen had said began to eat at me. I tried not to think about it by attempting to tie several number 28 Griffith's Gnats. A number 28 hook is so small that thirty of them on my fly-tying table look like a pile of metal dust and although the Griffith's Gnat is a simple, two-step process, even with the aid of my magnifying glass, it takes considerable concentration.

Wally Murray called at four-thirty. "We have the court order, Max," he said. I could picture his eyebrows jumping up and down.

I told him about my visit from Collari this morning.

"Fifty thousand? How did they leave it?"

"Collari says I have until tomorrow at noon to make up my mind."

"When's your friend the geologist coming in?"

"Tomorrow night."

"You're going to have to move reasonably fast, Max," he said. "It won't take long for Claremont to find out about this court order."

"How fast is fast?"

"I don't mean run right up there to the clear-cut from the airport." He chuckled. "Let your friend get his bearings. Decide how he needs to do it. Just remember, Max, you're only going to get one chance."

I went back to trying to tie Griffith's Gnats. I heard Stephanie return around five and, after pulling her hair into a ponytail and changing into jeans and a loose, red moleskin shirt, she poured herself a glass of white wine and joined me. She sat and pulled her legs under her in the corner of the couch behind me and patted the cushion beside her for Spotter, who happily jumped up, laid down, and put his nose in her lap. She didn't say anything and I didn't turn around. I could feel her eyes on my back and hear the jingle of her bracelet as she sipped the wine. The clock ticked in the hallway. Stormy started making cooking noises in the kitchen and a red squirrel began a staccato scolding in a tree behind the lodge.

"At least you're not so mad you didn't come back," I said without turning around.

She didn't say anything.

"But, you are mad at me."

"Yes."

I swiveled on the stool and faced her. "It's not my fault, Steph," I said, taking off my glasses.

She chewed her lower lip and slowly moved her head from side to side. "You turned down fifty thousand dollars," she said. Her tone was disbelief.

"How do you know that?"

"Al told me."

I nodded. "He's not going to buy me off."

"No one was trying to buy you off, Max. That's business."

"This isn't about business."

"Max, you don't do that much business in two years."

"I said, this isn't about business." I turned back to the magnifying glass and lit a cigarette. We were both silent again. I stared at the tiny, buggy-looking thing in my tying vise.

Her bracelet jingled and she said, "What about me, Max? What about my business? My order?"

I turned back to her. "I can't do anything about that."

"If the mill closes, it's never going to happen."

"Why can't your friend Al get his logs somewhere else?" I said. "He has in the past."

"Dammit, Max!" She stood up. Spotter jumped back, his eyes wide. "There is nowhere else. Nowhere close enough anyway. That land belongs to Collari. You can't tell him what to do with it."

"I'm not telling them what to do with it," I said.

"Bullshit, you aren't." She threw the wine glass at the fireplace where it exploded on the hearth. "What the hell are you doing, then?" She clenched her fists at her sides. She was trembling.

"I'm not telling them what they can do." Spotter slinked out of the room. "I'm telling them what they can't do."

"And where do you get off? Who are you?" She stomped to the doorway, stopped, and turned. "You're one person, Max. And hundreds of people are going to be affected by this, this . . . snail-darter, spotted-owl mentality of yours." She slapped the doorjamb. "Where do you get off being so selfish?"

I didn't say anything. She stared at me, breathing hard. Finally, she sighed and said, "Take the fifty thousand, Max. While you still can. I know you're going to wish you had."

I listened to her footsteps cross the dining room floor and then heard the screen door slam. For a second I considered going after her and apologizing. Giving the whole thing up and calling Collari and taking the fifty thousand. Maybe, I thought, I can work with them. Establish some guidelines for the logging. Work with Wally and Claremont and find a compromise. Some way to fix it. But then I remembered Red and what he had said up in the woods. "It ain't right, cuttin' like this," he'd said. "You can't fix it. You gotta stop it."

I snubbed the cigarette, got the fireplace broom, and swept the broken glass from the hearth into the dead ashes.

At dinner, Stephanie acted like nothing had happened. She was charming and animated, joking with Rayleen one minute, and the next, thoughtful and interested as she listened to Chad and Tonya describe their day of sightseeing.

It had begun raining just as Stormy started serving her famous baked swordfish in mustard sauce and, as the front swept across the lake and up the mountain, lightning flashed and loud cracks of thunder rattled the windows. The lamps above the long table dimmed twice and, just in case, I lit several candles and put the flashlights by the phone in the hall. Spotter, who was afraid of lightning and perhaps could sense the intense thunder, retreated to my bedroom and cowered beside my suitcases under the bed.

"I hope this doesn't mean I won't get my casting lesson," Tonya said, breaking off a chunk of Stormy's homemade bread.

Rayleen chuckled into his beer and shook his head. "Front like this with all this thunder? Coming from across the lake? Nah. It'll be gone by mornin'." He smiled at her. "It's when we get it from the nor'east and you can barely hear it, that's when it rains for days." He looked at me. "Good chance this warm front'll put an end to the mud, Max. Your buddy's gonna be takin' cores at just the right time."

Stephanie's head whipped around and she looked at me, her face hardening. "What cores?" she said.

"Can't stop the clear-cuttin' for good without 'em," Stormy said to her, standing and going to the window.

"Only wish finding Red was as easy." She peered out just as the lake lit up like someone was out there taking pictures. The flashbulb brightness was followed instantly by a violent crack of thunder and another dimming of the lights. "Sure hope he's someplace outta this weather," she said.

After dinner, Rayleen pulled on a slicker and limped out through the growing puddles to the workshop to continue dismantling the Harley. After Stephanie called her voice mail and then a friend to check on her apartment and cat, she disappeared upstairs to her room. Stormy, Chad, Tonya, and I built a small fire in the reading room fireplace and, sharing the six-pack of Loon Lager Special Dark Chad had purchased at the brewery, we watched *A River Runs Through It*. Stormy soon tired of my constant stopping and restarting of the video as I replayed the casting sequences in slow motion for Tonya. Finally she took her pack of cigarettes and went to the kitchen to make a couple of cherry pies. "One of these days, Maxwell Addams," she whispered, as she passed my chair, "I'm gonna take that remote gizmo out to the lake and drown it."

By midnight we were all in bed. The *Loon Sentinel* had been delivered this morning and I read the report on Red's disappearance. A Gordon Miller "UpCountry Insider" report concerning my T.R.O. was under a picture of the town and an inset of the mill. The headline read CLEAR WATER CLOUDING OUR FUTURE? I folded the paper in half and read what the "insider" had to say.

Whitefork Lodge, the tony retreat for wealthy fly-fisherman out on Route 16, two days ago filed a temporary restraining order against Loon's largest employer, Boston-based Collari International's

Northeast Regional Pulp Division. In the T.R.O., Whitefork alleges Collari's logging has polluted nearby watersheds, killing fish, vegetation, and other wildlife.

Collari attorney, Claremont Taylor, told the *Sentinel*, "It was a simple spill of a few gallons of diesel fuel. Certainly, no Exxon Valdez. The problem was quickly rectified by Collari." Wallace Murray, the Montpelier lawyer representing Whitefork Lodge owner, Maxwell Addams, hinted that a permanent injunction is possible, stopping Collari's logging operations in Loon altogether.

One paper company employee, who asked not to be identified, told the *Sentinel*, "Unless we can get logs, the mill's going to have to shut down. And we lose our jobs." When logging in the area, as well as creating pulp for paper, Collari employs between five hundred and six hundred Loon citizens and pays $1,135,000 a year in township taxes.

Loon Mayor and longtime friend of Mr. Addams, Ruth Pearlman, claims her office is closely following the situation but refused to comment, "until all the information is in."

But, for this Insider, the potential economic impact of a Whitefork Lodge injunction is clear. In a state where one in every ten people receives food stamps, the seriousness of closing a facility like Collari's is obvious. What's really at stake here is Vermont itself. The Vermont of the past has been lost to newcomers like Mr. Addams who have developed a social and political agenda that seems to emphasize environmental protection even when it means loss of jobs. In many places in our beautifully preserved Green Mountains (which this editor feels is becoming a theme park for the wealthy), many of us are living in frightening poverty. Claremont Taylor puts it more succinctly, "Sure the scenery up here is great. But folks can't eat it."

I threw the paper across the room, clicked off the light, and, tossing and turning as I attempted to compose my rebuttal, finally fell asleep.

By three A.M. the rain stopped and three-quarters of a bright moon lit the lake and the front of the lodge, spreading pale white rectangles across my bed.

The door to my room opened and Stephanie stepped in, closing it softly behind her. "Max?" she whispered and sat on the bed. "Max? Are you awake?" She gently shook my shoulder.

"I'm awake now." I rolled over and looked at her. The moonlight frosted her hair and etched a thin, pale blue highlight around the shoulders of her nightgown. "What's wrong?" I said.

"Me." She shivered and sat on the edge of the bed. "I'm wrong."

"You're cold," I said and lifted the covers. "You want to get in under here?"

"No." She shook her head and pulled part of the quilt up around her shoulders. "I just wanted to tell you I don't want to fight anymore," she said. "Okay?"

"Okay." I looked at the clock. "It's late," I said.

"I couldn't sleep." She pulled the quilt tighter around her shoulders. "Why didn't you tell me about Red?" she asked.

"You haven't exactly been around," I said. "And we didn't think it was anything very serious at first." I felt for my cigarettes, found them, and fumbled one to my mouth.

"Don't you think he'll show up?"

I lit the cigarette and for a second the room exploded with light. "I hope he does," I said, putting my head back down on the pillow and exhaling through a shaft of moonlight.

"What about this other stuff?"

"What? My sign and the pickets and the cancellations?"

"Yes."

"I don't know."

"It might get worse, Max."

"So everyone tells me."

"How much are you going to take before you give in?"

"I don't know."

She was silent for a while and I watched the tip of my cigarette pulse orange in the darkness. "What's this about taking cores?" she asked.

"You won't like it."

"I said I don't want to fight anymore." I heard her take a deep breath. "Tell me."

She was silent as I told her about John coming to take the cores and the injunction I hoped to get. When I finished, she still didn't say anything. "See?" I said. "I told you that you weren't going to like hearing it."

She shook her head slowly. The quilt fell on the floor. "You're going to back everyone into a corner, Max," she said, standing and turning toward the door. "There's no choice." She put her hand on the doorknob and opened it.

I snubbed the cigarette in the ashtray. "No choice of what?"

She didn't answer and quietly closed the door behind her.

I heard the stairs creak under her feet and I fell back onto the pillows and stared into the darkness.

At four-thirty I was awakened again. This time it was Spotter. He was whining at the door. Still half asleep, I shushed him, rolled over, and put my head under the pillows.

CHAPTER ✦ NINE

Saturday was one of those sun-bright, rain-washed, clean-smelling, start-again-and-nothing-can-go-wrong kind of mornings. I felt great and although I didn't exactly whistle in the shower, Spotter could sense it and wagged his tail every time I walked by him as I dressed. I was optimistic about Red's return. After all, he'd only really been missing a little over a day. I'd stopped the logging, the river was running clearer, the trout weren't dying, and John was coming.

Stormy and Rayleen were up. I could hear her in the kitchen and had caught a glimpse of him scratching and stretching in his long johns in the workshop doorway.

I poured two coffees and, with Spotter zigzagging nose-down around the yard, carried the mugs out to the workshop.

"Tell the old buzzard not to forget his pill," Stormy yelled from the kitchen window.

Not a ripple disturbed the lake. It was like a sheet of plastic food wrap pulled taut and held or staked down at the shore by boulders and budding trees.

Although most of my guests prefer to fish the waters of the river, fifteen-acre Sweet Lake is really the jewel of the property. Actually not a lake, it is a classic forest pond created and maintained with almost religious fervor by hundreds of generations of beavers. Only fifteen feet at its deepest point, Sweet Lake itself is home to the largest and probably oldest trout on the property, as well as loons, osprey, and several species of migrating ducks and geese. Its irregular shoreline hides white-tailed deer, bobcat, pine martin, otter, black bear, and, more recently, several moose that have wandered down from Canada. This time of year, just after the thaw, the lake is perfect for fly-fishing. Later in the season, however, as the water warms under the summer sun, it becomes better spin cast or bait fisherman's water. Since I allow neither at Whitefork Lodge, Sweet Lake becomes our reflecting pool and the background for quiet, after-dinner conversations on the lodge porch.

Rayleen and I sat in the warm sun on the bench against the front of the workshop and sipped our coffees. The air felt more like a June morning than April.

"Looky there," Rayleen said, pointing at the lake. "Trout're startin' to rise."

He was right. Bullseye rings were appearing everywhere.

"Too bad them kids ain't out there right now," he said.

"I'm giving casting lessons this morning."

"The girl?"

I nodded.

"On the dock?" He squinted toward the dock and the canoes upside down up in the grass.

"On the river."

"What's on the bottom of that canoe there, Max?" He pointed to the Old Town.

I looked. The way the morning sun angled across its dark green surface, it appeared deeply scratched or cut.

We both got up and walked over to the canoes. "Lordy!" Rayleen said. "Will ya look at this mess."

I dropped my coffee mug. The dark green canvas skin on the antique Old Town had been slashed in a dozen places, some spots torn back exposing the pale ribs like a partially skinned water creature that had been dragged to the beach for quartering.

"And, will ya look at this!" Rayleen was squatting at the smaller red fiberglass canoe now, his fingers tracing one of the two dozen punctures in its shiny bottom. "They couldn't cut this one," he said, "so they just stabbed it." He looked up at me. "Who'd do a thing like this, Max?"

"Must have come in the night," I said. "I should've paid more attention to Spotter. He was whining at the door around four this morning." I walked around the fiberglass canoe. Scratched deeply in the opposite side were the words NO T.R.O. "Here's who did it," I said, stooping and feeling the deep cuts that formed the letters. "They carved their calling card over here."

He stepped over the canoe and joined me. "No T.R.O.? Hell, Max," he shook his head, "that coulda been left by 'bout half the folks what live 'round here."

"I know." I stood and looked up at the lodge. "Help me get the canoes into the workshop, huh?" I stooped and lifted an end of the fiberglass one. "I don't want the Harpers to see this. They've had enough happen since they got here."

We put the fiberglass canoe on a pair of sawhorses on one side of the workshop and went back to get the Old Town. "I can fix 'em both, Max," Rayleen said as we wrestled with the heavy old canoe. "Though, this one'll be the nastiest to get right. Gotta strip it right downta them ribs."

We put the Old Town on another pair of sawhorses beside the fiberglass and were standing there discussing how to repair them when, my coffee mug in her hand, Stephanie stepped into the workshop. "I found this mug out there in . . . my God," she said. "What happened to the canoes?"

"Somebody snuck in and slit 'em up," Rayleen said.

She looked at me and I nodded. "Just another attempt to get me to change my mind," I said.

"Max," she went to the Old Town and ran her hand over one of the slash marks, "this is not only serious, it's frightening. What if they start cutting people? Or Spotter. Or God knows?" She looked at Rayleen. "Did it happen while we were asleep?"

He shrugged. "Musta," he said.

"Max, this has gone far enough," she said. "Surely you'll rescind that restraining order now."

I shook my head.

"Why?" She pointed at the canoes. "These people mean business. For all we know, they could be dangerous."

I continued to shake my head.

"Dammit, Max!" She tossed me the coffee mug. "Don't say I didn't warn you!" And she turned and stomped out of the workshop.

"Lady's got a point, Max," Rayleen said. "These here incidents do seem to be getting bigger, if you know what I mean."

I heard a car door slam and an engine start. Without warming up, gravel sprayed under spinning tires and it roared away. I didn't have to look out the window to know it was Stephanie.

There was still no news of Red at breakfast.

"I called Wilba first thing," Stormy said. "Poor woman's outta her mind with worry." She sighed. "Least her momma's with her now, though. Helpin' with them boys and tryin' to keep her spirits up."

I could feel Rayleen looking at me. I looked at Tonya

and smiled. "Anytime you're ready, Tonya," I said, "we can start your casting lesson."

"Should I wear all my gear?"

I nodded. "We're going to be in the river. You get it right, we'll try to catch something."

She turned to Chad. "Will you go fish somewhere else? Please."

"Sure. That is, if you don't mind, Max," Chad said, "Tonya thinks I'll make her nervous, so I'll fish somewhere upstream."

"You actually might want to try downstream," I said. "Where the river runs into the lake. It's not unusual for some big trout to be laying in there." I smiled. Tonya was self-conscious enough. Having him watching would only make even more difficult what I imagined was going to be hard enough.

Spotter and I met Tonya in the yard and we walked to the river, then, ducking under branches and climbing over rocks along the bank, we worked our way upstream to a place I call the Meadow Run. It is a lazier, wider, and deeper stretch of the Whitefork that meanders through a three-acre, alpinelike meadow. Trees are sparse here and I felt the open area would give her the kind of unhindered back-cast room she needed while she learned.

Spotter went immediately upstream, stood on the lip of a grassy overhang, and stared down into the river where it cut deeply under the bank.

Tonya and I waded into the thigh-deep water at the tail of a long run ten yards below Spotter. It was cold and the current was strong. "It feels like an undertow in the ocean, doesn't it?" she said, struggling against the current. "The way the water pushes so hard on your legs?"

"The best thing for you to do," I said, "is stand here and watch for a couple minutes." I'd tied a number 10

Dead Princess on six feet of 5X tippet before I left the workshop and false cast a few times while I stripped some line out onto the water. "Now, watch the way I move my rod when I'm casting."

"Ten to two," she said with a smile. "Ten to two. Ten to two."

"That's right. Where'd you learn that?"

"Joan Wulff," she said smugly. "In one of your *Fly, Rod & Reel* magazines. Chad got me a whole stack from the reading room."

"Watch me anyway," I said and waded carefully out in the faster moving water a couple yards away from her.

She watched patiently as I cast and recast several times. My thought was to quickly get her comfortable and reasonably accurate with a basic cast and then teach her, as part of pick-up technique, the all-important roll cast. As far as I'm concerned, too much emphasis today is put on double hauling and distance casting when, unless you're on a big western river, trout are found in close quarters on small rivers. Without the ability to roll cast, your chances of catching them are zero.

Finally, I decided it was time to let her try.

I've taught a lot of people to cast over the years and invariably it's the women who master it fastest. Men always seem to want to muscle the rod, using their strength to literally throw the fly out on to the water. On the other hand, having nothing to prove, women seem to instinctively let the rod do the work.

Tonya was no exception and, although she wasn't getting much distance, it took only fifteen minutes or so before she was casting beautiful tight loops out over the water in front of us.

"That's perfect," I said, as her line whistled by our heads. "Perfect. You're good, Tonya. Real good. I thought . . ."

"I told you, Chad makes me nervous," she said as she

shot the line, watched it settle perfectly on the water and then reeled in. "Do you think I could have a fly tied on my line now?" she asked.

"I don't see why not." I hadn't tied a fly to her leader because I'd anticipated her hooking it in trees, grass, or one of us as she learned. I pulled a box of flies from my vest and selected a number 8 olive and black woolly bugger.

"That's the fly Chad always gives me." She made a face as I began to tie it to her tippet. "Why can't I have one of those sparkly kind you're using?"

I shrugged, put the woolly bugger back and took out a Dead Princess. "You're a lot better than I thought you'd be, Tonya," I said, tying it on her leader, "but these sparkly things, as you call them, are really difficult to cast." I bit the tag end from the knot. "They're heavy so you'll have to slow down your cast. Wait for your rod to load up before starting your forward cast." I dangled the Dead Princess out in front of us.

"Why don't I just cast it a few times before I try to catch a fish with it?"

I shook my head. "Because how many times do you think you can splash this thing out there in the water before the trout figure it out?" I smiled. "Up 'til now, you've been casting. With this on your line, you're going to be fishing."

"Where should I aim?"

Spotter was still above the cut in the bank staring into the water. "Put it," I pointed, "about six feet upstream from where Spotter is."

She took the Dead Princess from my hand, stripped line from her reel and began false casting upstream.

I stepped back to give her room. The Dead Princess would leave a nice welt if it hit someone in the head. "And don't false cast so much," I said. "There are only three reasons to false cast. Get more line out, change direction, or dry a fly."

She playfully stuck her tongue out at me and shot the fly out over the water. It splashed into the water thirty-five feet in front of us, five feet upstream from Spotter, and sank immediately. It was closer to the bank than I would have liked. I watched her line begin to slowly drift back at us and hoped the Dead Princess wouldn't snag on anything down there.

Spotter looked at us.

"Lift your rod tip as your line floats toward us," I said. "Lift and strip in the slack. You want to keep enough tension so you feel the strike."

"I'm trying," she said, yanking on the line. "But it won't pull. It's stuck, Max."

"Damn," I said and helped her get what slack there was onto her reel. "Lift your rod tip, Tonya." She did and all that happened was the rod bent alarmingly. I nodded. "I thought this might happen. It's hung up on something."

"I'm sorry, Max."

"It's not your fault," I said and waded by her to the bank. "Just don't pull too hard or you'll break the fly off. Keep the line taut." I climbed up into the calf-deep grass and walked up the bank to where Spotter stood. He began wagging his tail. The tight line dug into the current just below him and disappeared down into the cloudy water. I nudged him aside with my knee. "Look out, boy," I said.

"What are you doing?" Tonya shouted.

"I'm going to see if I can free it," I yelled back at her and laying my own rod on the grass, knelt at the water's edge. "No sense losing the fly if we don't have to." Spotter laid down in the grass at my side and put his nose over the bank. I rolled up my right sleeve. "Just keep the line taut, okay?"

"Okay," she yelled.

I grabbed the line and followed it with my fingers down into the cold, murky water. With the water at my bicep I could feel the nail knot that attached the leader to the line. The fly was snagged farther under than I'd thought and I pushed my sleeve higher and laid down on my stomach.

"Don't fall in, Max," she yelled.

I strained and stretched my arm deep into the water, my fingers now carefully following the thin leader. Just as the cold water swirled around my armpit, I felt the hook eye on the Dead Princess. "I've got it," I yelled over my shoulder. "Keep that tension." I felt my way over the fly to the hook trying to determine what it was snagged on. What my fingers touched next made me shout, "Jesus!" and leap back from the river. I sat in the grass staring at my wet hand. Spotter whined but didn't move.

"What's the matter, Max?" Tonya yelled.

"I just felt a face!"

"A face?"

"Yeah! A person's face! Your fly is hooked on a face!" I crawled back to the water's edge.

"C'mon, Max. That's not funny."

"I'm serious." This time I peeked into the cloudy current, straining my eyes. At first I couldn't see it, then little by little I could begin to make out the faint red and black plaid of fabric pulsing in the current. It was a jacket or a shirt.

"What is it?" she yelled.

I didn't answer because it was taking just about all the will power I had to reach back into the water. I lowered my hand to the red and black blur and grabbed a handful of soggy wool. Then I lifted hard and, inch by inch, the weight in my hand came up through the water toward me. When it was close enough, I grabbed with my other hand and pulled hard.

Red Crosley's distorted white face popped out of the water a foot from mine. His red hair was matted black to his head and his bulging eyes were milky green. The Dead Princess was hooked through his left eyebrow. Spotter barked and I recoiled and dropped Red back in the water where he rolled over in the current, spun slowly, and headed downriver toward Tonya.

"Oh my God, Max!" she screamed, "It's floating this way!"

I jumped to my feet, narrowly missing my rod, ran back down the bank, jumped in, and waded to where Tonya stood. The body tumbled through the tail water and slammed heavily into my knees. I grabbed the collar of the shirt, tore the Dead Princess from Red's eyebrow and dragged him to the river's edge. "I need some help, Tonya," I said, beginning to wrestle him out of the water. "He's heavy." Spotter was barking.

She waded tentatively toward me, reeling in the line. "Do I have to?"

"Don't look," I said. "Just grab and pull."

It took us almost five minutes to drag him out of the water, up the steep bank and into the grass. Tonya staggered a few feet away and dropped to her knees. Her back was toward me and it shook like she might be throwing up. I toed Red onto his back. His face was pale blue-green. Water gushed from his nostrils. His swollen black tongue protruded from his twisted mouth like one of the rotting potatoes Stormy had thrown away. He was long beyond CPR.

Again, for the second time in a week, Stormy, Rayleen, and I sat at the long plank table in the dining room with Darren Foley standing at the end, taking notes in a small spiral-bound notebook. This time, however, not only were Chad and Tonya with us, but the *Loon Sentinel* was there too. Mister "UpCountry Insider" himself, Gordon Miller, sat on a chair by the fireplace with a small tape recorder in his hand.

"Sit down, Darren," Stormy said, blowing her nose in tissue. "You look like a waiter standing there." Like the rest of us, she was tired of all the questions.

He blushed, pulled out a chair, and sat. "Just a couple more things," he said. "And then we'll leave all of you alone."

We had a yard full of people, paraphernalia, and vehicles.

I had stayed with Red's body while Spotter and Tonya ran to the lodge to get Stormy and call the sheriff. Stormy joined me at the body. She was a nurse. "Damn. Damn. Damn," she had said after one look. "Poor Red." She knelt by the body, tears welling in her eyes. "Oh, you poor boy." She took one of his bluish hands in hers and was still holding it when the sirens screamed down the access road.

Darren's squad car was first. It was followed thirty seconds later by the orange and white EMT truck and Loon's biggest hook and ladder. Behind that was the *Loon Sentinel*'s black Jeep Cherokee with Gordon Miller salivating at the wheel and "staff photographer" Bruce Eichner riding shotgun. It looked like a circus act as all three vehicles skidded to stops at crazy angles, doors flew open, and everyone piled out.

With Bruce flashing pictures of every move, Red was pronounced dead at the scene. After the county medical examiner had done his preliminary poking and prodding, the body was wrestled inside a black, rubbery plastic bag, zipped up, and slid into the back of the EMT truck. It roared away with all lights flashing and we went into the dining room with Darren to answer a few questions.

We'd been in the dining room an hour. Tonya, her face still ashen, leaned on Chad's shoulder, twisting and retwisting a tissue in her hands. I felt sorry for both of them. Their stay at the lodge was quickly becoming the honeymoon from hell.

Rayleen was slumped at the table, his greasy hands folded prayerlike before him. Stormy sat in her place behind an ashtray with a small mountain of cigarette butts. I sat with one hip up on the sideboard.

"You sure Red said he was comin' here, Max?" Darren was looking at the notebook. "Had some information?"

"I told you, Darren. We only talked a couple minutes. He was on the two-way radio. The reception wasn't good. He said he'd found out something about the clear-cut. He thought it was important. Someone else is involved. Something like that."

"But, he didn't say what that was, right?" He narrowed his eyes. "Or who?"

"No."

"He didn't even hint?"

"Godammit, Darren!" Stormy slapped the tabletop. The pile of butts jumped. "What's your point?"

Again, Darren blushed. "Stormy," he said, "I know this is hard. Hell, it's hard on everybody. But we gotta do it. It's my job to figure out how and why that boy got in that river." He sighed. "Look at it from my side. You folks are just one little piece of this puzzle. I gotta go question Wilba and the boys yet." He shook his head. "How d'you think I'm gonna feel 'bout doin' that?"

"Wilba?" I stood up. My patience was running thin too. "What's his wife got to do with this? It's Collari you should be questioning," I said.

"I intend to question many of Mr. Collari's people, Max," he said, narrowing his eyes at me. "When it seems appropriate."

"Appropriate? Jesus, Darren! Red told me himself he was afraid because he'd shown me the clear-cut."

"And just what was he afraid of, Max?" Darren's tone was condescending.

"Well," I shrugged, "his job," I said. "For one thing."

"Of course he was afraid he'd lose his job. So's everyone else in this town." He sighed. "That don't mean anybody did him any harm."

"It weren't no accident, Darren," Stormy mumbled. "And you know it."

Darren leaned forward on the table. "I don't know anything of the kind," he said. "And you don't either." He looked at me. "Neither of you." He looked back at her. "And, if I hear tell that you're goin' around saying that Red was murdered by someone who works for Mr. Collari, which is what you're hintin' at—" he pointed his finger at each of us "—I'm gonna come out here and arrest each and every one of you for interferin' with a police investigation." He shot a look at Gordon Miller. "That means you too, boy. That paper of yours prints one thing that I ain't personally okayed, I'll shut you down."

"What about us?" Chad asked. "I mean," he attempted a smile, "I know we have to stay around until you say we can leave but," he glanced at me, "do we have to stay at the lodge? I mean, would it be okay if we stayed in town until this was over?"

Darren nodded. "Long as you let my office know where you are," he said.

"Sorry, Max," Chad said. "I hope you understand."

I understood. I felt like leaving too. Going back to Key Largo and then starting this spring all over again.

Deputy Richards clumped into the room, came around the table and up to Darren. We all watched as the young man leaned and whispered something in the sheriff's ear. "Good." Darren nodded. "I'll be right out." Mark exited and Darren closed his notebook. "Found Red's truck," he said to us. "Way up in the clear-cut." He stood.

"You mean, this is the first time you looked up there?" Rayleen said.

Darren shrugged. "Looked myself, Rayleen," he said. "Guess I didn't look good enough. Anyway, from the sound of it, Red had been havin' himself quite a little party up there the other night. Beer cans and booze bottles all over inside the cab."

"That's impossible!" Stormy shot to her feet. "Red wasn't a hard drinkin' man. You know that, Darren. Everybody knows that."

"She's right, Darren," Rayleen said, shaking a greasy finger. "We all've had beers with him. You even. When'd that boy ever get through more'n two?"

"I know, Rayleen. But that don't mean he ain't capable." He walked to the door. "I tend to believe what I see. And since I ain't seen it yet, I'm goin' up there and take a look right now."

Gordon Miller was out of his chair and right behind him.

Darren pointed his finger at Gordon. "Where you goin', boy?" he said.

"Up to Red's pickup, of course."

Darren pointed at Gordon's chair. "You just go right back over there and sit 'til I say it's alright for you to come look. I don't need you trompin' all over a possible crime scene, now do I, boy?"

Darren clumped out of the lodge and, smiling sheepishly, Gordon retreated to the chair and sat. Short and chubby with thin blond hair always in his eyes, Gordon Miller looked closer to fifteen than his midtwenties. To compensate for his cherubic boyish face, he had grown a moustache when he'd taken over the *Sentinel*. To me, the result looked exactly like a cherubic little boy who'd attempted to grow a moustache.

He pointed the tape recorder at me and clicked it on. "Notice how the sheriff said, 'crime scene,' just then, Max?"

It hadn't registered on me, but I nodded as if it had. The kid did have a reporter's ear.

"Kind of interesting, wouldn't you say?" He smiled. "I mean considering how hot under the collar he got when you suggested Red's death wasn't an accident."

It was interesting, but I wasn't going to comment on it. I didn't trust Gordon. "Shut that tape recorder off, Gordon," I said.

"But, I hear you've had a lot of things happen out here at the lodge since that T.R.O. went into effect, right?"

I nodded. "So?"

"So, maybe Red's another one."

I looked at Stormy. Her eyes were red and swollen. After the EMT's had arrived, I'd had to physically hold Stormy to keep her from jumping in the Jeep and driving into town to confront Collari. "Turn off the tape recorder, Gordon," I said again.

He didn't. "So, how you feeling about that T.R.O. of yours now?"

"Gordon," Stormy said, "whyn't you just shut that toy off like Max asked you and shut your mouth?" She lit a cigarette. Her hand shook slightly.

"I don't think you have to sit here anymore," I said to her. I looked at the Harpers. "Or you guys."

The Harpers looked relieved and stood. Stormy just shook her head. "I'm stayin' 'til I know what they find up there in the clear-cut." She waved the honeymooners toward the door. "You two go on. Take a walk. This don't need to concern you no more."

Tonya went to Stormy and put her hands on her

shoulders. "We'll just be upstairs," she said and looked at me, "packing. Let me know if I can help with anything, Stormy."

"Thank you, honey." Stormy patted her hand. "If you're still here for lunch, you may be helpin' yourself to that. Okay?"

"Can I ask one last question, Max?" Gordon said, sliding his tape recorder into his breast pocket. "Off the record?"

I shrugged.

"Miss Wilcox is staying here, correct?"

"As a matter of fact, yes."

"And you're aware she's a friend of Alphonse Collari's?"

"Now what's your point, Gordon?" Rayleen grumbled.

"Yeah. What's your point, Gordon?" I lit a cigarette, went to the window and looked out into the yard. "What's who Stephanie's friends with got to do with all this?" Foley's squad car came skidding to a stop in front of the porch. Mark Richards jumped out, put on his Smokey hat and came up the steps.

"It just seems odd," Gordon said. "You and Collari being enemies and all. Whose side is she . . . ?"

Mark stuck his head in the room. "Gordon? Sheriff says you and your picture guy can go up to the pickup now."

Gordon jumped to his feet. Mark turned to leave.

"Wait just a damn minute, Mark Richards," Stormy said. "I want to know what you found up there."

Mark sauntered into the room, the leather belts on his tan uniform squeaking. He walked up to Darren's end of the table, took off his Smokey hat, and, in a pretty good imitation of the sheriff, put his foot up on the chair. "Well," he said, flicking at something on the crown of the hat with his finger, "I suppose it wouldn't hurt."

"Quit that damn posturin', Mark Edward," Stormy said. "Tell us about Red's pickup. And get your dirty boot off that chair!"

Mark blushed. "Yes, ma'am." He dropped his foot to the floor.

"Well?"

He lowered his eyes and fingered the brim of his hat. "Well, it's Red's pickup alright. Looks like he drove it up in there pretty fast and hung it up on a rock. You can see where he tried to get it unstuck. I mean, the tires is all dug in and like that." He looked up. "Truck has four wheel drive but it didn't do no good with that big rock wedged under the frame."

"What's all this garbage about booze?" she asked.

"Yes, ma'am. There's a lot of it. Maybe three, four six-packs of empties on the truck floor. Bottle of Canadian Club on the passenger seat, mostly empty. Another one, broke, over by the river where it looks like Red was when he slipped and fell in."

"Fell in?"

"Yes, ma'am. That's the way Sheriff Foley reads it."

"Darren thinks Red slipped and fell in the river?" She shook her head in disgust.

"Well, it seems pretty likely maybe he was drunk, ma'am," Mark said. "And, of course it was dark and—"

"Bullshit!" Stormy's fist hit the table. The ashtray jumped. "I've known Red Crosley since he was seven years old. Babysat him just like I done for you and your brothers, Mark Edward. He wasn't no drinker. Don't you clowns listen?"

"We ain't sayin' he was, ma'am." Mark looked very uncomfortable. "The county medical examiner will have to tell us that for sure." Mark started for the door. "It's just that, well, that's how it looks to Sheriff Foley."

"Look like Red was alone up there?" Rayleen asked.

"That's a tough call, sir. As you'd expect, there's boot prints and tire tracks all over in the mud up there. 'Cause of that it's kinda hard to tell what's old and what's new."

Stormy sighed. "It ain't right," she said. "It ain't right."

"One thing's strange, though," Mark said. "Red's wallet ain't on him. Not up at the pickup either."

"You mean, he was robbed?" Her face was hopeful.

" 'Course," Rayleen said. "Somebody done robbed him."

"No, I ain't sayin' that. Sheriff Foley thinks the wallet probably fell out in the river. All that current roughin' Red up the way it did carryin' him all the way down here." Mark looked at me. "A couple of us'll be stayin' to search the river, Max. Be here the rest of the day, I suppose. Hope you don't mind."

I shrugged. "No," I said. "Look all you want." I knew I'd never get Tonya in the river again.

"Sure hope we find that wallet." He smiled at Stormy. "Musta been a wad of money in there since he cashed his paycheck and all. Sheriff Foley says Red's wife could sure use it."

Stormy frowned. "Then you see that she gets it, Mark Edward."

He blushed. "I have to get back, ma'am," he said quickly, putting on his hat. "If that's all, I mean."

"Go on, Mark," I said. "Thanks."

Mark and Gordon were out of the dining room like it was on fire. We listened to the squad car roar back up the hill. When the sound was gone, Stormy blew her nose and said, "Never liked that kid. I think he used to steal from my purse."

CHAPTER ✦ TEN

Once the squad car was gone and the lodge was quiet, the empty space that would be Red for some time became painfully apparent. Rayleen went back out to the workshop, I think to lose himself in Harley parts. "Slipped and fell in," Stormy mumbled as she went to the porch and sat in a rocker and, gripping the arms, stared out at the lake. I stood for a while at the screen door and watched her. She didn't rock. She didn't smoke. Occasionally, her shoulders would shake and I'd hear a small animal whine.

I went to my fly-tying table, sat, and stared into the magnifying glass but all I could see was the way Red's distorted, dead face had looked when I first pulled him from the river. For me, the anger would not go away. In fact, it continued to build.

I let Stormy sit that way for an hour and then, using a sweater as an excuse, joined her. "Here," I said, slipping the sweater over her shoulders. "It's getting cold." I sat on the railing and faced her. "You going to be all right?"

She looked up at me. Her eyes were dry, her face set. "I'm okay now," she said, brushing a loose strand of wiry hair from her face. "You think maybe I oughta go to town and help Wilba?"

"If you're up to it." I shrugged. "And, if you think she needs it."

"Nah." She shook her head. "She's got kin comin' outta her ears here in Loon." She smiled weakly. "Prob'ly got enough casseroles to last her a year already." She hung her head. "Them poor little boys," she mumbled.

I stood, kissed her on the forehead, and went out to the Jeep. I climbed in.

"Where're you goin'?" she called after me.

"Airport."

"You're lyin', Max Addams. Your friend John don't come in 'til this evenin'."

I pressed my forehead against the steering wheel. When I looked back at her she was standing beside the rocker. "I can't let Collari think they got away with this," I said.

"Max," she said, "don't do nothin' stupid. I can't afford to lose you too."

"I'm just going to talk to them," I said.

"What's it gonna help?"

"It's going to help me feel better." I started the Jeep.

"Findin' somethin' in them cores is what's gonna make us all feel better, Max. Goin' to the mill ain't gonna do nothin' but get you arrested."

"I'm not going to be arrested for talking."

She shook her head. "Just see that talkin's all you do."

"I'll go from the mill to the airport," I said. "I should be back with John around eight."

She nodded. "I'll try to cook up somethin' nice for him," she said. "God knows I could use somethin' else to think about."

In thirty minutes I was parked in Collari International's Northeast Pulp Division's parking lot beside an obscene, two-story pile of dead maple and spruce logs that I was sure were from Morning Mountain.

"Mr. Collari's in a meeting, sir," the plump redheaded woman just inside the door marked OFFICE told me. "If you had an appointment, I'm sure he would be glad to—"

I went around her desk, yanked open the door behind her, and stomped in. It was a big room, more like a rich man's den than an office. The lights were low, the blinds drawn. The walls were paneled in what looked like highly polished wide planks of birdseye maple. The desk was massive. Ornately carved into the heavy wood front panel was a logging truck loaded high with logs. In a large alcove to the right, illuminated by two recessed spotlights, Alphonse Collari and Claremont Taylor leaned over a long conference table spread with topographical maps and engineer's blueprints.

They looked up, their eyebrows going from surprise to frown in a nano-second. "What the hell?" Collari balled a fist. "Addams! Who let you in? What the hell are you doing here?"

"Red Crosley is dead," I said, going up to the table, leaning on it with both hands and putting my face in his. "We just found him floating in the Whitefork. Although, I suppose you already know that."

"My, my," said Claremont. "You aren't inferring that anyone here had—"

"The only thing I'm doing here," I said, lowering my voice, "is telling you that if there ever was a chance that we might resolve this thing without a permanent injunction, it's gone now." I slammed my fist on the table and Claremont jumped back. "Gone!"

"Addams, for God's sake, calm down," Collari said. "We don't know what you're talking about. Who is this Red?"

I looked from Collari to Claremont. "Tell him, Claremont," I said. "And once you've explained that, tell him how I'm going to shut this mill down! For good!" I turned and went to the door but just as I reached for the knob, it opened in and there stood Bull Turlock with a shotgun in his hands.

"I figured it was you, Addams," he said, pushing me back toward the table with the muzzle. "You got a thing for trespassin', don't you?" He looked around me. "What do you want me to do with him, Mr. Collari?"

"Bull." It was Claremont's voice. "Put that damn gun down!"

Bull looked confused.

"He said put it down, Bull!" Collari said.

Bull pointed the shotgun at the floor. I looked at Collari and shook my finger. "Red wasn't an accident," I said, my anger building again. "I'm going to find out who killed him. And meanwhile, I'm going to stop you dead."

"Get out of here, Addams," Claremont said. "Now! Or I call the sheriff!" He reached for the phone.

I didn't wait for him to say it twice.

Burlington, Vermont, is a college town and its airport reflects the needs of the hundreds of University of Vermont students and their families. Over the years I've been using it, it's gone from basically a waiting room in an old hangar to a pretty sophisticated little airport complete with a restaurant, bar, and delayed flights. The runways have been enlarged and now can accommodate the small and medium-sized jets of all the major airlines. You can fly into Burlington from just about anywhere, only not direct.

John's flight from San Francisco came in via Chicago, Cincinnati, and Pittsburgh, the planes unfortunately getting smaller with each successive stop. Nevertheless, his twin-engine, twenty-six-passenger commuter from Pittsburgh was due in right on time. Problem was, I was four hours early.

I went to the bar, bought a beer for almost the price of a six-pack and stared at my reflection in the mirror between bottles of exotic liqueurs.

Like I always did after a display of anger, I felt stupid. What the hell had I done that for? As usual, Stormy had been right. Why had I thought it would help to confront Collari like that? Other than almost getting shot I had accomplished nothing. Collari hadn't even known what I was talking about. Curious thing was, I believed him. His surprise was genuine.

I looked down at the wet circles on the bar from the bottle. This whole thing was turning me into someone I almost didn't recognize. And worse, I was beginning to forget the reason it had all started. Mr. Macho. Me. Defender of nature. Bullshit!

I looked back at my reflection in the mirror. Honestly now, Max, I said to myself. What's this really all about? Trees? Ecosystems? Come on! My motives for stopping the logging were purely business. Just like Stephanie had said. My trout were threatened and therefore so was my income. Would I have been so quick to throw down the gauntlet if Collari had been clear-cutting on the other side of Morning Mountain?

I sipped the beer, remembering an article about saving America's trout water I'd read in one of the fly-fishing magazines I subscribe to. The guy who wrote it made the point that the only way trout water, or anything else in the natural world, for that matter, stood a chance of surviving was if ways could be found to make it profitable for someone to protect it. "Conservation," he wrote, "has to respond to the bottom line, just like exploitation. We have to find ways to make saving

America's resources as financially lucrative as destroying them."

I drained my beer and ordered a new one. I slid another five-dollar bill to the bartender, watched him ring up the sale and return with two quarters. I stacked them with the other two. I suppose it doesn't make much difference anymore what my motive is, I thought as I sipped. I'd made sure of that in Collari's office. And Red's death? Who was I kidding? I wouldn't know where to start to prove it wasn't an accident. I shook my head and looked back at myself in the mirror. No, Stormy was right about the cores too. All I could do now was hope they came up loaded with bad news for clear-cutting.

I met John at the baggage claim. At five ten, John was a couple of inches shorter than me, but what he lacked in height he more than made up for in bulk. In a word, John was beefy. He had thick forearms, a broad, hard chest, and big muscular thighs like an aging college football player who still went to the gym every day. We'd been friends for twenty years and, although he'd added a drooping handlebar moustache, he still wore his hair in a short military cut. He didn't smoke or drink, but agreed that his addiction to rich food was probably the source for his sky-high blood pressure. His permanently flushed face had made my ex-wife once comment, "John reminds me of a tick ready to explode." It was typical of the acrimonious comments she had for all my friends toward the end of our marriage, but in John's case it was a pretty good description.

"Jesus, I hate those puddle jumpers," he said, shaking my hand. "The final approach was like a strafing run." He was carrying his rod cases over his shoulder and his beat-up leather duffle was the first down the chute and onto the carousel. I grabbed it. "One more," he said. "The core-taker. It's in a red leather golf bag." He took the duffle from my hand. "You look beat, Max." We watched the bags, boxes, and suitcases slide onto the carousel and his fellow passengers crowd in to claim what was theirs.

Tonight John was wearing a Denver Broncos cap, a pair of faded jeans, black cowboy boots, a black T-shirt and a leather-sleeved black athletic jacket with the word ROCK in four-inch-high letters on the back.

The golf bag was the last piece of luggage down the carousel and I hefted it to my shoulder. "Car's right outside," I said, staggering under the weight. "What did you do," I laughed, "bring a couple granite cores with this thing?" It felt as if it weighed at least one hundred pounds.

"I told you it's new." He shrugged. "I wasn't sure what I'd need so I brought every attachment it had."

We threw everything in the back of the Jeep, swung through a McDonald's, and got a couple coffees. I filled him in on the past week as we headed back east on Interstate 89. He frowned as he listened, sipping his coffee through the lid and when I was finished, said, "Your assistant drowned? Jesus, Max. I didn't come here to get caught in some sort of Hatfield, McCoy thing." He shook his head. "How the hell are you going to get me permission to take cores up at that clear-cut with this kind of shit going on?"

"We've got a court order," I said, exiting the big highway and starting up the two-lane Route 16 toward the lodge. "It's legal. As long as we move reasonably fast."

"How fast is fast? I've got to look over the core-taker. I'm not even sure I know how this one works."

"I think we've got a day or so." I told him about my confrontation with Collari.

"You're lucky you're not in jail," he said. "Or dead yourself. Who's this guy with the shotgun?"

"Among other things, he's the logging site foreman."

"Well," he drained his coffee cup, "at least you've got the court order. There are places in Colorado where landowners shoot trespassers."

"This isn't Colorado."

"It doesn't look much different," he said, looking out the window of the Jeep. "Not at night, anyway." The only thing we could see in the peripheral light from my highbeams were the vertical white slashes of birch trees in the dark spruce along the road.

We drove another ten miles in silence. Finally he said, "What do you really think happened to Red?"

"Stormy's got us all thinking he was murdered," I said. Ahead of us, one pair of headlights approached. I lowered my highbeams. It did the same. It was a truck. A line of small orange lights defined the top of its cab.

"But by who?" he asked.

The headlights were fifty yards away. "Two days ago," I said, "I probably could've told you. Now the whole damn town's against us and I can't tell . . ." The headlights were now one hundred feet away and approaching fast.

"What the hell's with this guy?" John said, just as the truck clicked on his highbeams again, swerved into our lane, and came directly toward us. "Look out, Max! This bastard's going to hit us!"

I stood on the brakes and cranked the wheel to the right and we plowed over the shoulder, spun, ricochetted off a few small saplings, and finally skidded to a stop pointing back toward Burlington. The truck's airhorn blared as it screamed by and swerved back into its lane. Then, with a flash of brake lights, it disappeared around a curve.

"Son of a fucking bitch!" John said, gingerly touching the place where the bridge of his nose had connected with the dashboard handgrip. It looked like it was bleeding. "He could have killed us."

"It was a Collari truck," I said.

John forced his door open and got out. I dug the flashlight out of the glove box and did the same. Both sides of the tough little Jeep were scraped and it took both of us to pry the right front fender away from the wheel, but it restarted and seemed to run like nothing had happened once we were in fourth gear. I could feel him eyeing me in the darkness. "How many of those bozos you accosted this afternoon knew you were picking me up?"

"There's no way any of them knew," I said. "No way."

It was eight o'clock when we got to the lodge.

"No way they knew, huh?" John said, pointing through the windshield at the trees surrounding the entrance to the access road. He was still holding a McDonald's napkin to his nose.

My headlights illuminated several poster-size signs stapled to the trees that hadn't been there when I left. "Damn," I said, stopping the Jeep. The signs were handmade and crude, but the messages were pretty clear. JOBS NOT FISH! one of them said. COLLARI YES. WHITEFORK NO. another said, with the FORK crossed out and FUCK written in its place. The third sign obviously had been lettered to look like it had been done by a child. It read MY DADDY WAS LAID OFF SO RICH MEN CAN FISH. The fourth was the nastiest. In big block letters it read, RED DIED FOR YOUR SINS. I stopped the Jeep, got out, and ripped the signs down. I tossed them behind the seat and climbed back in.

"You better hope I find something in those cores," John said.

I didn't say anything and we continued down the driveway to the lodge. The Harpers' car was gone. I parked in front. The air was balmy and sweet with woodsmoke. John climbed out of the Jeep, stuck the napkin in his pocket, and stood with his hands on his hips looking at the building.

"Not bad," he said. "Not bad at all." He turned and looked out at Sweet Lake. It was a sea of reflected stars. "You fish the lake?"

"Sometimes." I pointed toward the Whitefork. "River's what most sports come for."

The door opened and Stormy stood behind the screen. "You two gonna stand out there all night?" she said. "Me and Stephanie's got pork chops ready to grill." She squinted at the Jeep. "What happened?" she said.

"Truck ran us off the road," I said as I grabbed John's duffle.

"You okay?"

"Yeah, we're fine." I turned to John. "We'll get the core-taker later," I said, leading him up the steps to Stormy who opened the screen door. "This is John Purcell, Stormy. John, Stormy Bryant. The brains and brawn of Whitefork Lodge."

John and Stormy shook hands. "Sure heard a lot about you over the years," he said.

"Yeah," she laughed, "your name's come up once or twice, too."

We entered the hallway. "You okay?" I whispered to her and she nodded. I carried John's bag up the stairs to the second floor. He followed, carrying his rod cases. "We'll be right down," I said to Stormy over my shoulder. "Chad and Tonya leave?"

"Yep. 'Bout three hours ago," she said. "We're going to eat in the readin' room. You want beer?"

"Coke for me," John said.

I put him in the big double in the front overlooking the lake and dumped his duffle on the smaller bed. "Bathroom's right back down the hall." I started for the door. "See you downstairs. Just follow your nose."

"Tonya? Stephanie?" He smiled and leaned the rod cases against the wall. "Who are they?"

"Tonya's the wife of a paying guest. Stephanie's a friend of mine," I said. "She's staying here for a while."

He smiled. "A friend, huh?"

"Yeah, an old friend," I said, ignoring his look and going back downstairs. Stormy came out of the kitchen carrying a Loon Lager and a Coke.

"Where's Rayleen?" I'd noticed his pickup was gone too. "He's not joining us?"

She shook her head. "He's downta the Starlight. He and some of the boys are puttin' together a fund or something for Red's kids."

"Good for him," I said.

"Yep. Old buzzard's okay if he wants to be," she said. I turned and started for the reading room. "Oh, I almost forgot. Wally Murray called. Said for you to call him as soon as you got in. No matter what time." She pointed to the phone. "Number he give me's right there."

Wally answered on the first ring.

"Max," he said, "we've got trouble."

"Now what?"

"They've succeeded in closing the clear-cut."

"How . . . ?"

"This thing with Red Crosley dying up there. Sheriff's closed it down. The clear-cut's off limits until the investigation is over."

"Now what am I supposed to do? My geologist just arrived. What about *our* court order?"

"I'm afraid our court order's not worth very much right now."

Neither of us said anything for a full minute. Finally he said, "Max, Claremont called me screaming about what happened in Collari's office this afternoon. You're lucky he isn't pressing charges."

"It was dumb, I know."

He didn't comment. "Look," he said, "whatever you decide to do, be careful. The sheriff's deputized some of Collari's people. They're going to be guarding the clear-cut day and night. With guns, no doubt. It could be dangerous."

I didn't tell him about almost being hit by the truck, and we hung up and I joined Stephanie in the reading room to wait for John to come down. She was sitting in the chair by the fire with Spotter at her feet. She got to her feet and embraced me as I entered the room.

"Oh, Max," she said. "I'm so sorry about Red."

I held her away from me at arm's length. "It's all right," I said. "Things were pretty bad around here for a while today but I think we're coming to grips with it."

"I was at the mill today," she said, pulling away and sitting back in the chair. A glass of red wine sat on the small table beside her and she picked it up and looked at me over the rim as she sipped. "You'd just left."

I sighed and sat on the couch. "I kind of lost my temper."

"So I heard." She nodded. "You lost the fifty thousand, too."

"I never had it."

"Al was quite upset."

"So was I."

"He's very powerful, Max. After today, things are going to be different."

"They already are," I said. "The clear-cut's been closed."

"See? You're not going to win this thing."

John stepped into the room. He'd obviously been outside the door a few seconds. "This is cozy," he said, looking directly at Stephanie. "I'll bet you're Stephanie."

Her face lit up and she smiled coyly. "And who are you?"

"I'm the guy who's going to make sure Max *does* win this thing," he said, stepping across the room and taking her hand in his. "I'm John Purcell, famous geologist, ardent fly fisherman, and dedicated bachelor." He bowed slightly and laughed.

Stephanie lowered her eyes and blushed.

He stood at the fireplace and leaned on the mantel. "What's this about closing the clear-cut?" he said to me.

I told him.

"That's all?" He smiled. "Max, I'm a rock hound, remember? Finding ways to get onto private property is part of my job description."

My daughter Sabrina and her husband David live in New York City. Both work. She is a television commercial producer with a medium-sized advertising agency. David does something with bonds on Wall Street. Every October, just after fishing season, they spend a week with me at Whitefork. Sabrina and I reconnect as father and daughter while David spends most of his time buying and selling stock via the cellular phone that never leaves his hand. Between them, I think, they make a lot of money. Or, at least, a lot of money for a couple kids in their midtwenties. Very much like her mother, Sabrina is a thoughtful guest and every time she and David arrive they bring a gift. Most are hapless electronic gizmos that I can never make work or use after they leave. Last year, however, they gave me a thing called the Tuscan Grill. It's not electric and has only the most basic of moving parts. It's a uniquely engineered cast-iron device that slides in between any fireplace's andirons, instantly making it possible to grill meats, fish, poultry, and vegetables over the coals of a hardwood fire. Stormy uses it all the time and tonight, the thick, center-cut pork chops she'd grilled on it in the reading room fireplace were nothing short of fantastic.

We ate on trays before the fire and listened to John talk about the New England of millions of years ago. It was fascinating, but I'd seen him do this before. It was standard operating procedure when he found a woman attractive, and nine times out of ten, it was successful. It was working on Stephanie and she hung on his every word, smiling and occasionally touching his arm or knee and laughing more enthusiastically than Stormy or I when he would say something amusing. I watched Stormy's reaction too and, for the first time since Red disappeared, the worry lines in her face softened and she seemed to genuinely relax as we listened to stories of Triassic lowlands and the Border fault and how Vermont's Green Mountains were once thousands of feet higher than the Himalayas. John might have been a glib, unabashed flirt, but tonight, he was just what we all needed.

Later, when the conversation turned to the European cities John and Stephanie had visited, I stifled a yawn, left them comparing museums, and went to the kitchen to help Stormy load the dishwasher. I actually don't think they saw me leave.

"Guy's a real charmer, ain't he?" she said, sliding our plates into the top rack. "Makes even an old broad like me feel as though I ain't lost it yet."

"He doesn't sleep alone very often." I laughed, pouring soap in the little cups in the washer door. "I thought you knew that."

She smiled. "You just better be careful, Maxwell Addams," she said, closing the machine and clicking it on. "Case you ain't noticed, your friend Stephanie's ga-ga already."

I shrugged. "She's a big girl," I said.

"That she is," she said, lighting a Camel. "And she's stayin' right down the hall from him too."

I lifted the Camel from her lips, took a drag, and put it back. "So are you," I chuckled.

CHAPTER ⚘ ELEVEN

At five-thirty the next morning I was awakened by a tapping on my bedroom window. It was John. He was on the porch dressed in waders, a green and black plaid wool shirt, and his vest. He smiled and gestured with a steaming mug of coffee in his hand. I threw some water on my face, dressed, and then Spotter and I joined him in the dining room. He had made a pot of coffee and built a small fire.

"You're up early for a Sunday," I said. "I thought you'd probably sleep 'til noon." I poured myself a mug of coffee. "What time is it in Colorado? Three-thirty?"

He wasn't listening to me. "I know how we're going to get those cores," he said, kneeling and giving Spotter's head a good scratching. "We're going to sneak up there tonight." Spotter's tail drummed on the floor.

I smiled in spite of myself. John had once parachuted into a heavily posted Wyoming ranch with a rock pick and a fly rod strapped to his back. "You're nuts," I said.

"I told you I'd think of something."

"Yeah, well, think again," I said. "My lawyer told me it's being guarded around the clock. With guns."

"So," he shrugged, "I'll just have to go up there today and see how guarded it really is."

"I repeat, you're nuts."

"No. Think about it, Max." He sat on a chair. "Vermont is one of the states with a Moving Water Shared Use Law, right?"

I nodded. A couple years ago several river rafting organizations had pushed through a law that made all Vermont rivers public domain as long as you didn't set foot on the private property on either bank.

"And, the Whitefork comes right down through the clear-cut, right?"

"Right."

"So, it's legal for me to fish it," he said. "I'll fish my way up there this afternoon and check it out. They see me, screw them. They don't know who I am anyway."

I looked into the fire. "I can't have you taking that kind of chance for me."

"You don't have any choice, Max. I came here to get you the cores. And that's what I'm going to do." He drained his coffee cup. "I can't wait around until the time is right. I've got to be in Boston next week, remember?"

"All right. But why not go up and look right away this morning?"

"You mean, instead of this afternoon?" He smiled. "You must be kidding, Max. I'm going to catch some of these brook trout submarines you've told me about all these years." He lifted Spotter's head and looked in the dog's eyes. "And I want to see Wonder Dog here do his thing."

I wrote him a license and got my things while he filled a thermos and grabbed two metal mugs from the kitchen. Then, with Spotter off at a trot in front of us, we walked to the river, where we sat on a log beside the Cobble and rigged our rods. The forecast was for rain but right now the sun was just washing the sky pink and chickadees flitted through the budding limbs near our heads almost as though we weren't there. Although Mark Richards and another deputy had been up and down the Whitefork several times yesterday looking for Red's wallet, the river seemed no worse for the experience.

"I'd forgotten how good an eastern forest smells," John said, tying a new piece of tippet to his leader. "Out West it doesn't smell like this, does it?"

He was right. It did smell good. The damp morning air this close to the river was deliciously thick with the sweet decay of spring. "Did you two stay up late last night?" When I went to bed at eleven, John and Stephanie were still in the reading room talking.

"I didn't look at the time." He shrugged and looked at me from under his cap brim. "She sure thinks she's getting screwed by all this, doesn't she?"

I nodded and poured myself a half mug of coffee from the thermos. "Her big order from Collari was the first casualty," I said.

"Way she talks though," he stood and brushed off the back of his waders, "she seems positive you're going to eventually see the light and drop this whole thing."

"Not much chance of that," I said, pulling a cigarette from the pack in my pocket and lighting it.

He smiled down at me. "That's what I told her. Said she should've seen you on the Ruby two years ago."

I laughed. I had spent the entire week John and I were on Montana's Ruby River knee deep in one twenty-foot stretch, trying everything I knew to catch one very big, very smart rainbow trout. "You tell her I never caught the trout?"

He shook his head. "She's pretty well connected with this Collari guy, isn't she?"

"She says he wants to get her in bed."

"I can identify with that."

"I'll bet you can."

"You mind?" He eyed me as he opened a fly box.

"Would it make a difference?"

"She was coming on pretty strong, Max."

"So were you."

He laughed. "Hell, I was just doing my thing. I didn't mean anything by it."

"She's looking for a commitment," I said.

"Aren't they all." He opened a fly box. "What do you suggest this morning, guide?"

I pulled two sizes of the Dead Princess from my drying patch and handed them to him.

He took the flies and frowned. "What the hell are these?"

"Something I made the other day," I said. "The Dead Princess. Try the smaller one first."

"Kinda heavy, aren't they?" He hefted them in his hand and smirked. "You're sure these aren't for a spinning rod."

"Just tie it on and shut up." I laughed. "In water this fast and deep you'll be glad."

He hooked one Dead Princess to his vest drying patch and tied the other to his tippet. "Okay, Spotter," he said, walking to the edge of the river, "show me where they are." Spotter didn't look up. He was already staring across the river at the spot where Chad and I had caught our first trout.

I snubbed my cigarette, put it in my pocket, and then joined Spotter. I let John wade into the river and pick his spot first.

"Spotter sees them in that seam along the right bank," I shouted over the roar of the water.

"I see where he sees them," he yelled back and then put his finger over his lips indicating he wanted me to be quiet. I mouthed, "Sorry," and waded in about ten yards downstream and stood watching him.

John's casting was more than flawless, it was like ballet. He seemed almost motionless as he half crouched in the water under the low hemlock limbs and faced upstream. Only his wrist moved, the nine-foot Sage doing all the work as his first cast shot out over the river. It was a side-arm cast and his accuracy was amazing as he reached his rod across his body and put a big upstream mend in the line before it settled on the water, the Princess plopping, practically splashless, two inches from the overhanging bank.

We both watched the line drift back down in the current and when he lifted his rod tip the Sage bowed and shook. In less than a minute, John had just caught his first trout on the Whitefork River.

He didn't believe in playing small trout and very seldom put one on his reel. True to form, he quickly stripped in the fish and, letting his line coil on the water around his knees, scooped the brookie into his net and slipped the hook from its mouth. He carefully held the fish in his hand for a second before sliding it back into the water. It was about a foot long. "Not a bad-looking brook trout," he shouted. "What is he? Big or average?"

"Small," I yelled back.

The second trout was mine and I slipped the hook from his jaw and released him wet, never taking him from the water.

John moved farther upstream, casting and placing the Princess as he went. I waded after him. As we always did on rivers, he took one side and I took the other, taking turns casting as we moved. The sun rose above Morning Mountain and streamers of pale yellow light angled through the trees, gilding the rocks and turning the tumbling water into blinding avalanches of diamonds. Spotter moved with us, staying just far enough ahead to be able to sit and be pointing when we arrived.

Above the Meadow Run, we climbed out of the water

and took a break. I poured the coffee and we sat on the high bank in the sun-splattered grass with the current hissing around our wading boots. I lit a cigarette. I considered mentioning that this was where we'd found Red, but instead, said, "Not bad, huh?"

He sipped at the hot metal cup. "This is a hell of a lot more fun than fishing the Madison," he said. "There's something about wild brook trout, isn't there?"

He was right. Not only were brook trout smart and difficult to catch, they were beautiful. Stormy called them "our jewels" and with their dark backs, bright red-orange spots, pale bellies, and fins edged in creamy white, they really were.

John pointed upstream to where the river flowed from the dark spruce into the meadow. "Look, Max," he whispered, "something's hatching."

I looked. Like a sudden spring blizzard, hundreds of milky-winged caddis flies were rising from the water and into the air, silhouetted against the dark trees as they danced above the rapids. Immediately trout began rising up and down the river and swallows appeared from nowhere, swooping into and through the cloud of rising and falling insects as it moved over the water toward us.

As we quickly changed to longer and finer tippets and tied on tan caddis imitations with wings of buoyant elk hair, the tiny bugs swarmed around us, coating our clothing, the insides of our sunglasses and fluttering up our noses.

Not wanting to spook the feeding fish, we cast from our knees on the bank, me working the upstream, John the downstream, each of us attempting drag-free drifts through the tricky currents of the deceptively slow-moving water.

The water bulged and swirled around John's fly first, as a one-pound brook trout snatched it and charged downstream. As he scrambled on his knees along the bank to keep the fish in the center of the river, my fly was sucked into a cotton-white mouth and for several minutes we had two beautiful trout pulling us in opposite directions at the same time.

When the hatch moved back upstream and into the dark trees, we waded in and followed, casting above exposed rocks and letting the flies drift back into the pockets of slack water behind them. Almost every cast now produced a strike and many times we had to stop and exchange the waterlogged flies for fresh dry ones.

By the time the hatch had faded to only stragglers struggling to remain airborne and the trout had returned to their hiding places, John, Spotter, and I were just a hundred yards below the Route 16 bridge.

"Where the hell are we?" he asked.

"As the crow flies," I said, "only about a mile from the lodge."

"Christ. It seems longer than that."

"It was. We fished about six miles of river."

"Your land stop there?" He pointed at the bridge.

I nodded. "That's Collari's from there on."

"Who owns the bridge?"

"The state."

"How far up is the clear-cut?" he asked as we changed from dry flies back to the Dead Princess.

"A mile and a half."

"Then I'll start from here this afternoon," he said, snipping off a piece of tippet.

"I'm coming with you."

"Christ, Max, they know you."

"They won't see me," I said, pointing at the thickening dark clouds above us. "It's going to rain this afternoon. Besides, I'll stay a couple hundred yards behind you. But if there's trouble, there'll be two of us."

"Great," he said as he waded into the water and began casting. "Both of us can get shot. Who'll be left for Stephanie?"

I waded in after him. "She'll still have Collari," I said, stripping out my line.

We'd only cast three or four times when I saw Stephanie making her way down through the trees. She looked at John and smiled. "You going to stay out here all day?" she shouted, picking her way through the low blueberry bushes to the river's edge. "Aren't you going to eat?" She was wearing a very snug pair of jeans, a forest green sweater and her golden hair had been carefully arranged in an exotic twist behind her head.

John's face lit up and he reeled in, waded by me and up to the bank at her feet. "What's on the menu?" he asked. I'd never seen John leave a river midcast for anything except lightning and I stood there watching them talk. I couldn't hear their conversation over the sound of the river but from the expressions on their faces, I could see it wasn't what was being said that was important.

I reeled in and joined them.

"Stephanie's made us a lunch, Max," John said. "Let's take a break, huh?" He climbed up out of the water to her side, turned, and extended his hand to me.

I ignored it and stumbled up onto the bank on my own.

"Don't be such a grump, Max," Stephanie said, hooking her arm through John's. "You've got to eat something. It won't take long."

"Yeah," John said, handing me his rod. "A little time off won't hurt."

As I followed them up through the trees away from the river toward the lodge, I watched the way the back of her jeans moved as she gingerly stepped over logs and ducked under branches. I smiled to myself.

It was silly, but I felt a faint twinge of jealousy. Not of

John, but of Stephanie. With her carefully chosen clothes, deliberately styled hair, and big brown eyes, she was trying to steal my friend.

During lunch, John explained his plan to get the cores. As I assumed they might, Rayleen and Stormy thought it was a great idea, although Stormy didn't understand why I would risk discovery by accompanying John during the afternoon's reconnoiter. It was Stephanie, however, who surprised me. She not only thought it was a good idea, but couldn't seem to get enough information on how and why cores were taken.

"Why do you have to take samples from the land up on the clear-cut?" she asked. "What's wrong with down here? This is where Max is so worried about anyway."

"These mountains are made up of vertical strata," John said. "You know the plates I told you about last night? How they collided? How these mountains were once flat land?" He held his two hands, fingers up, out in front of him. "And how they're tilted up like this now?"

She nodded like a pre-schooler with a favorite teacher.

"Well, the kind of pollution we're looking for, if there is any, just doesn't run downhill. It can't, because this vertical rock acts like a series of dams. Instead, it runs straight down the cracks between the stratifications until it finds a place to collect. Like the aquifer. It takes time. The mess Collari's made is new. Most of the crud he's created is still up there seeping down into his land."

"Then how'd that diesel get down here so fast?" Stormy asked.

"It was still Mud Season then," he said. "The permafrost was still frozen. The diesel couldn't soak through, so it took the quickest route. Just like snow melt does."

"What are you hoping the cores will find?" Stephanie asked.

"I'd settle for pathogenic bacteria, trace algae, or diatom colonies," he said with a smile.

"What's a diatom?"

"Tiny little organisms that suck oxygen out of fresh water."

"How do they get in the land?"

"Like I told you, they seep there."

"No, I mean, what causes it?"

"Sunlight." He shrugged. "Clear-cutting exposes a hell of a lot of ground to unfiltered ultraviolet that hasn't seen it in hundreds of years. The result is almost instantaneous. Chemical reactions happen. Everything changes. Ground water warms. The Whitefork warms. It's like a bathroom. Bad things grow in the heat. Like diatoms. Eventually the river and lake will turn into a soup."

"Then, how come everybody always talks about the erosion clear-cuttin' causes?" Stormy said.

"Because it's the most obvious," he said. "Tree leaves are like sponges, Stormy. They collect almost eighty percent of the water when it rains." He shrugged. "Cut all the trees down and suddenly a hundred percent of the water hits ground that can't handle it and," he snapped his fingers, "you've got major erosion." He smiled warmly at Stephanie. "Still, it's the insidious little things like diatoms that are the real culprits. And that's why we have to use the core-taker."

"How much noise does that core-taker thing make?" Rayleen asked.

"I don't know. I've never tried it. The machine's brand new," he said. "It's basically a weed-whacker engine hooked to a bit. A couple horsepower, I think. Like a giant drill that runs on gasoline."

"That don't sound too silent to me," Rayleen said. "I

mean, if you intend to sneak up there and get these things without nobody knowin' 'bout it."

"No, it doesn't," I said. "It's not the kind of noise we have in the woods up here at night."

"Maybe we could disguise the sound somehow," Stephanie offered.

"You have an idea?" John asked.

"Maybe," she smiled mischievously. "What if a woman was to get her car stuck in the mud up there on that road that leads into the clear-cut? I mean really stuck. What would she do?"

We all just looked at her.

"She'd yell for help, right? Loud."

We nodded.

"And when all those big strong men guarding the clear-cut came down the mountain to help push her out, she could keep gunning her engine and making it worse." She smiled. "Not to mention the noise her car would make."

Rayleen nodded. "It'd make a ton a noise if her muffler was missin'. Or fulla holes."

Rayleen and Stephanie smiled at each other. "And while my car is making all that noise," Stephanie put her hand on John's bicep, "you could be making noise with your thing at the same time."

John put his hand on hers. "It would work, Max," he said.

"No," I said to Stephanie. "I can't have you taking that kind of chance. I don't want you involved in this."

"Why not, Max?" She frowned. "It's a good idea."

"Yeah," Stormy said, looking at me through her cigarette smoke, "what's your problem?"

I sighed. "A lot of those people know you, Steph," I said.

"So what? It might even help." She smiled. "I'm a friend of Al's, remember?"

"All right, we'll try it." I sighed. "John and I will go up this afternoon and check things out. If it looks like we can pull it off, we'll drill the cores tonight." I looked into Stephanie's big, brown eyes. "Let's just hope they remember you're a friend of the family."

We all cleared the lunch dishes and then Stephanie went to the phone saying she had to call her office in Boston and a couple customers in New Hampshire she planned on seeing later in the week. John, Spotter, and Rayleen went out to the workshop to see how complex the core-taker was, get our fishing gear together, and check out a topographical map I had of the Whitefork River. I went with Stormy up to the newlyweds' room to help her flip the mattress so she could change the bed. She always insists upon each new guest having a different side of a mattress. I think it's a pain. She says it's just common courtesy. "Who wants to sleep in someone else's dents," she says. "And 'sides, mattresses last longer that way, too."

She grabbed an end and I grabbed an end. "On three," I said. When the mattress was flipped, we straightened it on the frame and I sat on it.

"I can't make it with you sittin' there," Stormy said, shaking out a bottom sheet.

"What do you think's going on with Stephanie?" I asked.

"You mean, her all of a sudden becomin' so helpful?"

I nodded.

"Seems pretty plain to me," she said, pushing me off the bed and spreading out the sheet. "Now that there's no stoppin' this thing, I'd say she's thinkin' maybe she's found another way to get that baby she wants so bad. Tuck that corner in there."

"John?" I laughed and folded the corner of the sheet under the mattress. "Never."

"Only man I ever know'd who said 'never' and made it stick is Rayleen," she said. "And not 'cause of what happened at Normandy neither. That war took a lot more'n his leg from him."

A car horn honked out in the yard and I went to one of the two windows and peered down. A big, red Jeep Cherokee was stopped in front of the porch.

"Who's that?" Stormy said from the bed.

I shrugged. "I don't recognize the car. A red Cherokee."

"Sounds like Ruth's."

She was right. The driver's side door opened and Ruth Pearlman got out. She was wearing a pair of snug, faded blue jeans, hiking boots, and a red sweater. "You're right," I said. "It is Ruth."

"Go talk to her, Max." Stormy waved another sheet over the bed. "She's probably here to see you anyways." The sheet settled. "I'll be down in a few minutes."

Ruth Pearlman and I met at the screen door. "I'm so sorry about Red," she said, as I stepped out onto the porch. "I just found out about his accident this morning."

I'd forgotten how sexy her voice was. In fact, I realized I'd forgotten a lot of things about her in the excitement of the past week. Her chestnut hair seemed looser and softer around her face than the day I was in her office and it had gold highlights sprinkled through it. She took my arm and we walked down the steps and across the yard toward the dock. "How's Stormy? Are you all right, Max?"

"It wasn't an accident," I said.

She stopped and faced me. The breeze ruffled her hair. Her green eyes were the color of the new grass coming up in the yard behind her. "I didn't hear that part. The sheriff just said . . ."

"Darren Foley only believes what he sees. You should know that much by now."

"But, how . . . ?"

"I don't know how, but I know Red."

She sat on the empty canoe rack. I sat down beside her. Our thighs touched. "I had another reason for coming out here," she said, crossing her legs. Her legs were longer than I remembered. I lit a cigarette. "Claremont Taylor brought Alphonse Collari to my office this morning," she said.

"And?"

"They're going to call an emergency session of the city council to put an end to this."

"What do you mean, put an end to this?"

"They're going to vote to get the logging started again."

"They can do that?"

She nodded. "With something like this, they can. Now that the mill's closed, the economy of the town is in jeopardy." She smiled wanly. "Thing is, they need my cooperation. The mayor has a line-item veto on anything and everything the council does. All I have to do is say no to starting the logging when it crosses my desk."

"So, what's the problem? You just say no, right?"

"I wish it were that easy, Max." She shook her head. "This is a non-partisan issue. Just about everyone in Loon wants the logging started again. I'm the mayor. Mayors who buck the city council on things like this don't have much chance to get reelected."

"So, you're saying that you don't have a choice?"

"Claremont said he won't run for mayor if I agree with the decision of the council."

"And if you don't agree with the decision? If you veto it?"

"He and Collari will make sure I don't get reelected."

"They're blackmailing you, Ruth."

"I know. But I also know that one two-year term isn't enough to do anything in this town," she said. "I have plans for Loon, Max. I need that second term."

"But what they're doing can't be legal."

She shrugged. "It's politics, Max."

"When would this happen?"

"Next day or two. Some of the council members are out of town and they all have to be present for an emergency session."

I leaned on my knees and hung my head.

"I'm sorry." She put her hand on my thigh. "I came to warn you, Max," she said softly. "You have to get the evidence you need for your permanent injunction as soon as you can." She removed her hand.

I dropped my cigarette between my feet and stepped on it. "My geologist is here now," I said, looking at the taut jean fabric on her thigh. "He's going to take the cores."

"Soon, I hope."

I nodded.

"Just be careful, Max." Her hand was back on my leg. The spot was still warm from the first time.

"It's nice to know you care."

She removed her hand, brushed the hair from her eyes, and looked at me. "Are you being facetious?" She frowned.

"No. No," I said. "I'm serious."

A smile replaced the frown. "Well, I do care." She stood up and straightened her sweater. "So, be careful."

"Yes, ma'am," I said and stood also. I smiled.

She studied my face. "Did I ever tell you how my ex-husband had pale blue eyes like yours?"

I shook my head.

"I was a sucker for them. When I finally got up the courage to tell him I wanted a divorce, I had to do it with mine closed. I wouldn't have been able to go through with it, otherwise." She smiled. "I'm going to go say hello to Stormy." She turned and walked back up the lawn toward the lodge.

There was something in the way her hips moved in her jeans that told me she knew I was watching.

CHAPTER TWELVE

The Route 16 bridge had originally been covered. I'd seen pictures of it in a couple of the older books I'd inherited with the lodge. A fire in 1953 caused by an automobile accident midspan had destroyed the wooden superstructure but the beautifully laid rip-rap foundation of granite boulders still remained. Several well-worn paths snaked down to the river on both sides of the bridge from the highway and it wasn't uncommon to see as many as a dozen bait fishermen clustered on the banks or hanging over the bridge rails on a Saturday or Sunday during the summer. Although, technically, my side of the bridge was catch and release, rather than hassle anyone, I let those fishing in my water keep what they wanted. It was Stormy's idea. "Public relations," she called it. It didn't bother me. I figured what trout they caught and killed had to be pretty dumb to be hanging around under all those guys on the bridge anyway. It was good to get them out of the gene pool.

John and I rigged our rods, crossed 16, and waded into the river on the upstream side of the bridge. The high water had left a couple beer cans and three or four styrofoam bait boxes tangled in the underbrush at the water's edge.

"The ever present bait container," John said, shaking his head. "What do you suppose these idiots think when they toss this stuff? That it's going to go away?"

"Usually it does," I said. "I come up here and pick this place up at least three times a summer. Pisses me off."

"Just be glad they don't fish with spray paint."

I laughed and ducked under a maple branch studded with swelling buds. A tangle of nylon line was knotted around it. "They certainly have a way of telling the world they were here," I said, holding the branch up out of the way as he ducked under and waded ahead of me.

Ten yards farther and the river turned away to the left. It tumbled toward us down a steep grade and into a narrow cut with twenty-foot-high shale cliffs on each side. The water was too fast and deep in the small canyon to wade, so, hugging the slender ledge at the cliff base, we worked our way into it and around the corner. We were now in Collari territory.

I pressed my mouth to John's ear so he could hear me over the roar of the water. "That's Collari's land directly above us," I said.

"Let's stop up there." John pointed to a slight depression in the cliff ahead of us.

We scrunched ourselves in the hollow and squatted facing the river. Wet mist from the tumbling waves hung in the air and coated our faces. My beard dripped cold water down my neck.

He ran his fingers over the water-worn, gray rock above our heads. It was studded with lighter-colored things the size of golf balls. "A good example of biotite orbicules in granite," he said.

I looked up and water dripped in my face.

He pointed upstream. "I'll go first," he said. "You

follow about fifty feet or so back. That way if someone gets seen, it'll be me, not you."

I nodded.

"You pissed about Stephanie?" he asked.

I shook my head.

"It just happened, you know what I mean?" He shrugged.

"What happened?"

"She didn't tell you, did she?" He rolled his eyes. "She was supposed to tell you when I went out to the workshop with Rayleen."

"She was on the phone," I said. "Then the mayor showed up."

"Jesus." He scaled a stone across the current. "We slept together last night, Max."

All I could say was, "That was fast."

"I kept telling myself," he said, "this is Max's girl." He looked at me. "But . . . it just happened, you know?"

"She isn't my girl," I said. "I told you. We're friends. And we still are."

"How about us?" He studied my face from under the dripping bill of his Bronco's cap.

I laughed. "I'll wait and see what kind of stuff you get with those cores."

"Yeah." He laughed too. "If I get a chance to drill them."

We both watched the water. A kingfisher flew by, low over the waves, saw us, squawked, and banked up and out of the canyon.

"Then how serious is this thing with Stephanie?" I asked.

"I don't know," he said. "It is kind of sudden, isn't it? It's different, though. Really different from anything else that's ever happened to me."

"She's a wonderful woman. Special."

"That she is." He looked upstream and then back at me. He smiled. "You sure you're not pissed?"

"I'm not pissed, dammit!"

He laughed. "All right then, let's go count the enemy."

"Lead the way, general."

He stood carefully. "Watch your head," he said.

I stood and banged my head.

We worked our way along the cliff to where the river widened and calmed down. I stayed on the narrow ledge while John waded in, stripping line and beginning to false cast.

"What if I catch something?" he mouthed back over his shoulder.

I shrugged.

He began wading upstream, casting ahead of himself, placing his fly into the current just above exposed rocks and letting it swirl around and into the eddy on the downstream side. Then he'd lift it from the water, roll cast to get the line moving and place it behind the next rock. I don't know what fly he had on, but if he wasn't careful, he was going to catch a fish.

When he was about fifty feet ahead of me, I waded in, got my line out and moving, and began placing my fly along the far bank. I stuck close to the left side of the river. The water had cut deep into the hill here and, although it was almost chest deep, I knew the overhang of time-worn rocks and exposed roots would give me a hiding place should someone see John and come down to the river. I kept one eye on my fly line and the other on him.

For me, moving against the strong current of the deeper water was slow going and John quickly increased the distance between us by another fifty feet. He didn't look back and occasionally I lost sight of him behind boulders or low-hanging spruce limbs. To my left, over the edge of the bank, I could see the clear-cut through the thin screen of remaining trees. I couldn't see any people.

We fished on like this for about five minutes when I saw John raise his hand, signaling he wanted me to stop. I reeled in and moved as close to the bank as the water depth would allow. My vest was soaked and water lapped at my armpits. It was deepest right against the eroded ledge. I couldn't hear anything over the river sounds and watched John turn and begin moving back downstream toward me, casually casting across and down as he came. He looked at me and nodded. He'd obviously seen what we'd come to see in the clear-cut.

He was fifteen feet away from me when a loud explosion fractured the damp air and a geyser of water erupted between us. Instantly it was followed by a second explosion and a second geyser, this one close enough to where I huddled against the bank to soak me. John's eyes were wide and staring at something directly above me. His line, now untended, drifted into my hiding place and piled up against my chest.

"You're on private property!" a man yelled from above me. "This here's a no trespassin' area!" It was Bull's voice and a shotgun shell dropped into the water a foot in front of me, spun in the current, and floated by.

I watched John raise his hands up away from his body. "Hey!" he yelled. "I'm just fishing. Jesus. Be careful with that gun." He gave Bull the best innocent look I'd ever seen. "I didn't see any no trespassing signs."

"How'd you get up here?" Bull shouted. A couple stones dropped into the water at my shoulder as Bull moved around on the ground above my head. I pushed myself farther back in under the bank and several quarts of freezing water flooded over the tops of my waders, soaking my chest and belly, running down into the legs and numbing my feet.

"I came up the river from the bridge," John said, now slowly wading toward shore. "Guy down there said the big ones are up here."

"He did, huh? What guy?"

"I don't know. Some guy fishing with his kid on the bridge."

"Where you from?"

"Burlington."

"You ain't stayin' at that Whitefork Lodge, are you?"

"No." John shook his head vehemently. He was at the bank ten feet from me. "No. I drove up for the day. Parked down the road a ways. Walked up to the bridge."

"Damn good thing you ain't," Bull said. "That White-fork place ain't gonna be around long."

"What's the matter?" John relaxed his arms and let them slowly drop to his side. "They going out of business?"

"Yeah," Bull said. "Real sudden like."

John put one foot up on the bank.

"Get back in that water!" Bull roared and John jumped back. "Told you. This here's private property." I didn't have to see what Bull was doing. The look on John's face reflected the shotgun pointed at him.

"It would be easier for me to leave," John said, "if I walked back down to the road on land. It took me an hour to wade up here in the river."

"Tough shit. Stay in the water," Bull said. "Get that damn fish line reeled in and get the hell outta here."

John attempted a smile and began reeling in his line. By now, however, it was tangled securely around my right arm and to free it I would have to extend my arm from under the overhang. John glanced at me and I knew he instantly could see the problem. He turned the crank on his reel slower.

"C'mon, goddammit," Bull shouted. "Get that line in and get the hell outta here."

I frantically felt around the line to find where it was snagged and watched in frustration as it pulled taut. John looked from me up to Bull and smiled sheepishly.

"Oh for Chrissake," Bull yelled. "Just yank it free."

John lowered the rod tip and yanked. My feet were barely touching bottom and I was almost floating in the deep water. His yank just about pulled me from under the bank. I grabbed at a root and hung on.

"Fuck," I heard Bull say. "Hold it tight, goddammit." And to my horror, accompanied by a shower of loose soil and pebbles, his big hairy hand, wrist, and bare forearm reached down from the overhang above my head, the fingers working, feeling for the line, inches from my face. "Fuck!" he grunted. His hand swung wildly. I ducked under the water and it pawed at the air where my head had been.

My ears ached and had it not been for the gallons of water now filling my waders, I know I would have begun to float. I frantically felt the front of my vest for the little clipper tool that hung there.

By now Bull had a grip on the line and was yanking, trying to free it. John's six-weight, floating line held and it felt as if, any second, Bull was going to lift me straight up out of the water.

I've never been much good at holding my breath. Cigarettes probably. And my lungs were bursting just as my fingers found the clipper. I frantically snipped at the fly line, cutting it everywhere my fingers touched and suddenly the tension disappeared. The line was free. Separated from my tether I sank like a Dead Princess and was pushed hard by the strong current roughly along the wall of the deep cut, down the river. I fought my way to the surface, not knowing if I was going to pop up in full view of Bull and not caring. Another second under water and I was going to drown anyway.

I surfaced ten yards downstream. I felt gravel under my knees. I was facing away from where John and Bull stood and, keeping only my head above the water, slowly turned to look.

John was already picking his way around the boulders coming toward me. I could see Bull standing on the lip of the bank over where I'd hidden, his right sleeve wet and still rolled to his bicep. The shotgun in his hands was moving slowly, following John's progress. Neither one of them were looking in my direction and I quickly crawled behind a large granite boulder, dug my fingers in some cracks, and hugged it. It was then that I realized my rod was gone. I looked at the foaming water around me. Nothing.

"Tell that asshole on the bridge," Bull yelled, "that I'll come down there and kick the shit outta him and his kid if he sends anyone else up here."

John's wader-covered legs appeared on my right. I tilted my face up and he glanced down at me as he stepped around the boulder. "Don't move," he said. "Wait."

I mouthed, "Now I'm pissed." And he slogged on downstream.

I waited. I twisted my wrist and watched the hands on my watch move. Fifteen minutes. A half hour. I was beginning to shake. It wasn't the cold. Only my ears and hands were cold. Although not intended for the purpose, neoprene waders are a lot like a wet suit. Water that gets inside warms to your body temperature. My problem was the position and the strength of current nipping at me as it swirled around the boulder. I couldn't feel my knees. My thighs were cramping. I was losing my grip on the granite. The water was only four feet deep, but it was moving fast. If I didn't stand up soon, I knew I could really cramp and lose my grip. If that happened, I'd tumble away downstream like a beach ball. If the rocks banging on my head didn't kill me, I would drown.

I pushed my feet against the bottom and slowly lifted my head above the top of the boulder. Bull was gone. I could see a group of five men clustered around two pickups in the low end of the clear-cut but, because of the trees between us, couldn't tell whether he was one of them. I looked downstream. He wasn't behind me either.

It was as I started to stand that I saw the wallet wedged in the crotch folds of my waders. My fingers were so stiff that I almost dropped it as I lifted it to eye level. The wallet was tooled leather, soaked black with water. A heavy brass zipper enclosed three sides. I jammed it down in the bib of my waders and slowly stood, pain shooting through my legs and up the small of my back. I took a step. With the water in the waders my legs must have weighed close to a hundred pounds a piece.

I had gone about ten feet when the rain that had been threatening all day started. It fell lightly at first and felt warm on my face, then the sky opened up and sheets of it came down, hissing on the river and obliterating everything except the roiling water at my feet.

I still had no choice but to stay in the river and continue slowly and painfully downstream, stumbling and falling just about every third step.

It was going to be a long, hard walk back to the lodge.

It was almost dark by the time I got to the bridge. John was huddled underneath, squatting on a rock.

"Over here, Max." He clicked on the little penlight he carried fastened to his vest.

I slogged to him.

"Christ," he said. "That was hairy. You alright, Max?" He took my arm and helped me sit on the rock beside him. "I was beginning to think that moose had caught you. I didn't know what to do."

I tried to speak but my lips were so cold they wouldn't work.

"I picked up your Loomis," he said, shining the light on it. "It floated almost all the way down here."

I could barely smile but I was glad. I had paid three times what it was worth at an American Museum of Fly-Fishing auction one year down in Manchester. I had stretched at the wrong time and no one outbid me.

"I counted five of them," he said. "Looked like they all had guns."

I could only nod.

"C'mon," he said, putting my arm over his shoulder, "let's get the hell out of here and get you warmed up."

There was a fire in the dining room fireplace and Stormy put me in a chair directly in front of it. It took John and Rayleen, yanking and pulling, to get the waders and my pants off. My hands still didn't work. As the waders inched off, a couple gallons of river water poured to the floor between my legs. The wallet splashed into the puddle. Spotter sniffed at it.

"What's this?" Stormy said, picking it up.

"I think it's probably Red's wallet," I said. I'd forgotten I had it. "Somehow it ended up in my lap after I was under the water."

"Let's see that." Rayleen took it from Stormy's hands. He nodded. "Yep, it's Red's alright. Seen it enough times at the Starlight." He turned it in his hands studying the zipper. "Think we should call Darren?"

Stormy snatched it back. "I'm for openin' it," she said.

"I think we should do both," I said, struggling out of

my wet shirt. "Although, we should probably open it first. Make sure it's Red's before we call."

"I'm tellin' ya, it's Red's," Rayleen muttered.

"Okay." Stormy laid the wallet on the hearth. "We'll open it when Max's warmed up." She took my arm and tugged me to my feet. "Right now, you go take a good, long, hot shower. You're blue as a newborn."

The shower was bliss and I stood in it like I was drugged. When the hot water began to run out, I shut it off, grabbed a towel and went into the bedroom. Stephanie was sitting on the edge of my bed.

"I've always thought you had the cutest butt," she said.

"Yours isn't bad either." I smiled and rubbed the towel in my hair.

"Are you mad at me, Max?"

"About John?" I shook my head. "No, I'm not mad, Steph. I'm happy you're so happy. I can see it in your face."

"John said he talked to you. I'd hate it if I'd done anything to damage your friendship."

I wrapped the towel around my waist and sat beside her. The bed squeaked and we looked at each other and laughed. "It certainly seems to know when we're on it, doesn't it?" I said.

She looked at her hands. "I'd like to stay here at Whitefork, Max," she said. "At least, until John leaves." She seemed to glow in the backlight from the bedside lamp.

"That's all right with me."

"I might move into his room."

"That makes sense."

She looked at me. "You're sure you're not mad?"

I shrugged. "I think I was jealous at first."

"I really like him, Max."

"So do I."

She kissed me on the beard and stood. The bed squeaked again. "It is a nice sound, isn't it?" she said.

I nodded.

She leaned, kissed me again, and then was gone.

I gave the bed a bounce and listened to its *squeak, squeak* in return.

I pulled on a pair of jeans and an old tan moleskin shirt and returned to the dining room. Stormy had wrapped the wallet in paper towels to help dry it and the five of us took it to the reading room and put it on my fly-tying table under the bright circle of light from my gooseneck halogen. We clustered around the table like doctors doing brain surgery. Now, partially dry, you could see the leaping deer tooled into one side and the crossed hunting rifles on the other. It was nice leather. "Who wants to do the honors?" I asked.

"You open it, Max," Stephanie said. "You found it." She picked up the wallet and held it out to me.

"No, Max." Stormy knocked it from her hand. "Not like that. Hold it by the edges. What if there's finger-prints?"

I frowned at her and gingerly picked it up by the edges and carefully unzipped the zipper. Then I laid it on its back in the light. It was Red's wallet alright. His face stared back at us from a Vermont driver's license in the first of several plastic sleeves.

Stephanie turned away.

"Steph?" John touched her arm. "What's wrong?"

"Nothing," she said, her voice muffled by her hand. "He was just . . . just such a nice guy. It's his face in the picture is all."

Stormy opened a drawer in the tying table and handed me a dubbing needle. "Use this to turn them plastic pages, Max," she said.

I took the dubbing needle, which is nothing more than a thick piece of long, sharpened wire stuck into a wooden handle, and carefully lifted the plastic pages one by one. The first one held Red's MasterCard, the next had a picture of his boys. The next two pages were stuck. I pried and they popped apart. In one was a picture of his wife and his Collari International identification card was in the other. The next two pages held a Sunoco card and his union card. "That's it," I said, letting the pages fall back into place.

"But there ain't no money," Stormy said. She took the dubbing needle from my hand and pried open the money compartment. "See. It's empty. His paycheck's gone." She slammed the needle on the table. "Just like I thought, dammit. They killed him and stole his money too."

"What's this about money?" John asked.

Rayleen told him how Red had cashed his paycheck before going to the Starlight. "Even if the boy bought everybody in the place a drink, which nobody's said he did, he still woulda had, hell, a hundred and fifty—or more—in there."

Stormy's fist hit the table. "He wasn't killed for the money," she said. "Somebody just saw it and took it. And I bet only the guy who took it knows it's gone. Slipped it out when nobody was lookin', zipped the wallet back up, and tossed it in the river. Red was dead and floatin' away by that time."

"Good God," Stephanie said. "What if Stormy's right?"

"I am right," she said. "I can feel it." She looked at the wallet. "And look there, Max." She pointed to the driver's license. "What's that?"

We all looked. There was a smudge. Stormy pulled down the gooseneck magnifying glass my eyes needed to tie anything smaller than a number 14 and held it over the wallet. She peered through. "It's a big, fat fingerprint," she said, lifting her head away. "Take a look at that, Max."

I looked. She was right. Just as clear as if it had been permanently embossed, there was one large fingerprint dead center on the plastic.

Rayleen took a peek. "Yep. That there's a fingerprint all right."

John and Stephanie looked. "It's certainly a fingerprint," John said. "But so what? This thing's probably loaded with them. It is a wallet, you know."

"I'll bet my boots," Stormy said, "that there fingerprint was put on that plastic by the last person to open Red's wallet. And I'm tellin' you, the last person to open it weren't Red Crosley."

There was no denying that Stormy could be right. What we were going to do with the wallet, however, did create some disagreement.

Stormy wanted to call Darren Foley and get him up to the lodge immediately. Stephanie and John cautioned that we should agree on where it was found, preferably somewhere closer to the lodge and definitely not where we'd been, because we were trespassing on Collari land. I disagreed with all of them. "Whether you're right or not about the fingerprint, Stormy," I said, "really isn't what's important right now. We need the cores. If we call the sheriff now, he'll be all over that clear-cut within the hour looking under every rock." I looked at John. "John and I won't be able to get within ten feet of the place much less onto the land to take those cores."

John nodded. "I agree," he said.

I tipped the wallet closed with the dubbing needle and pushed it toward Stormy. "You can give this to Darren first thing in the morning. Say you found it walking by the river. Okay?"

"All right." Stormy nodded. "I'll put it in a plastic bag," she said. "It'll be in the refrigerator. One night ain't gonna make no difference. The scum that did this think they got away with it. I can wait 'til tomorrow to find who they are." She smiled sadly. "Just hope it ain't no one I babysat."

CHAPTER ⚓ THIRTEEN

Alfonse Collari telephoned about a half hour after Stormy had put the wallet in the refrigerator. We were all in the reading room, going over the fine details of our plan when the phone rang. Stormy went and answered it. When she came back into the room, she said, "Guess what? It's Collari." She looked at Stephanie. "And he wants to talk to you."

Stephanie looked from John to me.

"Talk to him," I said.

"Yeah," John smiled. "What the hell? See if he sounds suspicious of anything."

When she came back, I thought she looked a bit shaken. "You okay?" John asked. "What did he want?"

She sighed. "Nothing important," she said. "He just wanted me to know that we're still friends." She walked to the magnifying glass and ran her finger around the rim. "He said he can guarantee that they'll be logging by next Tuesday. Something about the mayor and the city council."

Everyone looked at me. I nodded. "He's right," I said. "Ruth told me about it today. That's why it's so important we get those cores tonight."

John stood and went to her side. "What about you?"

he said, putting his arm around her shoulders. "You're not changing your mind about tonight, are you?"

"Of course not." She shook her head and looked down. "I just don't want anyone else to get hurt." She flicked at something on the magnifying glass with her finger. "Al says he doesn't either."

"Tell that to Red," Stormy snorted.

"I know," Stephanie said. "I know."

John and I pulled Stephanie's car into the workshop where Rayleen crawled underneath and pounded a couple fist-size gaping holes in her muffler with one of our hammers and a chisel. Then I climbed in behind the wheel, started the engine, and gunned it. John stood back, stroking his mustache, evaluating the deafening roar. He looked satisfied.

Rayleen lifted his cap and scratched his head. "Hell, that damn noise'd drown out a seven-forty-seven," he said.

We pulled the car back out in front of the lodge. The rain had tapered off and bright little specks of stars were beginning to show in the black spaces between the rapidly dissolving clouds. "Gonna clear," Rayleen said as John and I went up the steps onto the porch. "But don't fret none. Be plenty a mud for her to get stuck in up in that clear-cut." He sat on the steps.

"I just hope it's not so much that Stephanie won't eventually get unstuck," John said, holding the screen door for me. "I think I'll only need about thirty minutes to pull the cores. I don't want to leave her up there with that Bull and his shotgun."

"I doubt he'll even be there," I said. "The last thing he'd expect is us up there tonight."

Stephanie was coming down the stairs as we entered the lodge. Stormy stood at the top watching her.

"Wow," John and I said in unison. Stephanie wore a

very tight, very short black wool skirt, no hose, and very red, backless high-heeled shoes. She had a sweater on that made her look like she'd been dipped in red paint. Her hair was teased up big and frothy and her lipstick matched the red of her sweater.

"The sweater's not too tight, is it," she said, pushing at her breasts with her palms.

We shook our heads.

"I don't want this one to be too noticeable." She pushed down on her false left breast. "It kind of wants to slide up because of the pins in the back." She turned slightly to show us the vertical line of safety pins pulling tight and securing the bulk of the sweater down the middle of her back.

"You look great," John said, extending his hand and taking hers as she came down the last two steps. "In a trashy sort of way."

"Good. The trashier the better." She beamed. "Stormy helped me do it." She did a pirouette. "We altered some of the clothes I had with me."

"Them bozos at the clear-cut're gonna fall all over themselves tryin' to help this woman," Stormy said, clumping down the stairs. She still had a thimble on her finger.

John looked at me and smiled. "It almost seems unfair, doesn't it?"

Stephanie took her trenchcoat from the rack in the corner and slipped it on, shaking her Dolly Parton–esque hair out over the collar. "There," she said, turning one more time. "The safety pins show?"

"They're about the only things that don't," I said, laughing.

"Hey," Stormy said. "I thought you two was gonna get ready."

Although most of it was a little tight on him, I found enough dark clothing in my closet and drawers for both

John and I to wear. Stormy pulverized a couple charcoal
briquets with the mortar and pestle in the kitchen and
mixed the black powder with olive oil.

"Feels like I'm going trick-or-treating," John said as
we smeared the paste on our faces and necks.

The core-taker was essentially a sectional diamond
drill bit around which sections of four-foot-long steel
pipe would be slid as it bit deeper and deeper into the
rock. Once the drill had cut to the proper depth, it was
pulled out of the pipes and then the pipes, which now
contained a core sample, were pulled up. The whole
thing was run by a small gasoline engine that sounded,
as John had predicted, just like a weed-whacker. We
split the core-taker into two piles and zipped each inside
one of the two big canvas duffles I had. Both had shoulder straps and I hefted mine. It was heavy but manage-
able.

We were going to wade back up the river to just above
where John had been confronted by Bull and we all
stood on the porch as John and I pulled on our chest
waders.

I looked at my watch. "I know it's a cliché," I said.
"But synchronize your watches. It's eight forty-five."

"What do you think, Max?" John said. "An hour?"

I nodded. "Give us an hour," I said to Stormy, "to get
up there and in position. Then you and Rayleen take
your truck and lead her over to Hooker Hill Road and
the entrance to the clear-cut." I looked at Stephanie.
"Then you drive that car of yours in and stick it good.
Honk the horn and yell for help. Then as soon as we
hear your engine indicate that they're trying to help you
get unstuck, we'll start to work."

"If there's any problem," I said, "lean on the horn
and keep leaning on it like it's broken."

"And take this." Stormy handed Stephanie a small
canister the size of a small can of insect repellent. It was

mace. "If one of them bozos starts anythin', spray him right in the kisser."

"Where in the hell did you get that?" I asked.

"Found it under the bed today in the newlyweds' room. That Tonya musta dropped it," she said. "I was gonna toss it."

"No." I took the canister from Stephanie and slipped it in the pocket of my black-hooded sweatshirt. "You're going to be in a car, Steph. You could end up spraying yourself."

"But, Max."

"He's right," John said. "Forget the mace. You get in trouble, it could just make things worse."

I hefted the duffle to my shoulder, went down into the yard, and stopped. John was still on the porch. He and Stephanie embraced. I looked away.

The air was cold and the duffles were heavy. Even so, wading back up the river wasn't that difficult. We knew where the bad spots were and with occasional use of our small flashlights were able to avoid them. In the deeper water we were able to float the duffles behind us. The darkness and the roar of the river made it almost impossible to communicate, so before we'd left the shelter of the bridge, we had devised a simple signaling system; one tap on the shoulder meant look right, two meant look left, three meant stop, and four meant trouble. For that reason we attempted to stay as close as possible.

It took us a little over forty-five minutes to get to the spot John had picked for us to exit the river, and we crawled out of the water and up through the trees to the hay bales at the edge of the clear-cut. He tapped me twice on the shoulder and I looked down the cut to our left.

Four men bundled in heavy parkas stood or squatted around a small fire. Two of them were drinking beer.

Two pickup trucks reflected the flames a few feet beyond. Leaning against the grill of the nearest truck were four rifles, and what looked like a spotlight lay on the hood.

John tapped me once on the shoulder and I looked up to the right. The beam from a flashlight came down the edge of the trees we were hiding in, illuminating the boulders, hay bales, and piles of cut branches. Occasionally, it was shined into the woods. Fifteen feet away I saw it was Bull, the shotgun cradled in the crook of his arm. John tapped me four times and I nodded. We pressed ourselves into the dead leaves against the hay and I held my breath. The light passed over us. I cautiously raised my head and looked. Bull had gone by and now was walking out into the clear-cut toward the fire. I heard one of the men shout his name and then laughter.

We got to our feet and, crouching low, started up the hill following the hay bales just inside the tree line. In the darkness it was difficult to see every limb and several slashed at my face. Low bushes clung and tore at our wader legs. We'd gone a hundred yards when John grabbed my arm. He pointed at the duffles and then out at an exposed granite ledge the size of a compact car in the middle of the clear-cut.

"What's wrong with closer to these trees?" I whispered.

He shook his head.

"Jesus," I whispered again. "We'll be sitting ducks out there."

He shrugged, tapped me three times on the arm, and sat down. I sat too. Now we'd wait for Stephanie.

It didn't take long. Even with the sound of the river in the background we could hear the stock car roar of the punctured mufflers as she gunned the engine and powered the car up into the road to the clear-cut. Her headlights shone up through the trees toward the men at the fire, the cocked beams clearly visible in the wood smoke. Then we listened as she floored it again several times, obviously spinning her wheels deep into the mud. The men were on their feet and grabbed their rifles. One switched on the spotlight and trained it in the direction of Stephanie's car. Her horn began honking and I was positive I could hear her shouting.

John grabbed my arm. "Let's go," he said, and running at a crouch we carried the duffles out into the clear-cut to the granite ledge. As John quickly began to sort out the pieces of the core-taker, I looked down at the fire. Bull's bulk was obvious and he looked like he was directing traffic. He pointed to the men and then pointed to where Stephanie's car was stuck. Two of the men climbed in a pickup and backed down into the woods toward her headlights. He gestured to the smaller of the four who threw up his arms, turned, and sat back down by the fire. Then Bull trotted down the hill after the pickup. The sound of Stephanie's mufflers rattled up the mountain in regular spurts and I could imagine the men straining and pushing at her hood, trying to rock her out.

"They've left one guy behind," I said to John.

He glanced quickly down the hill over his shoulder. "Shit," he said and handed me the assembled core-taker. "Hold this upright while I start it." He grabbed the short starter rope, fiddled with a switch on the engine and pulled. The little engine coughed blue smoke, sputtered, and caught. As the core-taker whined to life, the sound of the car roared. We both watched the man at the fire. He didn't move.

"Okay," John said. "I'll guide it in. You give it gas in sync with her mufflers." He placed the end of the drill in the dirt at the base of the ledge. The little engine idled quietly.

"Now," he said, as the roar of the car echoed up the mountain. "Now!"

I opened the throttle wide and the engine screamed and I watched the drill head disappear quickly into the ground.

When the car stopped, I closed the throttle. When it started, I opened it.

When the drill bit had cut about eight feet down, John removed the engine, slid two steel tubes over the drill, and tapped them down into the hole. "Lift out the drill, Max," he said. "Carefully." I did and then, even more carefully, he removed the tubes, closed the ends of each with styrofoam corks, and put them in his duffle. "Now, over here," he said and we moved ten feet farther out into the clear-cut. Stephanie's car was still roaring. I was sweating and could taste the charcoal from my face.

We took the second two samples the same way and just as John finished corking them, all the sound from below us stopped. I cut the idling engine and looked toward the man by the fire. He was on his feet, looking in our direction.

"Duck," I said, dropping to my belly. "He's looking right up here." John fell to his stomach beside me and we watched the man by the fire walk to the spotlight, turn it on, and shine it up at us.

"Don't look at it," I whispered and we buried our faces in our arms.

The harsh, bright light swept over us several times and then it was dark again. I peeked over my arm. He was coming up the hill. His rifle was in one hand, a flashlight in the other. "Jesus, he's coming up," I said, getting to my knees.

"C'mon," John said, "let's get the hell out of here." He scrambled to his feet, threw the core-taker's parts in the duffles and hoisted his to his shoulder. By the time I was up and had mine, he was almost to the trees.

As I entered the trees, the sound of Stephanie's car began again. This time the growl was steady and looking back down the hill, I could see her headlights moving. "They're getting her out," I said.

"Good," John said. "Let's hope we can get out, too."

I peered through the trees. The man was almost to the granite ledge, his flashlight beam already playing on its surface. Something metal glinted as his light swept over it and then shone as he quickly pointed it back again. "Oh Christ," I said, "we left one of the tubes."

We stood for a second and watched the man stoop and pick up the tube. He studied it in the flashlight beam and then raising his rifle above his head, squeezed off two shots. The sounds were still echoing around the mountain as we plunged into the river and started wading downstream. The last thing I heard before the roar of the river obliterated everything was the sound of Stephanie's car and a friendly *toot toot* as she drove away.

John and I never stopped until we were under the Route 16 bridge and then we both collapsed on the rocks at the base of a rip-rap piling. We were breathing hard.

"Jesus," he said, leaning his head back against the boulders. We were both breathing hard. "This is why they use young men to fight wars."

"I wish I'd just looked around once before I ran," I said. "I would have seen that pipe."

"It's not your fault, Max. I should've counted."

"Still . . ."

"Screw them. We got the cores, didn't we? They can have the damn pipe. What the hell are they going to do with it?"

* * *

Stormy dug a bottle of champagne from the bottom back of the refrigerator, Rayleen built a fire in the dining room, and, although it was only Stephanie, Rayleen, and myself drinking, we all celebrated our assault on the mountain. John and I had washed and changed, but Stephanie, like a kid after her first school play, was still in costume.

"You should have seen those guys falling all over themselves trying to help me," she giggled. "I might just start making sales calls in this stuff."

"We saw Bull up there," I said. "Did he recognize you?"

She shook her head. "He stayed in front of the car," she said, fighting back laughter now. "And you should have seen him when they finally got me moving." She doubled over with laughter. When she got control of herself, she continued. "He just disappeared."

"Disappeared?" Rayleen frowned.

"Yes, my wheels spun and mud shot out and he just disappeared." She started laughing again. "He just turned gooey brown. From the top of his head to his feet. Gooey brown mud!"

"Bet he was ready to kill somebody," Rayleen said. "Sure woulda liked to see that."

By ten-thirty, the events of the day had taken their toll. Not to mention the second bottle of champagne we opened. Rayleen wandered back out to the workshop and Stormy went up to bed. John wanted to get the cores wrapped, so I cut apart some cardboard cartons and we fashioned a long, padded container.

The full core tubes were leaning against the wall by the fireplace and Stephanie picked one up and unscrewed the styrofoam cork. She peeked inside. "It looks like plain old dirt to me," she said.

"It is," John said as he lettered a name and address on the cardboard. "But it won't be once this guy gets his hands on it." The package was being sent to an Ivor Smith in Boulder. "This guy owes me, Max. He can get top line back to me within forty-eight hours. If he finds something you can use in court, an official document can follow in five working days."

Stephanie picked up one of the five empty tubes we hadn't used. There had been ten. We'd filled four and left one behind in the clear-cut. "Want me to put these away for you?" She pointed to the golf bag in the corner. "Do they go in that thing there?"

"Yeah," he said. "Just stick them in anywhere. I seriously doubt any of us will have any use for them again."

At seven the next morning I was awakened to the sound of someone pounding on the lodge front door. I pulled on a pair of jeans and yawned my way to the door. It was Darren Foley and Deputy Mark. They looked serious.

"Sorry to wake you so early after a weekend, Max," Darren said, holding out a piece of paper. "This here's a warrant for the arrest of your guest, John Purcell of Boulder, Colorado."

I didn't look at the warrant. "What? What for? What the hell are you talking about, Darren?"

"Just get him for me, will ya, Max? I'm tryin' to do this nice."

"But . . ."

Darren's face tightened. "Get him. Please."

I went to the bottom of the stairs and shouted, "John? You better get down here." I heard some sounds from upstairs and a couple minutes later, a door opened and John and Stephanie appeared at the top of the stairs. He had on a pair of sweat pants and sweat shirt. She was wearing her robe. "What's going on?" he yawned. "There's a cop car outside." He started down the stairs. Stephanie followed, her hands on his shoulders.

"You John Purcell?" Darren asked around me.

John nodded and walked up beside me.

Darren nodded his head at Mark who quickly stepped into the hallway behind John and, pulling his hands behind his back, clicked a pair of handcuffs on his wrists. "What the hell?" John said.

"What are you doing?" Stephanie pushed Mark against the wall.

"Stand back, ma'am," Darren said and looked at John. "John Wingate Purcell, I'm placing you under arrest for unlawful trespass, willful destruction of private property, and aggravated assault with a deadly weapon."

"Aggravated assault?" I said. "What aggravated assault?"

Darren held up his hand. "Relax, Max. One thing at a time." He looked at Mark. "Read him the Miranda, deputy." Mark took a tattered piece of paper from his pocket, carefully unfolded it, and slowly read John his rights. When he was through, Darren said, "Now, put him in the car."

"Jesus," John said. "I just woke up. Can I, at least, take a piss?"

Darren frowned. "You got a bathroom on the first floor, Max?"

I nodded and pointed to the dining room. "In there. Just outside the reading room."

"Go with him, Richards," Darren said.

"Max," Stephanie said, looking close to tears, "what's going on?"

Stormy shuffled down the stairs and up to the door in her bathrobe trailing a cloud of Camel smoke. "Darren," she said, "now what you tryin' to prove?"

Darren ignored her and looked at me. "You know as

well as I do, Max. Your buddy there was up on Collari's land last night taking cores. As if that wasn't enough, when he was asked to leave, he attacked one of Mr. Collari's employees with a steel pipe."

"He what?"

Darren nodded. "Pounded Whitey Laycock a couple good ones. Boy's in Loon Memorial right now in a coma. A mess. Fractured cheekbone and a broken jaw. Might lose his right eye. If he wakes up."

John came stumbling back into the hallway. "Get me some shoes somebody, huh?"

Stephanie ran up the stairs and Stormy headed for the kitchen.

"This is bullshit, Darren," I said. "He didn't hit anyone."

"I did what?" John struggled against the handcuffs.

"I've got four witnesses." He scowled at John.

I sighed and turned to John. "I'll call a lawyer," I said. "We'll have you back at the lodge by lunchtime."

"Wouldn't count on that, Max," Darren said. "Judge Emery won't be settin' bail 'til four this afternoon." He looked at John again. "And if that boy dies, there ain't enough money in Vermont to get you out."

"Don't worry about me, Max," John said, wincing slightly from the handcuffs. "Just don't forget me."

Stephanie returned with socks and his cowboy boots and helped John put them on. Stormy came out of the kitchen carrying the plastic bag containing Red's wallet. "You wanna arrest someone, Darren," she said, tossing the baggy at him. "Check into this."

He caught it and turned it over in his hands. He looked at us. "Red's wallet?"

"Damn straight." Stormy pushed by me and up to him. "And it ain't got no money in it either." She pushed her face to within inches of his. "Which is very interestin' considerin' it was zippered closed tighter 'n a pea pod when we found it."

He raised his eyebrows.

"And I'd handle it real careful, if I was you, Darren," she said. "There's a big fat fingerprint plain as day right inside on that first plastic page that I'm bettin' proves that boy was murdered."

"You tampered with the wallet?"

"Opened it, if that's what you mean," she said. "How else was we to know it was his?"

"And the fingerprint?"

"Seen it through Max's fly-tyin' magnifyin' glass." She thumped the wallet with her forefinger. "It's right there. First page. You check, Darren. That fingerprint ain't gonna be Red's."

"Hummm," he said. "Interesting." Then he looked at me. "Sorry, again, Max, to have to spoil your mornin'." He looked at Mark. "Let's go, Richards. Put him in the car."

I watched Stephanie follow John and Mark to the squad car. I put my hand on Darren's shoulder as he turned to leave. "Darren, don't you see?" I said. "This is all bullshit. It's a faked up deal."

"Then, how'd a steel tube with J. Purcell written on it come to be bashed into Whitey Laycock's head up there in the clear-cut?"

I shook my head. I decided I'd said enough. I knew I should talk to Wally before I said anything more about either of us being at the clear-cut.

"Go on, git, Darren," Stormy said. "And don't you dare forget about the fingerprint in that wallet. I don't hear somethin' from you by the time we come to town to get John, all hell's gonna break loose."

"Don't you worry, Stormy," he said. "I'm sure we'll find Red's prints on file at the plant." He turned and joined John and Mark in the car. John and Stephanie kissed through the back window and she slowly came back up onto the porch. Stormy gave her a hug and we watched the squad car drive away.

CHAPTER ⚲ FOURTEEN

s soon as Darren and Mark were gone with John, I found Wally Murray's card and called his office.

"Hello, Max," he said. "Hold on a minute, will you?" Then I heard him say to someone in his office, "Yes, three copies of that and would you close the door too, Milly? Thanks." Then back to me, "Sorry, Max. Kind of busy. We're preparing for a big trial tomorrow. Ordinarily you wouldn't even find me here this early. What's up? Did you get the cores?"

I told him everything in chronological order, from getting the cores to John's arrest for assault.

He sighed. "I suppose Claremont Taylor's representing the boy who was injured."

"Probably."

"Ruth know about this?"

"I don't know."

"How'd the core pipe get up there?"

"It was dark. We forgot it," I said. "It was stupid."

"How much money do you have in the bank?"

"I don't know. Maybe three thousand."

"That should be enough for bail," he said. "I'll talk to the hospital and the sheriff and then call Claremont and see what they've got. I'll meet you at the courthouse at four. You'll need something from the bank verifying your balance so the court will take your check."

"I'll get it."

"Good. Meanwhile, don't talk to anyone, Max. Especially the *Sentinel*. See you at four."

I put the phone down and it rang in my hand. It was Gordon Miller. "Would you like to give me your version of this vicious assault on Whitey Laycock?" he said.

"No comment, Gordon."

"The boy could die, Max."

"No comment." I hung up.

I was pouring another cup of coffee when Rayleen found me. "Max, you don't need me for any of this, do you?"

"No." I shook my head. "You've been a tremendous help already. What's up?"

"I figured maybe I'd get crackin' on the bike," he said. "You know, get serious 'bout it now it's apart and all."

"Go ahead."

"You don't mind then if I shoot downta Montpelier? To that Harley dealer there?" He showed me a greasy piece of paper. "Got me a list of some parts I need."

I shook my head again. "Talk to Stormy about the money you think you'll need."

"Thanks, Max," he said. "I should be back by supper."

"Say hello to Skip for me."

He smiled and limped toward the kitchen.

At one o'clock I slipped on my black hooded sweatshirt, put the package containing the cores in the Jeep, and drove to town. Stormy rode along. She had some things she wanted to do at home. I was going to mail the cores and then hang out until I met Wally. Stephanie stayed

behind at the lodge. She had her briefcase open on the
dining room table and said she needed to make some
business phone calls. She agreed to meet Stormy and
me in front of the courthouse at a quarter to four.

Her feet barely touching the floor, Stormy sat in the
passenger seat like a pile of flowered fabric with a head.
Cigarette smoke billowed over her thick forearm and
out the open window. In the rearview mirror it looked
like the Jeep was on fire. I hadn't been to town since the
day of the fish kill. Today I drove a little slower. I didn't
feel the same. I felt drained of purpose. I was confused.
I knew what the cores lying in the back of the Jeep
could make happen, but I also knew what they'd already
caused.

"You want one of these?" She held out the pack of
Camels. I took one, lit it, and rolled my window down.
The sun was warm but clouds were building out over the
southern mountains. We'd probably have more rain by
evening.

"You're awful quiet," she said. "You worried about
John?"

I exhaled. "I feel responsible. Seems like a lot of shit
has happened because of me. Stephanie's order,
Rayleen's job, Red, Ruth's caught up in it." I glanced at
her. "Now this."

"It ain't your fault."

"Of course it's my fault. Who else?"

"Collari."

I shook my head. "If I'd just let him log, none of this
would have happened. All we'd have is a bunch of trees
gone."

"Max," she said, "you can't think that way. If it
weren't you it woulda been somebody else eventually.
Somebody woulda called him on it. Green Peace. That
there Sierra Club. Somebody else woulda stopped him."

I ground out the cigarette in the ashtray and I fought

back a sudden, uncontrollable sting of tears. "It's just so goddamn frustrating." I hit the steering wheel with my fist. "Dammit."

I could feel her staring at me. She put her hand on my arm. "What you done is right, Max," she said. "It's what Red wanted, ain't it?"

I nodded.

"And Rayleen too. And John. And you know how Ruth feels."

I nodded again.

"You didn't con 'em into this. Them people is involved 'cause they wanna be."

I ran the back of my hand quickly over my eyes.

"I've known you a long time, Maxwell Addams. And I know how you think. Why we're successful at the lodge is, you care 'bout folks. They can feel it. It's why they keep comin' back year after year. And I know that right now, you're thinkin' maybe you oughta just throw in the towel on this thing."

I took a deep breath.

"You can't quit, Max. You owe it to every one of us to take this damn thing to the Supreme Court if you hafta." She snubbed her cigarette. "Okay," she said, "that's enough preachin'." She crossed her arms over her bosom. "Now. How you handlin' this Stephanie and John business?"

I laughed. "You don't miss a trick, do you?"

"Not much to miss," she said. "She slept in his room last night."

"I gathered that."

"Well?" She looked at me.

"They're my friends. What can I say?"

"You can say it bothers you."

"It did," I said. "But not anymore."

She nodded slowly. "So, what's with Ruth? I seen the

look in her eyes yesterday after you two was out there by the lake."

I glanced at her. She was smiling. "You're too much," I said.

We laughed and then were silent for a few miles. Finally, she said, "Poor Whitey. Hope he ain't hurt too bad."

"You know him?"

"I knowed his family a little. His daddy run off with a waitress when Whitey was just a baby. Pauline, that's his momma, took up with Claremont for a while."

"Claremont? Taylor?"

"He was quite the lady's man back then 'fore he married," she laughed. "Wasn't so full of himself in them days. Anyway, Pauline musta thought Claremont was gonna marry her, 'cause when it didn't happen she up and left. Went to California, some folks said. I heard she died a year or so ago."

"Whitey have any brothers or sisters?"

"No. He lives in that trailer park across the bridge up near Mark Richards on Brimmer Road. By himself, I think."

I wondered if Whitey had been the man who Bull had left by the fire last night. If he'd been the one who'd come up the mountain and almost seen John and me and found the pipe.

"What do you think Whitey done," she said, "to get himself beat up so bad?"

"I was just thinking about that."

"Rayleen told you, that Bull's a nasty one. Don't take much to make him fly off the handle."

"I know." I nodded. "I've seen it first hand."

Stormy lived on the north side of Loon and, instead of going through town on Main Street and having to endure the interminable stop light at Beech Street and the other at High Road, I cut around to the east on

Whitefork Road. It followed the river directly behind the town and I was always amazed at how docile and domesticated the Whitefork looked where the buildings backed directly up to it. They were the classic, three- and four-story red brick with high, multi-paned windows. Typical of those built at the turn of the century. Every New England river town has them. They all perched straight up on the granite cliffs thirty feet above the water. Originally ours had housed shoe, carriage wheel, and chair manufacturing. Now, except for some inexpensive apartments and, at street level, a few retail stores, they were mostly empty.

Stormy's house was a small white cape with a big center chimney on the roof and two windows and a door in the front. It had been built by her father and set close to the road. The large stump of an elm that had housed Rayleen's boyhood tree fort was the only thing in the small front yard. There was no curb and not much grass and I stopped the Jeep near the stump.

"You goin' to the post office now?" Stormy asked as she opened the door and climbed out.

"Yeah."

"Tell Reba I'm home, will you?" Reba was Vermont's oldest postal employee and Stormy's bridge partner.

"I'll tell her."

"And, Max—" she shut the door and leaned in the window "—go back the long way, huh? Stay away from the mill. Somebody sees you, there could be trouble."

I nodded and watched her waddle to the house, fumble with her keys, and let herself in without a look back. I pulled away and headed for the post office.

I knew I shouldn't drive by the plant, but I was curious, and as I approached, I could see the difference my temporary restraining order was making. Where dozens of skyscraper piles of logs usually lay stacked waiting for the pulp machines, now there was only mud and parked forklift trucks. Steam billowed from only one of the three smokestacks and the high-pitched scream of the grinders, usually so loud you could hear it with your car windows closed, was gone. Other than a group of three men and two women smoking cigarettes outside the main office door, there was no one in sight. As I passed, one of the men saw my Jeep and, no doubt, the White-fork insignia on the door, because he yelled something at me and gave me the finger. As I turned left up Main Street I looked in the rearview mirror. The three men were walking rapidly toward the small parking lot beside the office and another had just appeared at the door. Even in the vibrating mirror I recognized him. It was Bull.

When the new town offices had been built only the library and post office elected not to move from their present locations. The library had been designated a state historical site and their desire to stay put made sense. The post office, on the other hand, was tiny and poorly lit with nowhere near enough post office boxes for the residents who wanted them. The waiting list for box numbers was exceeded only by the number of people waiting to be serviced by the two clerks.

I was lucky. Not only did I find a parking place directly in front, but only two people were waiting in line inside. I stood with John's package in my arms and studied the posters promoting stamp collecting on the walls. A woman with a baby in a stroller came in and took her place behind me. I smiled at the baby and it just stared back looking like it might cry.

I let the woman with the baby go ahead of me to the other clerk so I could be waited on by Reba.

Reba had recently undergone cataract surgery and although the half-inch-thick glasses had helped her keep her job, they did nothing for her vision beyond five feet.

She didn't recognize me at first, much less see me until I cleared my throat.

"Max?" She tipped the glasses back and squinted. "It's you."

"It's me, Reba, How are you?" She wore a lot of mascara and the reverse magnification of her glasses made her eyes look like little raisins.

"I got a bunion that's killing me," she said. "But otherwise I can't complain. How's Stormy?"

"I just dropped her off at her house. She wanted me to tell you she was home."

"Too frightening out at the lodge for her?"

"Nothing scares Stormy." I laughed. "You know that." I slid the package across the counter to her.

"You bet I do," she chuckled. "That's why she's my bridge partner." She squinted at the package. "Colorado, huh? Parcel post or first?"

"First class, please."

She hefted it onto the scale, weighed it, and I paid her. While I was counting my change, she gestured toward the window in the front of the building. "That's your Jeep out there, isn't it, Max?" She craned her neck and tipped back the glasses. "What's going on?"

I looked out the window. The three men I'd seen at the plant stood at my Jeep. One of them was repeatedly poking a knife into the rear tire and another was pounding the hood with a crowbar. "Jesus," I yelled and ran out the post office. "Hey, goddammit!" I ran down the walk. "What the hell do you think you're doing?"

They stopped what they were doing and faced me. I could hear the tire hissing flat. A crowd had begun to gather on both sides of the sidewalk. A couple of people came running across the street, saw the looks on all our faces, and stopped at the white line.

The men, all dressed in nondescript work clothing, stood shoulder to shoulder.

I looked up and down the street. Where's a cop when you need one? The guy in the middle wearing the John Deere cap spit on the sidewalk. "You're Addams, ain't you?" he said, a smile pulling one side of his mouth up.

"Hope you wasn't planning on goin' nowheres," the bald one with the sunglasses sneered. "Your Jeep here's been in an accident."

"Yeah," the younger of the three laughed. He held the crowbar. "A nasty accident."

I looked at the crowd for a friendly face. I didn't see one, but I did recognize Bull. His face was expressionless, his big arms folded over his chest. "You saw what they did," I said to the crowd. "Would someone call the sheriff for me?" As far as I could see, no one moved. "C'mon," I said. "Somebody want to help me here?"

"What've you done for us?" a voice from the back of the crowd yelled.

"Yeah, how about letting the logging start again," a old woman in the front shouted. "Stop this foolishness."

"Yeah! Screw your fish!"

"Yeah! Screw you, Addams. You made this mess."

"Hurt him, boys!" It was Bull's voice. "Like he's done to us!"

"Yeah, make him wish he wasn't born!"

"Yeah! Get him."

Encouraged by the comments from the crowd the three men swaggered toward me.

I'm not a fighter, but I've seen enough fights to know that the party who strikes first usually fares the best. As the men closed in, I picked John Deere as my target. My plan was simple. I'd hit him in the face with every ounce of strength I had. What I'd do after that, I didn't know. There's no dignity in running, but there were three of them, and not only did they have a knife and a crowbar, their fists were the size of cherry burls. I knew if I stood there trying to slug it out, I'd only last the length of time it took me to be pummeled to the ground.

"Go get him, P.J.!" someone in the crowd yelled just as the bald guy stepped ahead of the other two, working his shoulders like a boxer loosening up. He took off his sunglasses and tossed them into the crowd. They cheered. Obviously, P.J. was to be the designated battler and I sighed. Somehow, a one-on-one contest seemed more difficult than three-on-three. I would be required to fight fair and stick it out. Running was out of the question now.

I backed up a step, my arms at my sides. "Deck him, Max," I heard Reba shout from behind me and I felt, rather than saw, the crowd close in around us.

P.J. took a step closer. His fists were at his chest. He was in his thirties. What I'd thought was baldness was a shaved head. His neck was thick, shoulders large. He grinned. His teeth were crooked. "C'mon, Addams," he said, taunting me. "Do pussy fly fishers know how to fight?"

"No, we don't. . . ." I said and lunged forward, my right fist coming up fast from my hip as I moved. I had the weight of my entire body behind it and caught him dead center in the face. I heard bones crack as I felt his nose collapse beneath my knuckles. Blood spurted from somewhere and my forward momentum carried both of us to the ground, something else cracking as my shoulder crushed heavily into his rib cage and my elbow buried itself in his solar plexus. Someone yelled, "Sucker punch!" as I rolled off him and jumped back to my feet. P.J. didn't move. Pain shot up my right forearm and I couldn't clench the fingers on that hand.

John Deere jumped in from behind me, grabbed and bear hugged my arms to my sides. "Hit 'em, Lester," he said.

Without the crowbar, Lester wouldn't have scared me

at all. He looked about sixteen. He stepped up in front of me, took a stance, and did what he was told. He swung the crowbar like a baseball bat and it hit me hard just above the belt. I doubled over. "In the face, you asshole!" John Deere yelled, as he yanked me erect. "In the head, Lester. Hurt him!"

I twisted in John Deere's arms and, as the three of us jerked and struggled, Lester's next two swings were off mark, the first just clipping my forehead and the second glancing off John Deere's shoulder before grazing my cheek. Both drew blood and my left eye instantly clouded red.

"Goddamn you, Lester," John Deere yelled as he released his grip and spun me around, "Like this!" and he swung his fist. I was staggering and his fist caught me just above my good eye, sending me sprawling onto my back in the grass beside P.J. who still wasn't moving. I rolled and John Deere kicked for my groin, his big work boot connecting hard with my hip. He kicked again. I didn't feel it. I was still rolling, trying to escape the pursuing boot. The crowbar whooshed through the air and thudded to the ground by my ear as Lester swung again, just missing both of us. "Lester!" John Deere yelled. "Back off with that thing! I got him now!" It was then that I remembered the little insect repellent–size canister of mace in my pocket and, as John Deere grabbed the front of my black hooded sweatshirt, cocked his arm, and leaned over to pound me into the turf, I sprayed him in the face.

He gasped as the clinging mustardy cloud enveloped his head, grabbed his throat with both hands and stood upright. Then with his eyes bulging, he staggered backwards through the scattering crowd, stumbled on the library's steps and fell on his back, his head bouncing hard on the worn granite. I scrambled to my feet, spraying a staccato of spurts at Lester as I came. He tried to duck and dodge the haze of mace but was unsuccessful and dropped to the ground like he'd been shot, writhing and gagging and then beginning to vomit violently.

Like a crazy man, I spun in a circle, pointing the little canister at the crowd. "Who else?" I screamed and they backed away, covering their faces. "Who else? You sons of bitches! Who else wants it?" I stood there glaring at them, my heart pounding, pains from my arm, hand, chest, forehead, and hip all coming together at once. Blood dribbled from my chin to my shirt. I couldn't see out of my left eye. The acrid, nauseating smell of the mace hung in the air. I willed myself not to fall over and the citizens of Loon and I stared at each other as the sound of an approaching siren grew louder.

CHAPTER ✦ FIFTEEN

T he x-rays showed P.J.s' face had cracked my wrist. It was only hairline, but I was given an L-shaped cast from my fingertips to my bicep. "For only two weeks," the doctor on duty in the emergency room said. "After that, an ace bandage will do." The two cuts on my head were a little worse and took nineteen stitches. My belly was a giant purple bruise from Lester's first swing with the crowbar.

"You're lucky you don't have internal damage, Mr. Addams," the doctor had said. "Not to mention a concussion." He wrote me a prescription. "This is for pain." He tore the sheet from the pad. "You're going to hurt tonight."

I was now sitting on a gurney in a partially curtained-off section of Loon Memorial's brand new and, ironically, Collari-endowed emergency room. I was waiting to be told I could leave. Deputy Mark Richards sat on a chair beside the small, white cabinet near the wall. Lester and John Deere, whose real name was Luke, were on their backs, handcuffed to two gurneys in front of me, oxygen masks strapped to their faces. P.J. had just been taken to x-ray to confirm a split sternum and several broken ribs.

"Damn mess you've created now, Max," Mark said, shaking his head. "A damn mess."

"Me? I was just mailing a package."

He turned his hat brim in his hands. "Sheriff needs to know if you're gonna press charges."

I sighed and looked at Lester and Luke. "I don't think so," I said. I'd had enough of Lester, Luke, P.J., Mark Richards, Bull, and Collari. Where I'd been depressed in the Jeep coming to town, now the whole thing just made me tired to think about it. And I still had to bail John out.

"You sure?" Mark said. "You change your mind later it won't be easy to find witnesses who tell the same story."

I saw Luke open his eyes and roll them at me. "I'm sure," I said.

"Well," he said, "then that makes things a lot easier. I can now—" He was interrupted by a commotion behind me. He looked and I painfully turned. It was Stormy trailing Camel smoke and a short, very upset, redhaired, red-faced nurse.

"You'll have to extinguish that cigarette, ma'am," the nurse said. "Please. It's no smoking in the . . ."

Stormy tossed the cigarette to the floor, ground it out under her Bean boot, and kept coming. "Maxwell Addams. You idiot," she said, approaching my gurney. She looked from the cast to my face. "You're too old for this sorta crap." She touched the bandages on my forehead and turned to Mark. "He hurt bad?"

Mark shook his head and gestured to Luke and Lester. "I think they got the worst of it, ma'am. And there's a third guy down in x-ray right now."

She touched my cast. "How'd you do this?"

"A lucky punch," I said.

"Luck, huh?" She gestured Mark off the chair and sat

heavily. "If this is what you call luck, Max, then it's just about par for the course today."

"Meaning?"

"Meaning, the fingerprint's gone."

"What?"

"Reba called and told me you was in a fight and so I naturally hurried over to Darren's office. You wasn't there, of course. But Darren was." She shook her head. "He told me 'bout the fingerprint."

"How could it be gone?" I looked at Mark.

"I meant to tell you, Max," Mark said. "We didn't find any trace of any strange fingerprints in that wallet. None, anywhere."

"The page it was on is gone," she said bitterly. "That's why."

"What? The plastic page with Red's license in it?"

"Yep," she said. "Gone. Torn right out. Max, that wallet never left the refrigerator. Never for a minute." She glared at Mark. "There's only one way that plastic page with that fingerprint on it coulda got removed."

"Jeez, ma'am." Mark's eyes widened. "I was right there when the sheriff opened the plastic bag," he said. "So was two other deputies. You can't be thinkin' that Sheriff Foley . . ."

Stormy interrupted, "Then you explain where it went, Mark Edward." She thrust her stumpy finger at him. "And don't tell me it wasn't there when we found it, 'cause you know Red hadta have a drivin' license."

"Did you check it for other fingerprints?" I asked.

"Yessir, Max," he said. "It was full of 'em, only they was all Red's."

"Dammit. Five of us saw it, Mark," I said. "It was there."

"It's not me, Max." He blushed. "Heck, I believe you. It's the sheriff. He says—" Mark was interrupted by the short, redheaded nurse. "Excuse me, Deputy?" she said.

"Mr. Laycock's regained consciousness. The doctor says he can be questioned for a few minutes now." She pointed. "There's a phone in the office if you'd like to call Sheriff Foley."

Stormy and I stood as Mark headed for the office. "Wait there, Max," he said. "You too, Stormy. Let me find out how the sheriff wants to handle this thing."

An hour later, Sheriff Darren Foley came into the emergency room. His hat was in his hands. Under the fluorescents his hair was almost violet. "I got me a big apology to make to you two," he said, looking at the floor. "Whitey says it was Bull that beat on him. Says he was left to guard the clear-cut while Bull and the others went to help some tourist stuck in the mud. Says he found the core tube up on the hill and when Bull found out you'd been up there taking cores, he flipped and blamed him for it." Darren shook his head and sat on the gurney beside me. "I guess Bull threatened the others that they'd lose their jobs if they didn't say it was John who beat Whitey up."

"Is Whitey gonna be all right?" Stormy asked.

"Don't know, Stormy. Guess he's gonna lose his right eye. And the doctor says he may need plastic surgery to replace an ear." He shook his head. "That damn metal tube cut most of his left one right off."

"That Bull," she spat. "Hope you lock him up and forget where he is."

"That ain't all," he said. "Whitey's not real positive, but he says it mighta been Bull that killed Red, too. Says Bull was real angry when you filed that T.R.O., Max. Blamed Red for the whole thing."

"You better not let me near him when you get him, Darren." Stormy's jaw was clenched.

"What about John?" I said.

"Deputy Richards has already left to take care of it, Max. Your friend'll be free in an hour or so."

"No, I meant, what about the other charges? The trespassing and destruction of property?"

He shrugged. "Dunno yet. If Claremont wants to push on that, it'll have to wait. I ain't got time to mess around with mickey mouse. Right now, I gotta find Bull and bring him in." He stood and fitted his hat over his violet hair. He smiled. "Been quite a day, ain't it?"

I nodded and watched him walk away.

"Knew it all along," Stormy said when he was gone.

"I still don't understand the fingerprint."

"I do."

"Oh?"

"Bull had help killin' Red," she said. "And whoever it was took the fingerprint. It's the proof they was there."

"Then, it should be interesting to hear what Bull has to say, shouldn't it?"

She nodded. "If the sheriff gets to him first."

I looked at my watch. It was three-thirty. "Stephanie will be at the courthouse in fifteen minutes."

She stood and smoothed the front of her caftan. "We can walk it in ten," she said. "Unless there's somethin' wrong with your legs too."

John and Wally were sitting side by side on the courthouse steps as Stormy and I walked up. John jumped to his feet when he saw us. Wally stood slowly, his eyebrows rising and falling. I must have been quite a sight. Besides the cast and bandages, blood was caked to my sweatshirt and there were grass stains and mud on my jeans.

"Max," John said, coming up to me and putting a hand on my cast. "I just heard about what happened." He studied my forehead, my cast, and my clothes.

"Jesus, look at you. You won? What the hell do they look like?"

"They look like they ate a can of mace," I said.

Wally walked up. "Say the word, Max," he said. "And we can sue."

I shook my head.

"Why?"

"Yeah, why not?" Stormy said. "You coulda been killed."

"Consider it public relations."

She touched the bandage on my forehead. "Could be that knock on the head cleared up your thinkin', Max Addams," she said. "Whitefork Lodge damn well could use a little good PR right now."

"Okay. So tell us what happened," John said. "Who did it?"

"Yes," Wally said. "All we know is that Whitey identified his assailant. We don't know who."

"Nobody's told you?" Stormy said.

"No," John said. "They didn't say anything except sorry. They only let me go three or four minutes ago. I came out here looking for you and—"

"I introduced myself," Wally said.

Stormy told them what we knew.

"Well, well," John said to her. "You've been right all along."

Stormy laughed and shook her finger at him. "And don't you forget it, young man," she said.

John looked at me. "You get the cores mailed?"

I patted my cast. "Not a moment too soon."

"Coffee's on me," Wally said, peering down the street. "If Freddie's is still open."

"Where's Stephanie?" John asked.

I shrugged and looked at my watch. "She should be here." It was four-fifteen.

"We'll get a booth in the window and watch for her," Wally said, starting down the street. "C'mon."

Although filled with the odors of a long day of pot roast, roast turkey, and New England Boiled dinners, Freddie's was almost empty. The few clusters of people at the counter and in the other booths went silent and stared as we walked in and took the big booth in the window. Eyeing us, two muscular young men in coveralls stood and laid some bills on their table. Their faces set, they walked over to our table. I could feel myself tense.

The taller of the two looked down at me. "We're real sorry about what happened today, Mr. Addams," he said.

"Yeah," the other one said. "We should've given you a hand."

I attempted a smile.

The taller one touched my shoulder. "Just wanted you to know," he said. "Not everybody in this town's against you."

We watched them walk out, cross the street, and climb into a pickup. "That and twenty-five cents will get you a cup of coffee," John muttered.

"Better now than never," Stormy said.

A dark-haired waitress who acted like she could barely cover the distance from the counter to our booth slouched over. She looked directly at Wally. "Kitchen's closed, counselor," she said. "And the grill's going off in two minutes."

"I know. Just coffees, Brenda," Wally said. His eyebrows didn't move.

"Eat here a lot?" I asked him.

"Every time I'm in town."

We didn't say much until after the four coffees were in front of us. Two squad cars tore by with their blue lights flashing. We passed the cream. John watched the courthouse across the street. "Where the hell is she?" he said.

"Call her." Stormy pointed toward the back of the restaurant. "Pay phone's right back there somewheres."

"Outside the men's room," Wally said, sipping his coffee black.

John nodded and left to call the lodge. We drank our coffees. He came back shaking his head.

"That's strange," I said.

He didn't sit and pushed his coffee to the center of the table. "Max, let's go," he said. "This makes me nervous."

I shook my head. "Not until someone helps me change my tire."

"Already done it, Max," Stormy said. "Made the guys from over at the Sunoco do it." She smiled. "Lashed down your hood too. It was pretty bent up."

"How about you?" I said to Stormy. "Coming back to the lodge?"

"You two go ahead. I been away from my house too long. The dust bunnies is havin' babies. Now that this thing's practically cleared up, you don't need me tonight. I'll be out first thing in the morning." She lit a cigarette and looked at John. "Make sure he stops at the pharmacy and gets them pain pills," she said and then looked at me. "And don't you try to be no hardass. Take them. And get some sleep."

We all stood as she slid out of the booth and then watched her through the window as she went out to the sidewalk. She waved, then turned, threw back her shoulders and, with her arms pumping like a competition speed walker, chugged away, her caftan swirling around her ankles, a contrail of cigarette smoke trailing behind her.

Wally said goodbye. "I'll call you tomorrow, Max. We've got a lot of things yet to talk about."

I nodded.

"Thanks for the coffee," John said, as Wally went to the counter to pay.

John and I got the Jeep and went to the pharmacy and it was almost dark by the time we got to the top end of Gracey Gorge. As I downshifted and climbed the last fifty yards or so, I saw an orange glow above the trees straight ahead to the west.

"Look at that sunset," John said. "Kind of late, isn't it?"

For a second I thought it was a sunset too, but as I topped the rise, shifted into fourth and started down the hill, I saw the thick white smoke against the darkening sky. It was a fire. A big one.

"Something's burning somewhere," he said.

The closer I got to the lodge access road, the brighter the orange got, until, as I turned in I knew; the fire was at the lodge.

"Jesus, Max!"

I floored the Jeep down the mile of bumps and muddy ruts. Showers of sparks and smoke as thick as fog covered the road. I could feel the intense heat before I even rounded the corner and I slammed on my brakes, jumped out, and ran into the yard. John was right behind me. The entire lodge was engulfed in flames. Half of the roof had geysers of it shooting fifty feet in the air. Part of the porch was burning on Stephanie's car. It had obviously blown up and thick, oily black smoke rose from where the trunk had been, mixing with the white from the logs. Something else exploded inside. More windows shattered. I could smell my beard singeing. I threw my good arm over my face and backed away from the heat. I bumped into the blackened trunk on a birch, slid to my butt, and stared, horrified and sick, as the giant tongues of flame ate my dream.

I was helpless. I could only watch as Whitefork

Lodge, log by log, collapsed, exploded, then crumbled and disappeared on a million sparks in the howling updraft that rose into the smoke-clogged night sky.

John still stood staring into the flames. "Stephanie!" he yelled. "Oh, God, no! Max? Where's Stephanie?"

CHAPTER ✺ SIXTEEN

I found a bailing bucket at the dock and John and I filled and refilled it, ineffectually tossing water that only vaporized before it even hit the flames. We might as well have been standing there spitting. Finally, in anger and frustration, I heaved the bucket into the fire and retreated out of the heat.

John continued to run frantically back and forth around the perimeter of the blaze, silhouetted against the blinding orange flames, calling Stephanie's name. He was a wild man. His clothes and moustache were smoking, his blood-red face slick with sweat. Several times he tried to dart into the inferno only to be pushed back by the wall of heat. Finally, he dropped to his knees at my side. "Where is she, Max?"

It's a Tuesday I'll never forget. By sunrise the fire was out. Where Whitefork Lodge had once stood, a smoldering pile of wet black now filled the cellar hole. A thin haze of smoke was strung like fog across the damp clearing, its acrid, dead smell burning my throat and eyes. All of the trees closest to the lodge had been half burned, their scorched, blackened trunks still smoldering on one side. They would live. I could see a seared toilet bowl jutting from the debris and the melted top of the refrigerator. Several knots of twisted pipes with dripping loops of wiring hanging from them stood where walls had been. The two chimneys leaned at precarious angles and, at eight o'clock, the one from the reading room fireplace began to sway and, with firefighters running in every direction, toppled in a roaring avalanche of boulders.

Only the workshop still stood. The log wall closest to the lodge was charred black but, miraculously, it had not burned.

It had taken the Loon Volunteer Fire Department almost half an hour to get to the lodge. Who'd called them, I'll probably never know. They arrived with one big hook and ladder truck and one tanker truck. It took everything in the tanker to just get the flames under control and they had to refill it three times from the lake before every last flicker of fire was gone. By that time so was everything else that had once been the lodge. The firemen were efficient and well organized, many times narrowly missing serious injury as pieces of the roof collapsed, walls caved in, and things exploded. Ironically, I recognized many of them as the same people who earlier passively had watched the fight in front of the post office.

Rayleen had been a volunteer for fifteen years and when he came rattling down the access road, returning from his trip to the Harley dealer in Montpelier, he jumped from his pickup and, yanking on his firefighting gear, limped to the workshop and hauled the flamables out of harm's way. If he hadn't, the gasoline, solvents, paint, and kerosene we stored there would have exploded and probably blown all of us into the lake.

Stormy wasn't far behind the fire equipment. Darren and Mark were right behind her. And, of course, the *Sentinel*'s dynamic duo, little Gordon and photographer

Bruce, were behind them, their big black Jeep so close on the squad car's bumper it appeared towed. The orange and white EMT van from Loon Memorial came whooping down the access road about fifteen minutes later.

Stormy and I just looked at each other. I knew how much the lodge meant to her. It had been her home away from home for almost thirty years and once during the night, I saw her down on the dock with her head in her hands. When she came back up to the tree where we all were watching the firemen, her eyes were swollen and the neck of her caftan was wet from tears.

It was the biggest thing to happen in the Loon area since the massive search for five-year-old Stevie Hardy who'd wandered away from a religious tent meeting the previous summer and, by midnight, dozens of the town's people had gathered in a half circle in the yard to watch. I was told cars and pickups were parked up and down both sides of Route 16 for five miles.

While Bruce took pictures, Gordon came over to the tree and sat with me.

"This is sure a bummer, Max," he said.

I nodded.

"Mr. Purcell seems to think Ms. Wilcox was in there."

"We all do." I had been searching the crowd for her face ever since they began arriving. "I don't know where she is."

"That's her car, right?"

I shrugged. Unless you'd known, it was now impossible to determine the make of Stephanie's car. It was just a black, windowless, tireless shape under the pile of smoking rubble that had once been Whitefork's porch.

"Stormy said Ms. Wilcox stayed behind to do office work. Make some phone calls?"

I nodded again. It just didn't seem possible. But

where could Stephanie have gone? Why hadn't she come to the court house? Why wasn't she here?

"Sheriff Foley says investigators from the State Police Arson Squad will be coming up from Montpelier in the morning," he said. "Do you think the fire was deliberately set?"

I took a deep breath. Of course that's what I thought. What had Bull said when he caught John in the river? Whitefork Lodge will be going out of business very sudden? Something like that. As I watched the south wall of the lodge cave in with an explosion of sparks, I said, "I don't know, Gordon. I can't even think about that kind of thing now." I was suddenly very tired. Tired of the fighting. The hate. The death and destruction.

Darren had little to say to me while the fire was raging, but in the morning, when Mark brought us all coffees and donuts from the Starlight, he took me aside. "The arson squad will be able to tell us if it was torched, Max," he said, sipping his coffee through the lid. "I sure am sorry about this."

"I don't care about how it happened," I said. "I just want to know about Stephanie." My arm and head hurt and I swallowed three of the pain pills with my first sips of coffee.

"All of us here are gonna go through the rubble as soon as it cools down enough to walk on," he said. "If she's in there, we'll find her."

"If she isn't?"

"I don't know, Max." He shook his head. "Then I guess either we wait or try to figure where she'd go without her car."

Stormy joined us. "What about Bull? You get him?"

Darren shook his head. "But we will, Stormy. I've got an all points out on him. He can't get far."

She looked at me. "You seen Spotter, Max?"

I hadn't. In fact, in all the confusion I hadn't even thought about him.

"Nothin' better've happened to that old dog," she said with a sigh. "Don't think I could take that."

Spotter and Ruth Pearlman arrived at ten-thirty from different directions. Spotter walked slowly out of the trees from the river and Ruth, who had parked her car up on 16, walked down the access road. Stormy and I stooped and hugged and kissed the old dog's dirty, fire-singed head. The rest of Spotter was wet and muddy.

"Guess there are times you will go into the water, huh?" Stormy said to him. He licked her face, his wildly wagging tail throwing water on all of us.

I felt a little sorry for Ruth, who was standing patiently and watching us and the dog, so I let Stormy and Spotter talk and stood. Ruth touched my cast and then ran her fingers over my forehead bandage. "Are you going to be all right, Max?" she said.

"Yeah."

"I'm so sorry." She put her arms around my neck and hugged me. "You don't deserve this." Her warm lips touched my neck. "You just don't deserve this."

Stormy stood and the two women embraced. "Oh, Stormy," Ruth said, "what can I do to help?"

"There ain't nothin' anybody can do now." Stormy stepped back and lit a cigarette. "Nothin'."

"Nothing," I said, "except find Stephanie."

"Is that the woman who's missing?"

I nodded.

"Who is she?"

"A friend," Stormy said. "A good friend."

"Max? Stormy?" It was Darren Foley. He was standing calf-deep in the rubble beside what was left of the reading room fireplace. He waved. "Can you come over here?"

I nodded and Stormy and I started for what was left of the lodge. "Wait, Max," Ruth said, gripping my hand. "I want to ask you something."

"I'll go," Stormy said to me. "You come when you're ready." And she trudged up through the yard.

Ruth took my other hand and looked up at me through her fringe of hair. "Where are you going to stay tonight, Max? Stormy's?"

I shook my head. "Here, I think." I pointed at the workshop. "There's an extra room in there."

She nodded slowly and looked down at our hands. "You're welcome at my place." She said it so quietly I almost didn't hear her.

I sighed. "No," I said. "I've got to stay here."

She was still looking down and nodded her head again. "I understand, but if you . . ."

"Max!" It was Stormy's voice yelling from the rubble. "Max! Get in here! Mark found a body!"

Ruth dropped my hands and I waded into the debris. Mark was leaning on a tree behind the burned lodge, vomiting loudly.

"Watch where you step, everyone," Darren cautioned. "There's still some hot spots."

John walked hesitantly from where he'd been sitting on the bumper of the firetruck. Bruce Eichner and Gordon, who had been sharing a coffee at the hood of their car, came running. Bruce was screwing flash cables onto a twin-lens reflex bobbing on his chest.

There is nothing more grotesque in this world than a badly incinerated human body and this one was no different. The fact that it probably was Stephanie made it even worse. John stumbled through the wreckage and up to the body. I didn't want to look, but had to. There was a sour, burned grease smell of overgrilled meat. We pinched our noses. A flash went off.

It was on its side in what had been the reading room.

At first, I couldn't even see the body, it was the same black as everything else around it. Then I saw the shape. If it was Stephanie, there was no way I could tell. All the clothing had been burned off and the black flesh that remained had been so cooked and shrunken that resulting tightened muscles had bent the legs and arms and spine, curling it into a fetal-like position. The back muscles had been burned completely off and the exposed rib cage and spine were charred black. The lungs were dark gray like boiled meat. There was no hair, no ears, no nose. Eyeballs had popped and sunken. The lipless mouth was pulled open in a toothy silent scream.

Another flash went off as Bruce leaned in for a close-up. John turned his head and backed away.

Bruce circled the body, clicking off shots. I felt sick, turned away and walked to what was left of the fireplace. The mantel was gone and I leaned my head against the blackened stones. Something glinted yellow at my feet and I stooped and picked up what was left of a number 10 Dead Princess. The peacock herl, white goose biots, and hackle collar were gone, of course, but the hook and the three shiny brass beads remained. I slipped it in my breast pocket and then, with Darren, I waded out of the debris into the yard to where John stood. I put my arm around him.

"It's her, isn't it, Max?" he said.

"I don't know. I can't tell." Who else could it be, I thought.

"They killed her. Those sons of bitches killed her."

"We don't know that," Darren said.

"We know it," I said, the words coming out between my clenched teeth. "The only question is what we're going to do about it."

"Nobody's gonna do nothin' 'til we know how the fire started for sure, and are positive that body there's Ms. Wilcox," Darren said. "You gotta promise me, Max."

I nodded and said to John, "The building was old, John. The wiring was put in years ago. There were a lot of things that I should have fixed." Even though I didn't believe what I was saying, I hoped he did. "Hell, I hadn't cleaned the chimneys for three years."

"There weren't no fires in the fireplaces," Stormy said. She had come out of the rubble and now stood with Ruth. "This place was torched and you know it, Darren."

"Stormy." Darren looked about as serious as I'd ever seen him to look. "I want your promise, too. You're to do nothin', understand? Nothin' 'til we know for sure what happened here."

"How long will that take, Darren?" Ruth asked, putting her arm around Stormy and taking my hand in hers.

Darren shrugged. "Could know by early tomorrow 'bout the body if we can get her dental records faxed up from Boston." He smiled weakly. "Least we'll know if it's her. If it ain't, then it might take a while to find out who it is."

"I don't think I care who it is, if it isn't Stephanie," I said, knowing as soon as I said it, I didn't mean it.

Stormy put her hand on my arm.

Darren ignored me. "The arson squad might take a bit longer." He gestured toward what had once been Whitefork Lodge. "Lotta stuff to sift through in that mess."

By nine A.M. the crowd had left for their homes and jobs. The excitement was over. As they trickled out, many of the town's people stopped to tell me how sorry they were about the fire. "You didn't deserve this," I was told over and over again. Others gave me slips of paper with phone numbers on them. "You need help cleaning up, Mr. Addams, just call." Several families invited me to dinner. Jack Quinn, the impish owner of the

River Edge Inn, shook my hand and then held it. "I've always believed in what you were doing, Max," he said. "Should have spoken up before now, I know but, well, anyway, we're slow at the Inn right now, so if you need a place to stay until this gets sorted out, just let me know. Free, of course."

I thanked them all. It was gratifying. But it was also eerie. As they filed by, hugging Stormy and shaking my hand, I felt like I had as a twelve-year-old kid at my mother's wake. They were saying they were sorry for my loss and I hadn't accepted the fact that it was gone.

Little Gordon and Bruce had left as soon as the sun was up to put together the story for tonight's *Sentinel*. The fire trucks growled up the access road next and, after Darren and Mark assisted the EMT's in loading the stiff, charred body into the ambulance and it was gone, Mark cordoned off the foundation with yellow police tape and Darren came over to me. "You stayin' out here, Max?" He was dirty and looked tired.

"Yes," I said.

He nodded. "I'll put some pressure on the phone company," he said. "Get 'em out here right away to restring those lines." He pointed. The telephone and electric lines had burned down. "I'll also call Northern Vermont Electric for you, but you know how slow they can be. Least you'll have a phone." He smiled weakly. "That way you'll be the first to know when I know anything."

I thanked him.

"Also," he said, "we'll be sendin' a wrecker for her car. State police'll wanta go over that with a fine-tooth comb." He slowly walked up the yard to the squad car and, as he got in, Mark revved the engine and turned on the flashing lights.

Ruth remained and helped Stormy pick up Rayleen's things and clean the spare room in the workshop. Then, after one more attempt to get me to stay at her place in town, she left. "I've got a meeting with the city council this morning, Max," she said as I walked her to her red Cherokee. "It was supposed to be a preliminary meeting to set the agenda for that meeting I told you Claremont called for next week." She smiled. "But I think, because of this, they'll back off. Even Claremont's not going to push right now."

I watched the yellow tape flutter in the wind and then looked at her. I didn't have the heart to tell her that I really didn't care anymore what they did. I just thanked her again for her help and then watched her walk slowly up the access road.

Wally Murray came, looked at things, and left. What he said to me, I don't remember. I was too tired. I'd talked to too many people and heard too many words of sorrow and support.

Stormy and Rayleen talked John and I into having lunch at the Starlight. It was crowded and we took a table against the wall, where we were besieged by customers offering condolences, promises of help, and rounds of drinks. On top of that, Skip made it clear that lunch was on the house, as would be every meal I ate there until the lodge was rebuilt.

I hadn't thought about rebuilding. How could an antique like Whitefork Lodge ever be recreated? Stormy thought the suggestion was sacrilege. "Body ain't even cold yet," she mumbled and then realizing what she'd said, patted John on the hand. "Sorry."

When we got back to the lodge, the phone lines were up and strung to the workshop. "Well, I'll be damned," Stormy said, picking up the telephone they'd left for my use and extending the antenna. "Finally, we get a portable."

She and Rayleen went home at around four and John

and I ate at the Starlight again. Back at the workshop, there still was no electricity. It made no difference. We were so exhausted that we were in our sleeping bags and asleep by eight o'clock.

The ringing of the portable phone awoke us at nine Wednesday morning. For a minute I didn't know where I was and then, like Lester's crowbar in the belly, it hit me. My arm and head throbbing with pain, I rolled out of the bed, stepped over John in his sleeping bag on the floor, and found the telephone.

It was my daughter, Sabrina. "Daddy? Are you all right?" she said. "I just heard about the fire."

I gingerly rubbed my belly. "I've been better."

"What happened?"

"We don't know yet," I said. "How did you find out down there?"

"David," she said. "He's up in Hartford at a client's and heard it on the radio in his hotel room. He called me here at work. He said somebody died."

"We don't know who yet."

"Oh, Daddy, I was so worried it might be you. You must be sick about this. Do you want me to come up there?"

"No. There's nothing you can do."

"But, how are you eating? Where do you sleep?"

"We manage. The workshop was saved."

"Is Stormy okay?"

"She's home with Rayleen."

"Do you think I should call her?"

"I think she'd like that. You have her number?"

"Right here," she said. "But, Daddy, how did it happen? David said the news report said you've been in a fight about a lumber company clear-cutting above the lodge. You've stopping the logging, but a lot of people have lost jobs. He says that arson is suspected?"

"It's a possibility. We'll know in a day or two."

"And you don't know the dead person?"

"I hope not."

"Who could it be?"

"I don't know, sweetheart." I sighed. "I don't know." Suddenly I didn't want to talk about it anymore. "Listen, Sabrina," I said, "I really don't want to talk about it right now. And, anyway, David probably knows more about this than I do." John stumbled by me and into the small bathroom. "Just don't worry, huh? Believe me, all things considered, I'm fine, Stormy's fine"—Spotter walked around my legs and out the door—"and even Spotter's fine."

"But what's going to happen to your business?"

I forced a laugh. "I think this season is over," I said.

"David said to tell you, if you need money or anything . . ."

"Thanks." The last thing I wanted to do was borrow money from my son-in-law, the cocky little bastard. "Tell David thanks, but we'll be fine."

"You were insured, I assume." Now she sounded like her mother.

"Yes," I said. "We're insured." With a five-thousand-dollar deductible on the contents so I could keep part of the premiums down. "We'll be fine."

"Hang in there, Daddy," she said. "Don't let those lumber company jerks get to you. You're still right in what you're doing. People have to learn to find ways to have jobs and protect the environment at the same time."

We talked for a few more minutes and then with a promise to come up "on a moment's notice" should I need her, she hung up.

I used the bathroom, splashed water on my face, and then joined John out in the front of the workshop. He was sitting on the bench leaning back against the logs in only his jockey shorts, cowboy boots, and my hooded black sweatshirt.

"Cute outfit," I said, sitting beside him.

"Will you give me a ride to the airport this morning? I'm going down to Boston."

"You think you're up to giving your speech?"

"I've got to, Max. I'm the reason the conference is being held," he said. "I leave now, I'll make it just in time." He shrugged. "I've got to do something, Max. You don't need me here." He rolled his head back and forth on the logs. "It'll take my mind off all this, until we know for sure about Stephanie."

"What are you going to do for clothes?"

"I'll buy some."

Spotter wandered over and put his muzzle on my knee. He was hungry and I didn't have any food. I looked out at the lake. A flock of Canada geese sat dozing out in the middle. A faint breeze wrinkled the surface. "When do the planes run?"

"There's a commuter flight every couple hours," he said.

"Where are you staying?"

"The conference committee has me booked at the Ritz Carlton."

"When do you want to go?"

"As soon as I get some pants on."

We stopped at the mailbox on the way out. Rayleen had leaned it against a maple by the road. John jumped out and grabbed the *Sentinel.* It was yesterday's paper and the fire story covered the entire front page. What I could see of the photographs were actually quite good and very dramatic. John folded the paper lengthwise. I put the Jeep back in gear and then, with him reading aloud, we drove to the Starlight for some takeout coffees and raw hamburger for Spotter before going on to the airport.

"You want to hear this?" he asked.

"You're going to read it anyway, aren't you?"

He nodded and began to read.

"At two-thirty this morning, while dozens of Loon citizens watched, the last flames were doused on what once had been the exclusive Whitefork fishing lodge. By daylight, not only were questions of arson being thrown around like the sparks that flew all night, but a body was found among the charred timbers. As of press-time, the identity of the victim has not been determined. However, Loon County Sheriff Darren Foley confided to the *Sentinel* in an exclusive interview that, 'There's a good possibility that it's either Bull or Stephanie Wilcox.'

"Sheriff Foley is referring, of course, to Collari foreman Bull Turlock, who is wanted on suspicion of beating Whitey Laycock and perhaps Boston businesswoman, Stephanie Wilcox, who coincidentally is a friend of both Alphonse Collari and Whitefork Lodge owner Maxwell Addams. Both Turlock and Wilcox have been missing since before the fire late yesterday afternoon.

" 'It could be connected,' " Foley said. " 'Then again, we're not ruling out the possibility that the body is someone else entirely.'

"To this reporter that seems to be remote, since most of this spring's guests at Whitefork Lodge had canceled and everyone else in residence is accounted for."

"Nope," I said. "I don't want or need to hear this crap."

"Just listen to this part, Max." He found his place and continued to read.

"Far less remote and more interesting than the unidentified body or Bull Turlock or the fire, for this reporter, is the question, 'What now, Mister Addams? How much more will you put up with before you realize that people are more important than fish? How many more Red Crosleys, Stephanie Wilcoxes, Bull Turlocks, and Whitey Laycocks have to die or be injured, or God knows what, before you accept the fact that this is farming and lumber country and not a fly-fishing theme park for a few rich anglers?' "

I pulled into the Starlight parking lot and slammed on the brakes. "Fuck him," I said, hitting the steering wheel with my fist. "Dammit! I'm tired of being the bad guy."

John tossed the paper into the back seat and put his hand on my arm. "Relax, Max. Once the report on those cores comes back, you'll be a hero."

"I don't want to be a hero," I said. "All I want is what you want. I want Stephanie to not be the body we found in the fire."

I stayed in the Jeep and John bought the coffees and hamburger which Spotter gulped down on the back seat before we were even out of the parking lot.

At the airport, I pulled up in front. There didn't seem to be any sense in going in. John climbed out and stood holding the door. "Call me as soon as you hear anything," he said. "Anything."

I nodded.

"And don't let that two-bit newspaper get to you." He slammed the door and I watched him enter the terminal. Then I patted the passenger seat and Spotter hopped up front, sat on his butt, and stuck his head out the window.

"You were there when it happened, boy," I said to him, as I pulled away from the curb. "Who set fire to the lodge? Whose body did we find?"

Spotter didn't answer, of course. His nose was pointed back toward the lodge and his wet, pink tongue and black ears were already flapping in the wind.

CHAPTER ⚓ SEVENTEEN

I t was going to take a long time to get used to the lodge not being there and although I knew better, I was still shocked when I came out of the trees at the bottom of the access road and pulled the Jeep up in front of nothing.

A little before noon, two plain, maroon Ford sedans with State Police license plates pulled in. The four men and a fat woman identified themselves as being from the State Police Arson Squad. I watched them unload several big aluminum boxes from the trunks of the cars and then I told them, if they had questions, they could find me in the workshop.

I took the portable phone into the little bedroom, sat on the bed and called the sheriff's office. Mark Richards answered and I asked for Darren.

"Sheriff Foley's out, Max," he said.

I asked about Bull and the identity of the corpse.

"Negative so far on both," he said. "Although, I guess it won't hurt to tell you that this mornin' we found Bull's truck at the Burlington airport. But he musta bought tickets with cash and under an alias, 'cause there's no record of him takin' a plane anywhere."

I told him that the arson people had just arrived.

"I know. They were here first. I'm the one gave them directions."

"Anything on Stephanie?" I asked, holding the phone between my ear and shoulder while I attempted to scratch an itch under the cast.

"Be honest with you, Max. We haven't done much on that yet. Not even a missin' persons. Seein' as she could be right here in the morgue, sheriff thinks we should wait 'til we got the identity of the body first. Before we use taxpayers' money unnecessarily, you know?"

"How about the fire?" I couldn't reach the itch.

"We've asked a few questions," he said. "I was over at the mill at Collari's office this mornin' myself. But just routine. Right now, sheriff wants that kept low key too. At least, 'til we know for certain it was arson."

I thanked him, hung up and dialed Boston information. They gave me the number for Tear-Pruf and I dialed it and asked the woman who answered if I could speak with Stephanie Wilcox.

"She's not in the office today, sir. Can her secretary, Mrs. Bernard, help?"

I said yes and waited while I was patched through. "This is Pam Bernard," a woman's voice said. "How can I help you?"

I identified myself.

"Yes, of course. Mr. Addams. Stephanie has spoken of you often. How are you?"

I lied and told her that Stephanie had forgotten some important papers when she left the lodge the other day. "Could you have her call me when you talk to her?" I said.

"To be honest with you, Mr. Addams," she said, "I haven't heard from Stephanie since she first arrived in Vermont, five or six days ago."

"Really?"

"It's no cause for alarm," Mrs. Bernard said quickly.

"She does this sometimes when she's really wrapped up in something." She laughed. "Her father was the same way when he was working on a big deal."

"Well, if she comes in," I said, "have her call me."

"I certainly will. Good day, Mr. Addams."

I hung up and stared at the receiver in my lap. That's strange, I thought. I distinctly remembered, on at least two occasions, Stephanie telling us she was using the lodge telephone to call her office.

The phone rang in my lap, making me jump. It was Stormy. "How're you two men doin' out there?"

I told her John had left and that the arson squad had arrived.

"Poor guy," she said. "Well, least it'll give him somethin' to think about 'sides where Stephanie's at."

I told her about my conversation with Pam Bernard. "And she hasn't heard from Stephanie since she got here. Doesn't that seem strange?"

"Not to me," Stormy said. "Stephanie prob'ly just talked to somebody else is all."

"I talked to Mark." I dug my fingers down inside the cast. The itching spot was just out of reach.

"Me too," she said. "Sounds like they're draggin' their feet a little. As usual. So how you feelin' today? Takin' them pills?"

"Not that bad." I stuck a pencil down inside the cast. "If I could just get at the itch inside this cast, I'd be perfect."

"Try a pencil."

"I am." The pencil wouldn't reach.

"Get it?"

"No." I threw the pencil across the room. "If this keeps up I'm going to soak this damn thing off."

"Don't you dare, Maxwell Addams," she said. "You could end up with a crooked arm and then where'd you be? Huh?"

I didn't say anything.

"You comin' to Red's funeral tomorrow?"

"Tomorrow? What time?"

"Ten. At Saint Catherine's."

"Of course I'm coming."

"Wilba told me she didn't want you to be offended by not bein' a pallbearer, but she thought that with everythin' else you got goin' on . . ."

"I'm not offended."

"Rayleen's takin' your place."

"He mind?"

"Old fart don't like the idea of wearin' a tie, but he'll get over it."

I laughed. "Rayleen in a tie?"

"Dark blue suit too. I'm shortenin' the pants right now."

"The only clothes I have left are the ones I have on."

"Stores are open in town 'til nine, Max," she said. "What else you got to do?" And she hung up.

At five, the arson squad stripped off their rubber gloves and put away their gear. They had filled several small plastic bags with tiny, black, burned shapes and, as they were arranging them in one of the aluminum boxes, Spotter and I went out to see if they'd found anything significant.

"Can't say yet," the fat woman told me. "Although, it seems that ignition occurred about there." She pointed to where the hallway had been.

"We'll be back in the morning, sir," the taller of the four men said. "Another couple days and we should have an answer."

The woman gestured to Spotter. "You might want to keep an eye on your dog for the next forty-eight hours," she said. "We've sprayed some chemicals on parts of the burn that can be quite caustic until they've had a chance to soak in."

After they left, I loaded Spotter in the Jeep and went to town for some money and clothes.

I didn't get back to the workshop until after dark.

I'd bought a tweed sport coat, a couple pairs of khakis, jeans, shirts, socks, underwear, and toiletries. Then I'd gone out to the Starlight where Skip served me too much pot roast, mashed potatoes, and olive-drab green beans. A couple guys at the bar bought me three Loon Lagers and a shot of VO.

I stepped out of the workshop and sat on the bench against the front wall. It was a beautiful night. A full moon was rising over the eastern mountains and beginning to puddle like melted butter in the black, still lake. Peepers filled the balsam-scented air with their chirping and a loon laughed insanely out near the beaver dam. He was answered by another from the mouth of the river. Ducks quacked in their sleep out in the darkness and I heard a *hoo hoo, hoo hoo* from somewhere up on Morning Mountain as a great horned owl began its hunt. Spotter, full of Skip's ground beef and macaroni and cheese, lay on his side at my feet snoring. I'd brought a large black coffee back from the restaurant with me and sipped and chain-smoked. Mud Season was gone. So was the lodge. So was Stephanie.

"Where could you have gone, Stephanie?" I said out loud. "What made you run?"

I scratched my arm where the cast had been. Skip's wife, Lo Ming, had helped me remove it after dinner by submerging my arm in the deep sink behind the bar. She'd found an ace bandage in a drawer and wrapped the wrist. Stormy was going to be mad, but I didn't care. The thing had been driving me nuts.

Spotter suddenly raised his head and stared toward the lodge. I looked and saw nothing. Then I heard what he'd obviously felt; the sound of a car coming down the access road. The beams of its neadlights bounced in the darkness and when it came out of the trees, swung toward us and stopped, I was blinded. The engine was turned off, the lights extinguished and, after a minute the door opened, illuminating the interior and Ruth Pearlman in a bright green sweater as she got out and lifted a picnic basket into her arms. She hipped the door closed and it was dark again.

"Max?" she said. "Is that you over there?"

I stood. "Yeah," I said, taking the kerosene lamp from the nail on the wall. "Here, let me light a lamp." By the time I'd lit the wick, pushed the chimney back in place, and adjusted the flame, she was at my side. Spotter was on his feet, sniffing at her sandals and the hem of her ankle-length, flowered skirt.

"I brought you some things," she said, putting the basket on the bench and opening it. There were oranges, apples, bagels, instant coffee, bright red napkins, and the gleam of utensils in the lamplight. "And for you, Spotter," she pulled a plastic-wrapped rectangular shape from her skirt pocket, "a steak bone." Spotter, his tail thumping the ground, sat looking up at her. His tongue dripped from his open mouth. She unwrapped the bone and gave it to him and he trotted off out of the circle of light. She balled the plastic in her hands and smiled at me.

"I had supper at the Starlight," I said. "If I'd known I . . ."

"I know," she said. "Most of this is for breakfast. Only this—" she dug under the oranges and produced a bottle of wine, corkscrew, and two, long-stemmed glasses "—is for tonight." She put them on the bench and then, standing on tiptoe, pulled my face down to hers. "And, of course, there's this," she said and kissed me softly on the lips.

The coppery lamp light frosted her beautiful face and hair with gold. "Did you say breakfast?" I said.

"Well," she nodded and smiled softly, "if it works out that way."

I pulled her to me and we kissed again and, this time, her mouth opened on mine and her arms pulled me close.

The loons called to each other again as, hand in hand, we went inside through the dark workshop and stood in the shaft of moonlight by the small bed. Her hair was a halo of pale, white light and she smiled, stepped out of her sandals, and pulled the sweater over her head. I took off my shirt. Her flowered skirt floated down her legs and settled around her ankles while my fingers fumbled with the back of her bra and hers tugged at the buttons on my jeans.

"Oh, Max," she whispered, holding my head as I kissed her breasts. "My sweet Max." She slowly fell backwards out of the bright, milky light onto the dark bed and I followed and found her there, deep in the downy pile of open sleeping bags where she guided me onto her and between her soft thighs. She raised her knees to my shoulders and I felt her cool hand slide between our bellies, find and press me into her. Then, with her bare feet pointed into the moonlight above our heads and her mouth wet on my shoulder, the little bed began to creak beneath my knees and her arching back.

"It's supposed to fit tight, Max," she said. "It swells up in the hole and if you pull it out too hard, you'll break it off."

I laughed and handed her the wine bottle with the corkscrew jutting from the neck. "Here," I said. "You do it. I don't know from corks. Screw tops are my speed."

Ruth sat up on her knees on the bed in the lantern

light and gripped the bottle between her thighs. "You have to turn it slowly at the same time you pull." She expertly twisted and pulled. The cork popped free. "There. See?" We were both still naked and, in the flickering golden light from the kerosene lantern I'd brought in from outside, her skin looked as if she had been dipped in pale maple syrup.

I held out the two glasses and she poured each half full. She took one and we clinked the rims. "Ever since that day you were in my office with Wally," she said, sipping the wine, "all I've really thought about is doing this."

I sat beside her and kissed the tops of her breasts. Her green eyes watched me through the fringe of bangs. She had a dancer's body. Running and aerobics had made everything about her firm and smooth, sleek almost.

"And then," she said, stroking my hair, "when I heard your friend Stephanie was living out here, I was jealous." She smiled sheepishly. "Now, I feel so stupid. I'm here and she's maybe . . ."

"Shhh," I said and kissed her lips.

"But, Max," she sighed, set the glass on the bedside table, "coming here tonight like I did. . . ." She lay back in the sleeping bags. "Pretty tacky, huh?" She crossed her tiny ankles on my knee.

I put my glass on the floor and stretched out on my back beside her. Our hips touched. We looked at the ceiling.

"What is she like? This Stephanie?" She took my hand and held it on her warm belly. "Were you lovers?"

"A long time ago."

"Did you love her?"

"Not like you mean."

"What do you think happened to her?"

I shook my head. "I don't know," I said. "Half of me

can't figure it out. The other half doesn't want to. There are too many possibilities. The worst being that she's the body in the morgue."

Ruth raised herself up on one elbow and looked down at me. "When will they know?"

"In a day or two."

We were silent for a while. I shut my eyes. I could hear Spotter crunching the bone outside. The peepers had stopped and a chorus of frogs had replaced them. I heard the owl again. "Are you going to Red's funeral?"

I nodded.

She slid up on top of me. "Should we go together?" She straddled my pelvis and smiled down at me. Her thighs pressed against my hips.

"If you can afford to be seen with me," I said. "You're the one who wants to get reelected, not me."

She laughed, her breasts bouncing slightly in the lamplight. "Too late for that." She leaned and kissed me. "By now the whole darn town probably knows I'm here." Her breasts brushed my chin.

I laughed. "Then you're screwed."

"I know," she giggled, smiling wickedly. "And isn't it fun?" Then she covered my mouth with hers and, as her buttocks began to rise and fall under my hands, the little bed started creaking again.

The one hundred-fifty-year-old, classic New England, white building with its tall pointed steeple that now houses Saint Catherine's Catholic church originally had been Protestant. The Catholics bought it after the Presbyterian pastor had been caught teaching the specifics of procreation to a thirteen-year-old Loon Junior High School girl in the rectory's spare bedroom. Loon Presbyterians now drove to the neighboring town of Graniteville for Sunday services.

I'd always wondered, however, if it wasn't disconcerting to the parishioners the way the ornate and gaudy renaissance paraphernalia of Catholicism clashed with the austere and angular, whitewashed primitive interior. I didn't attend any church and had only been in this one on two occasions for weddings. Still, to me, it looked like a swap-meet for icons.

The church was more than two-thirds full when Ruth and I slipped into the right-angled discomfort of a well-polished wooden back pew. The casket, draped with embroidered white silk, sat surrounded by floral arrangements on a gurney down in front. Organ music played softly and I could hear occasional sobbing. I could see Stormy's braid and the back of Rayleen's tufted head in the second row. In front of them sat Wilba, Red's boys, and, I assumed, the rest of the family. I didn't see Darren but saw Mark Richards in uniform, Reba from the post office, Skip and Lo Ming, and, at the end of a row on the far left, Alphonse Collari and Claremont Taylor.

Ruth wore the flowered skirt and sweater from last night and, as the two priests came out and stood by the casket, she took my hand in hers and held it in her lap. She smiled at me and I wondered briefly if erections in church were sacrilegious.

The service seemed interminable and I felt for Wilba, struggling to keep the little boys calm.

When the casket had been carried out and the service was over, everyone milled around sober faced outside the church while instructions were issued and cars were lined up for the procession to Overlook Cemetery. Rayleen, the trousers of his shiny blue suit an inch too short, stood off to one side with the other somber pallbearers. Stormy was busy helping Wilba with the boys, so Ruth and I just stood and she chatted with people I didn't know about the weather and poor Red and what Wilba might do now and my unfortunate fire. Twice I caught Stormy looking at me and from the look on her face, I knew she was dying to find out what Ruth and I were doing together. If she noticed my cast missing, she didn't show it.

In his wrinkled suit, white hair ruffling in the breeze, Claremont Taylor was holding court to a circle of red-faced men with big bellies and badly tied ties. Alphonse Collari stood off to one side in a tweed sportcoat and big sunglasses. When he saw Ruth and I, he leaned and whispered something to Claremont and then wound his way through the crowd and up to us. He took off the glasses. "Hello, Ruth," he said, shaking her hand. He looked at me. "I have several things I need to tell you, Addams."

I gritted my teeth and didn't say anything.

"After the service at the cemetery," he said, "can we get together for a few minutes and talk?"

"Where?"

He shrugged. "The Starlight?"

"Fine." Then Ruth and I turned and walked away toward her Cherokee. I felt his eyes on my back. "I suppose I should thank you for not hitting him," she whispered.

"Thank Red," I said.

We were about twentieth in the long line of vehicles that wound from the church, through town, across Burney Bridge and up Spring Hill to Riverview Cemetery.

The ground was spongy and our feet were wet by the time we walked from the Cherokee to the grave site. Red's stone was already in place and the large mound of fresh earth from the grave seemed obscene under its carpet of fake, chartreuse grass. Wilba and the boys sat on folding chairs. The rest of us stood shoulder to shoulder, five deep around the perimeter.

Smelling of cigarette smoke, Stormy wormed her way

up beside Ruth and me. Her eyes were red and swollen. "Told ya not to take that cast off," she whispered and then smiled weakly at Ruth.

Ruth smiled back. "How is Wilba holding up?"

"She's a tough little girl," Stormy said. "She'll be better once this thing's over."

"It's nice she has you."

"I think you're right," she whispered and gestured with her head toward the crowd of people standing behind Wilba and the boys. "That's Red's family there," she said. "His momma's the one with the red hair. Nice woman. The rest of 'em are useless." She looked at me again. "Saw ya talkin' to Collari," she said. "What'd he want?"

"He wants to tell me something," I said.

"Bet he does." The minister stepped up to the side of the grave and held up his hand. "Gotta go," she said and she melted back into the crowd to reappear at Wilba's side. I watched her reach down and straighten the collar of one of the boy's shirts.

The ceremony was more of the same we'd heard in church, except this time tears were running down everyone's cheeks when Red's two boys, like stoic little men in their short pants, blazers, and ties, reached out and touched the casket one last time as it was lowered into the ground.

Then it was over and Ruth and I and, it seemed, about half of the population of Loon drove out to the Starlight. She let me drive and I could see Collari's dark green Range Rover five cars ahead of us. "I hope he didn't want this conversation to be too private," I said.

"Can we change cars at the lodge?" Ruth said. "I've got to go to the office." She ran her hand over the back of my neck. "You don't need me with you now anyway, do you?"

I shook my head.

"I can be back out to the lodge at about three. If you want me to."

"Sleep over?"

She smiled. "I'll bring my jammies this time."

"But I liked the ones you had last night." I kissed her goodbye, got my Jeep at the lodge, and drove on alone to the Starlight. The parking lot was half full and more cars and pickups were pulling in as I swung in off the road, spied Collari's Rover at the back of the lot against the trees, and pulled up beside it. It was empty.

I got out of the Jeep just as Stormy and Rayleen pulled in behind me. She hung her head out of the window. "You and Ruth sure got folks talkin' this mornin'," she said with a smirk.

I gave her a disgusted look and shook my head.

"I take that look to mean maybe folks is right in what they're sayin'?"

"What are they saying?"

"Her neighbors're sayin' she never come home last night."

"And what did you say to that?"

"She told 'em all to take a flyin' leap," Rayleen said. "And coupla other things I can't repeat."

"Damn busybodies got me riled. Like we need them talkin' after all we been through."

I smiled at her. "But you're dying to know, aren't you?"

"Well . . ." she shrugged and came the closest to blushing I'd ever seen. "Ruth's the mayor, Max. A single one, at that. Hell, remember poor Jerry Brown in California? Was datin' that there singer, Linda Rostart?"

"Ronstadt," I said.

"Whatever. Folks never give him a moment's peace."

"Let them talk," I said.

"Addams." Collari walked toward me. "I was looking for you inside."

"You still want to talk in there?" I said. "It's not going to be very private."

He shook his head. "Let's drive up to the Overlook," he said.

I said goodbye to Stormy and Rayleen and got back into the Jeep. Then Collari and I both backed up, turned around and I followed him out of the lot, onto 16, and west toward the Overlook.

Just before you get to Hooker Hill Road, you top out on a spot where, I swear, on a good day you can almost see all the way south to New York City. Because so many "leaf-peepers" stop there in the fall for photographs, the state had bulldozed a small parking area on the south side of the road, blacktopped it, and painted in three parking spaces. The ubiquitous handicapped icon was emblazoned on two of them. Under a winddeformed maple they'd chained a picnic table and a trash can.

Since it was spring, the Overlook was empty and Collari and I pulled in across all three spaces and shut off our cars. The clouds were moving in and the mountains rolled out toward the horizon like an appliqué study in degrees of fading pale green. In the farthest distance I could see the blacker, boiling clouds preceding a storm front as it pushed toward the northeast. It would miss us but it looked like Boston was going to get rain and lightning later this afternoon. I wondered how John was.

Collari climbed from the Rover, walked out to the picnic table, and sat with his back to the view. The air was still and warm and I took off my sportcoat and joined him. A red-tailed hawk soared behind his head a few hundred feet out. We looked at each other. I lit a cigarette. "Well?" I said, exhaling.

"You have to believe that I had nothing to do with your fire, Addams," he said. "You have to believe that."

"Maybe not you. Maybe someone who works for you."

"Maybe." He nodded and looked at his hands for a few seconds. I waited. When he looked back at me his eyes were full of tears. "I told her I didn't want her involved. I begged her."

"Who? Stephanie?"

"Yes. I implored her not to do those things. I told her the lawyers could work it out. I had her meet with Claremont. He told her the same thing." He sighed and looked back down at his hands again. He shook his head. "But she wanted that order so damn bad, Max." He looked back at me. "She wanted to adopt that baby so damn bad." He stood abruptly and walked to the cliff. "I told her," he turned, "I'd back her, for Chrissakes." He walked back to the table. "Hell, I said I'd buy her company if she'd just stay out of this." He sat down hard on the bench. "But, well—" he shook his head slowly, his eyes filling again "—you know Stephanie." He pulled a folded handkerchief from a trouser pocket and wiped at his eyes. "She's so goddamn independent. So goddamn independent. She was convinced you'd quit. Each time, she'd say, just once more, Al. He'll quit."

I took a long drag on my cigarette and exhaled slowly. "I don't have the slightest idea what you're talking about," I said. "What was Stephanie doing?"

His eyes widened. "You don't know?"

I shrugged.

"I thought that was why she ran away. Because you found out."

"Found out what?" I ground out the cigarette on the table top. "What did she do, dammit?"

"She did it all," he said. "She wrecked your canoes. She threw garbage in the river. She made the posters at the mill. The picketers. She organized them. She even—"

I held up my hand. "Whoa. Wait a minute." It was coming too fast for me. "One thing at a time. What do you mean, Stephanie wrecked the canoes? How could she?"

"I don't know exactly," he said. "She did it. At night. They were just the first in her campaign to get you to change your mind."

"And you knew?"

"I knew about all of it," he said. "But you've got to believe me, Addams, I implored her to stop. Yet, every day it would be something else." He sighed. "She even called your customers. Got them to cancel. And she took the fingerprint."

"Stephanie stole the fingerprint?"

He nodded sadly. "She was afraid it would belong to one of my people. The night I called and she said you had it, I told her I didn't care, but she wouldn't listen. She said, if one of my people was convicted of murder, the logging site would close for sure."

"Do you have the fingerprint?"

"No. I didn't want it. I told her I didn't want it. She kept it. I don't know where it is now."

I looked out at the view. The red-tailed hawk swooped through, going the other way. "Damn her!" I slammed my fist on the table and looked at him. "Why?"

"That's not all," he said.

"You're not going to tell me she set the fire?"

"No." He shook his head. "But that afternoon, she gave Claremont the cores."

"What?"

"She stole them for us."

I frowned. "That can't be," I said.

"It is." He nodded. "She called me and said she had

them. I sent Claremont to the lodge to get them and he brought them to me." He sighed. "I didn't want them, but both of them were insistent." He pointed to the Rover. "Hell, they're still in the back of my car."

I shook my head. "You couldn't have the cores, Al. We boxed them and I mailed them to Colorado myself."

He frowned. "When?"

"About two o'clock. Long before you say Stephanie gave them to Claremont."

"Are you sure?"

"I'll never forget it," I said bitterly. "That was when your men tried to kill me."

He stood, walked around the table and went to the back of the Rover. I joined him as he lifted the tailgate. Lying there side by side were four aluminum tubes with styrofoam corks. "Then, what are these?" he said.

I picked one up. It was heavy. I unscrewed the cork and peeked in. It was full of soil. I tipped it and poured some in my palm. It was loose loam with a few marble-size stones. It smelled strongly of dead fish. I put it down and opened another. Same thing. The other two also contained the same loose black dirt and strong dead-fish smell. I remembered Stephanie at the golf bag. Her interest in the empty tubes when John and I were wrapping the full ones. "These aren't the cores we took," I said. "These are extra tubes we had." I sifted the dirt through my fingers and smelled it again. "And, I'm almost positive, this is just soil from my house-keeper's garden."

He sat on the tailgate. "How do you know?"

"I can smell it. I buried all the trout you killed in that garden."

"But, but why? Why would she say . . . ?"

"I think she was doing a number on you too, Al." I sat beside him.

"But, why? Why me? I wanted to help her."

I shook my head and as we both stared at the asphalt, I lit another cigarette. "If she did all the things to me you say she did," I said, looking at him, "then she must have finally realized she couldn't change my mind."

"Yes." He nodded. "I think she did."

"Then maybe she thought she could get you to change yours."

"With the cores? How would they change my mind?"

"Maybe she thought you'd back off if you knew you had the upper hand. Maybe she thought you'd feel so confident of winning in court knowing you had the cores that you'd reinstate her order."

He nodded thoughtfully. "Claremont certainly was excited we had them." He rubbed his jaw. "He predicted we'd be logging again by next month."

"See?"

He nodded slowly. "I'm afraid I see too clearly." He put his head in his hands and spoke between them. "Then she didn't run, did she? You didn't scare her off. That is her body you found."

I put my hand on his shoulder. It was shaking. "Have you told any of this to the sheriff?" I asked.

"I hoped I wouldn't have to." He shook his head. "I wanted to talk to you. I hoped maybe . . . maybe, you would forgive her if . . . if I . . ." His shoulders shook violently. "I loved her, Max." He looked up at me. "Do you know that? I've loved her since she was a little girl. I would have done anything in the world for her. And she never knew."

"She knew," I said. "C'mon." I helped him to his feet. "I'll buy you a drink."

CHAPTER ✦ EIGHTEEN

I wanted to feel anger, but I couldn't. All the way back to the Starlight I thought about what Stephanie had done. And hard as I tried, I could only feel sorry. Sorry because I had joked about her wanting a husband and to be a mother. Sorry I hadn't seen or felt her desperation. Sorry I hadn't realized how much she'd really wanted that baby.

By the time Alphonse and I got back to the parking lot, he'd decided he didn't want a drink. He claimed he didn't think he could deal with all the people inside. I didn't argue. Sitting there in the Rover, he looked like he'd shriveled since the Overlook. Everything about him seemed older. His shoulders were bent and his head hung forward. The skin on his robust, tan face was ashen.

"You going to be all right?" I asked.

He looked at me through watery, red eyes and sighed. "I suppose you'll be telling the sheriff what I told you," he said.

"I don't know. What good would it do?"

He nodded. "It won't bring her back."

"We don't know she's dead, Al."

"I do," he said. "I can feel it." The electric window slid up and he drove away.

The Arson Squad was knee deep in burned rubble at the lodge when I pulled in and parked. "Anything yet?" I asked, as I climbed out of the Jeep.

They all shook their heads.

I went to the workshop, unlocked the door, and let Spotter out to go to the bathroom. I tossed my new sportcoat on the bed and took the portable phone down to the dock, where I took off my boots, rolled up my khakis, and dangled my feet in the clear water. I lit a cigarette and dialed the sheriff's office.

Mark Richards answered and, after saying hello and discussing the funeral, I asked to speak to the sheriff.

"He's still not here, Max," he said.

"Where in the hell is he?"

"Called in this mornin' and said he's followin' a lead on Bull."

"Did he say where he was?"

"No sir. But he wasn't far away."

"How do you know that?"

"He was on his two-way," Mark said. "That thing's only got a range of 'bout thirty miles."

"Any word on the body?"

"Well," he cleared his throat. "I did hear somethin' just before you called. In fact, I just hung up. Was writing the message for the sheriff when you rang."

"Well?"

"Well, I really should tell Sheriff Foley first, Max. You understand."

"Goddammit, Mark. That body was found in my lodge. It could be my friend." I was yelling into the phone. "You tell me what you know or I'm going to—"

"All right, Max, all right," he said.

"Who is it?"

"We don't know that part yet, Max. Not even what sex it is."

"What then?"

"The coroner called to say that the, ah, the victim had been shot."

"Shot?"

"Yes sir. With a gun. We got ourselves a for-sure murder here now. They found a bullet wound in its head."

"Jesus."

"Yes sir," he said. "Unfortunately they couldn't find no bullet though. Went right in the back and out the eye, they think."

I didn't want to hear any more. "Thanks, Mark," I said. "Have the sheriff call me next time you talk to him." I hung up and dialed Stormy's number. It took five rings before she answered. I said, "The person found in the fire was murdered."

"I'll be," she said. "How'd you find that out?"

"I just talked to Mark. Whoever it was was shot."

"Still don't know who it is though, huh?"

"No."

"I guess that part's good."

"Yeah."

"Hope that Darren's doin' somethin' 'bout this," she said. "This makes two murders by my count."

"He doesn't know about this yet. He's still out somewhere searching for Bull."

"Seems strange, don't it?"

"What?"

"Why Darren don't just turn catchin' Bull over to the state police or somebody. Why's he gotta run all over all by hisself? Hell, Bull could be in Hawaii livin' in a grass shack by now. Let the damn FBI find 'im."

"Mark told me Darren's somewhere nearby," I said. "So, maybe, Bull is too."

She let out a sigh of disgust and I heard the clink of

her old Zippo. "What'd Collari want this mornin'?" she asked.

"Are you sitting down?"

"No."

"Maybe you should," I said and then told her what Collari had told me about Stephanie.

"The bastard," she said. "He's lyin'. Stephanie would never do anything like that."

"No. I believe him, Stormy. You said it yourself that first day. She's a very determined woman. She wanted that order."

"Well, maybe. She sure wanted that baby, I know."

I didn't say anything.

"Then, where's the fingerprint?" she asked.

"Collari says, as far as he knows, Stephanie kept it."

"Well, we can kiss that goodbye. Damn thing's probably burned up with everythin' else."

"If the body is her."

"Must be, Max. Hell, face it. It's plain as the nose on your face. Somebody killed her for that fingerprint."

"And if the body's somebody else?"

"Then, if she's got that print, she better be hidin' good," she said. "She better be hidin' real good."

After we hung up, I sat with the phone in my lap and watched little tufts of breeze ripple the surface of the lake. The clouds were closing off the blue and I thought I could hear very distant thunder.

God, I thought. I started this. Look what's happened? If only I hadn't been so quick with the T.R.O. Collari doesn't seem that bad. He might have listened. That damn Gordon is right. This whole thing is my fault. If only I'd listened to Stephanie.

Spotter wandered out from behind the workshop down onto the dock, sat, and pointed his nose at the water about fifteen feet out.

I looked at his back and he wagged his tail, thrusting his snout insistently at the spot.

Spotter has what I call the Saint Bernard gene. Some dogs have it, some don't. However, instead of saving people from drowning, rescuing children from fires or carrying brandy to snowbound travelers, Spotter's method of salvation is different. Like the fish he sees when I can't, he seems to know when my stress level is reaching critical mass. More than once through our years together, Spotter has seemed to sense when I was troubled. He seems to know when I reach a point I don't know I've reached. I don't know whether he feels the bad vibes, or what, but, whether it was the week I was sweating my daughter's college tuition, the news of my wife's marriage to the yahoo in Florida, a bad season on the river, or now, he seems to feel my pain and his solution is always the same: "Focus on catching trout, Max."

I stroked his head. "You're right," I said to him as I got to my feet. "I should fish." I went up to the workshop, quickly rigged my old Cortland and tied on an olive woolly bugger. Whether Spotter's therapy worked or not, it was a good chance to try out my injured arm. As I walked back out onto the dock, Spotter gave me a quick glance over his shoulder, looked pleased, and then resumed his point.

My arm hurt a bit, but the ace bandage kept my wrist nice and stiff and I cast about fifteen feet beyond where he indicated so that by the time I'd stripped the fly up to the spot, it would be wet enough to sink slightly and I could jig it toward me, like something swimming about three inches below the surface.

Made with a palmered hackle over chenille yarn, the woolly bugger is about the simplest fly there is to tie. But it works. It's one of those flies that resemble nothing in particular to anyone except the trout that wants to eat it. And then it looks like what he thinks it looks like.

This one must have looked like something really juicy because, as I swam it through the place Spotter pointed to, the water suddenly bulged around it, there was a big splash, and a nice-size trout ate it for lunch. My reel buzzed as, realizing his mistake, the trout took off, shaking his head in an effort to dislodge the thing now biting him.

I didn't play him and quickly reeled him to the dock, stooped, and popped the barbless hook from his jaw. He was a very angry looking, sixteen-inch brook trout and, once he sensed his freedom, flipped his tail and finned haughtily away.

Spotter was already pointing to a shadowy place to the right under a low hanging spruce limb about four feet out from the shore. "Oh, thanks a lot," I said to him, as I attempted a sidearm cast intended to get the woolly bugger under the limb. "All the fish there are in this lake and you point out one that's impossible to even get a fly to." The woolly bugger landed on the limb, but I was able to yank it off without hooking it and I tried again. This time, it skipped in under the branch and, just as I was congratulating myself, the water erupted and the rod was almost yanked out of my hands as a very large trout pounced the fly and ripped the slack from the leader. My rod bent and my reel squealed as the fish ran with the line. He was on his way to the beaver dam. I have about seventy-five yards of line on this reel before the backing and there was only about five feet left when I finally got the fish to turn. I cranked about fifty feet back on the reel before he took a run at the dam again. This time he was a bit slower and when I turned him again and began reeling in, I could feel him reluctantly coming with it.

We have some real monster brook trout at Whitefork

Lodge and most of them, usually in the heat of summer, are in the lake. It certainly wasn't summer and it wasn't hot, so I was stunned at the size of this one when I finally got him up to the dock. It wasn't that he was long, he was only about two feet. It was his thickness, at least ten inches from dorsal to belly. As I slipped the fly from his lip, I estimated him to weigh somewhere between five and ten pounds.

Spotter kept me fishing like this for about half an hour and with every well-placed cast and every wiggling, tugging fish on my line, I felt the tension of the past few days slip away. It's like the friend of mine in town who repairs clocks and is dying of Lou Gehrig's disease says, "Concentration is the best way to forget."

Rayleen's old truck rattled down the access road and he waved as he parked beside the Jeep and the two state sedans. I reeled in, lit a cigarette, and watched him limp down the dock. He was carrying a six-pack of Loon Lager.

"It didn't take you long to get out of the suit and tie," I said with a laugh. He had on his coveralls, plaid shirt, and greasy cap.

"Yep. And it's gonna take some time 'fore I ever git back into it too, I'll tell ya," he said. "Stormy told me to come out here'n cheer you up."

"She did, huh?"

"Yep. Says you didn't sound too good on the phone earlier." He looked at the rod. "It don't look like you're hurtin' that bad, though. Catch anythin'?"

"Just enough," I said.

He gestured to the Arson Squad. "They findin' anythin'?"

I shrugged.

"Well, I thought maybe I'd do a little work on the Harley," he said, looking toward the workshop. "Unless you got somebody in there, of course."

I ignored the innuendo. "Maybe I'll give you a hand."

"Dunno 'bout that, Max," he said as I picked up the phone and my rod and we started toward the workshop. "Unless you know howta reassemble them carburetors."

"Can't do that," I said. "But I'll have one of those beers if you've got an extra."

He blushed. "Actually," he said, "I brought 'em for you."

I sat up on the workbench beside the hanging light, sipped the cold beer, and watched his gnarled, greasy hands work with the machined metal parts. He carefully inspected each piece and then after using a ball of steel wool to buff some blemish or burr I couldn't see, he carefully, with almost a brain surgeon's finesse, fitted it into its place in the carburetor. It was fascinating, like a puzzle without a box. But it was also disconcerting. Rayleen had the habit of holding his breath until he'd fitted a piece. Then he'd breathe. I counted to fifty-three before he felt the needle valve was in well enough to finally exhale and take a deep breath. I don't think he knew he did it.

The phone rang and I slipped from the workbench and took it in the little bedroom. It was Wally Murray.

"I just got a phone call from Claremont," he said. "He won't say how they got them, but claims they have the cores."

"I know," I said. And I told him briefly about my conversation with Collari and the tubes full of garden dirt.

He chuckled and then apologized. "I don't mean to laugh, Max. But it tickles me to picture that windbag when he finds out."

I laughed too. I wouldn't have before the fishing, but now it seemed funny.

"I also heard about the bullet wound in the corpse," he said. "That makes it murder for sure. You know, no matter who it turns out to be, you'll probably all be suspects."

"Sounds like you and I are going to spend a lot of time in court together before this is over," I said.

"The big one is still the injunction. Unless you've changed your mind."

"I haven't changed my mind."

"Good," he said. "Just hang in there, Max. A lot is going to happen in the next few days once the coroner's report is in and the arson investigation is over. I'm betting it's going to come out that more's been going on around here than clear-cutting trees and polluting the aquifer."

He had a call on his other line, so we said goodbye and I returned to the workbench and opened another beer.

"Who was that?" Rayleen said without looking up.

"My lawyer, Wally Murray. Why?"

He shrugged. "No reason. Only thought it might be the sheriff is all. Seen him on my way out here."

"Where?"

"I come around Hooker Hill way," he said. "So I could stop at the Starlight and get the beers? Well, sheriff was up there. Near the clear-cut entrance." He held a small, wedge-shaped metal part under the lamp and studied it. "Hell, I wouldn'ta knowed it was him if I hadn't seen his face. He was in that big van of theirs with all them whip-type antennas on top. Didn't recognize it."

"Probably doesn't want to be seen in the cruiser. Mark Richards told me Darren was tracking Bull somewhere close by."

"Well, if he's lookin' for him up in the clear-cut, that's pretty close, I'd say."

Rayleen had one of the two carburetors finished by the time Ruth pulled in. I wiped my hands on a rag and went out to greet her. She waved. She was wearing a short tan skirt and a pale blue blouse. A chocolate-colored sweater was tied around her shoulders. She was carrying a suitcase.

She kissed me and I took the suitcase from her hand. "What's in here?" I asked.

"Some things to wear for tomorrow." She smiled and took my other hand. "And my running clothes."

"How about jammies?"

She laughed and gave me a little hip-check.

"Excuse me, Mr. Addams?" It was the fat woman from the Arson Squad.

I turned and she climbed out of the rubble and walked up to us. She was carrying a strange looking flashlight. "Can I help you?" I said.

"You store kerosene in the hallway of the lodge?" she asked.

I nodded. "Lanterns. We lose our power up here a lot."

"Then we may have something. We've found kerosene all over what were the hallway surfaces. The walls and ceiling. Even the stair treads."

"You mean it exploded?" Ruth said.

The fat woman shook her head. Her face was streaked with soot. "No. It couldn't have, not and be spread like it is."

"You can detect something like that?" I said. "I'd think it would all be burned off."

"It is burned off, Mr. Addams. But everything burns with a different chemical reaction and what's left reacts to those chemicals we put in there yesterday." She smiled and patted the strange looking flashlight. "This is infrared. Shows a special shade of green for kerosene."

"That proves it was arson?"

She nodded. "If the density and saturation fits. We're

taking some surface samples back to the lab tonight. We should know by morning."

"Now if we could just figure out who did it," I said.

She smiled again. "Oh, we should be able to help you there too. The chemical combinations we find in a site are always unique. If someone broadcast that kerosene around in there and then ignited it, their hands will have definite traces of the same combinations. No matter how many times they washed." She turned, started back to the remains of the lodge and then stopped and turned. "We'll be leaving in a few minutes. Just thought you'd like to know."

When Ruth and I walked into the workshop, Rayleen looked up, fumbled with his cap, got it off and smiled sheepishly. "Hallo, Missus Mayor," he said.

"How are you, Rayleen?"

He wiped his hands furiously on his coveralls. "Been fine," he said and then looked at me. "Guess I better be goin', Max."

"Don't leave on my account," she said and pointed to the suitcase. "I'm going to go for a run anyway."

Rayleen looked a little confused.

"Finish what you're doing, Rayleen," I said. "You're not in our way."

He nodded and put his cap back on.

I carried Ruth's suitcase into the bedroom. "I don't know how I'm going to stand that gasoline smell he's got in there," she whispered. "Can we air the room out after he leaves?"

I nodded and shut the door. She began unbuttoning her blouse. "Where do you suggest I run?"

"How far do you need?"

She took off the blouse. "About five miles."

I put my arms around her and pulled her to me. "Let's see," I said, kissing her. "If sex is the equivalent of running up eight flights of stairs," I smiled, "then five miles would mean . . ."

"Max." She playfully pushed me away. "I'm serious."

The phone began ringing. I sighed. She picked it up. "Whitefork Lodge," she said, unzipping the skirt and stepping out of it. She listened a second and then said, "Oh. Yes. Of course. Just a minute." She handed the receiver to me. "It's your friend, John, calling from Boston."

"John?" I said, watching Ruth dig through her open suitcase. "How's the conference?"

"Max." His voice sounded strange. "She's dead, Max. They found her floating in the Charles River. Stephanie's dead."

CHAPTER ❦ NINETEEN

I sat hard on the bed. "What? What do you mean, Stephanie?" I had heard him but hoped I hadn't. "What happened?"

"Stephanie's dead, Max. Down here. Cops are saying possible suicide right now."

"I don't understand," I said. "When?"

"It happened last night, I think. I wouldn't have even known about it, probably, if my picture hadn't been in the *Boston Globe*. Andrea Shaughnessey saw it and called me."

"Who?"

"Collari's daughter. She's married to a doctor. Lives somewhere in what they call the Backbay here. She's Stephanie's best friend. They went to college together. She saw my picture. The article told where I was staying and she called."

"I know who you mean, now."

"She's petrified, Max. She says Stephanie was murdered. She had the fingerprint page from the wallet. She says Stephanie told her the fingerprint belonged to Red's killer and she knew who it was. You believe it, Max? Stephanie was the one who stole the fingerprint."

"I know about the fingerprint."

"How . . . ?"

"It doesn't make any difference," I said.

"Look, Max. This Andrea Shaughnessey has it now and she wants me to come to her place and get it. She doesn't want it. She's afraid."

"Stephanie gave it to her?"

"Yeah. Andrea says Stephanie told her she was being followed by the killer. She gave it to her for safe keeping."

Ruth was dressed in her running clothes and sneakers and gave me a questioning look. I indicated she should sit down and wait. "Why doesn't Shaughnessey just give it to the police?" I asked him.

"I asked her that. She says Stephanie made her promise that if anything happened, no police. I don't know. Evidently Stephanie had some sort of hangup about cops lately. Didn't trust them." I heard him exhale. "Look, Max, I don't understand all this. All I know is Stephanie's been murdered and Andrea Shaughnessey has the evidence that can prove it."

"What about Shaughnessey's husband?"

"Who knows? Jesus, Max . . ."

"Are you going to go get it?"

"Not without you I'm not."

"You want me to come down there?"

"Damn straight," he said. "As soon as you can get here, Max. Meet me at the hotel. I think we can walk to her place from here."

I looked at Ruth in her running shorts and tights. She raised her eyebrows. "I don't . . ." I started to say to him.

"Max," he said. "I came when you called. Now I'm calling. I don't want to do this alone."

"It'll take me a couple hours to get there." I looked at my watch. It was almost four. "At least."

"Thanks. I'll call and tell Andrea we'll be there tonight. Get the first plane you can. I'll expect you around eight or so. Room five thirteen."

I hung up and told Ruth what had happened and what I was going to do.

She stood and began pulling off her shorts. "I'll take you to the airport," she said.

"Will you make sure Spotter's fed?"

"I'll just stay here until you come back, Max."

"You'll be all right?"

"I'll be fine." She smiled. "I like this little bed."

When I first started flying in airplanes, nighttime was almost magical. Looking down from a few miles up in the inky sky at the cross hatch streets of small towns or the tangled sprawling web of large cities was like looking into a pirate's chest at the breathtaking sparkle of gold coins, diamonds, rubies, emeralds, and ropes of pearls.

Tonight, I could see none of it. The only thing I could see as I looked at my own long face reflected in the window was the Pandora's Box I'd opened with my temporary restraining order. I'd only intended to protect my river. To save the trout. Instead, Red had died. Then the lodge was lost. Now, hundreds of miles away in another river, Stephanie had died. Murdered simply because she, like me, had done what she thought was right.

I turned off the reading light and looked out my window. Through breaks in the thick clouds, I could see the lights of Boston. But, unlike jewels, these lights tonight pulsed dully like thousands of tiny, sooty fires under a sickly jaundice haze.

There were only five of us in the little commuter plane and, like a fighter on a strafing run, it banked, dropped between the clouds, and streaked toward Logan International's rapidly growing runway lights from low over Boston Harbor.

The terminal was almost empty and I had my choice of taxis from the long line idling in their own exhaust at the curb. The surly, overweight driver floored it away from the curb as soon as I climbed in and shut the door, and we were through the tunnel under the harbor and honking our way through Boston's crowded, narrow streets in less than fifteen minutes.

They say that spring moves north about fifteen miles a day and by the looks of the leafed-out trees in the Public Garden across the street from the Ritz Carlton's brightly-lit facade, Boston was easily two weeks ahead of northern Vermont. Even though it was dark, I could see the glow from seas of yellow and white daffodils behind the high iron fence work.

Ignoring disdainful looks at my boots, khakis, dungaree shirt, and frayed windbreaker from the crisply-suited and carefully-coiffed crowd in the lobby, I called John's room and he told me to come up.

The room was small and dirty, as if I'd accidently taken the elevator to a different hotel than the one represented in the lobby. The only window was thickly streaked with dirt and looked across a narrow alley at the small, cluttered windows in a sooty brick apartment building. He had eaten in the room and the tray of dirty dishes still sat on the end of the small bed. There was a carafe of coffee and two cups on the dresser.

"The coffee's still warm," he said, turning off the TV and closing the cabinet doors over it. "Want some?"

I did and he poured us each a cup. I sat on the bed with mine and he cleared a pile of newspapers from the only chair and sat there. "They say anything about Stephanie in there?" I pointed at the newspapers now on the floor.

He shook his head. "I looked for yesterday's newspaper everywhere, but in this town, old news is old news. They must pick up the unsold copies before the day is even over." He gulped some coffee. "Concierge downstairs said he'd try to find me a copy, though."

"No matter," I said and lit a cigarette. "What are we doing?"

"I called Andrea Shaughnessey. She and her husband live only three or four blocks from here, she says. Thirty-four hundred Beacon Street. A block west of Emerson College. She'll be there all evening. Her husband's out. Has rounds or something at the hospital. Jesus, she sounds frightened. Can't wait until she doesn't have that fingerprint anymore."

"When are we going?"

"Soon as we finish the coffee."

We both drained our cups and I dropped my cigarette in mine and placed it on the tray.

The walk felt good. The streets were still wet from the rain. We crossed the eastbound side of Commonwealth Avenue and as we cut through the grass between the massive sycamores of the parklike center median, I took the opportunity to tell him about my conversation with Collari at the Overlook.

He listened without comment, the shoulders of his corduroy sportcoat hunched up near his ears. When I finished, all he did was nod and say, "What difference does it make?"

Thirty-four hundred Beacon was a well-kept four-story brownstone with tall, sparkling windows in a long row of impressive turn-of-the-century brownstones. Magnolia trees in full bloom, small pin oaks, and silver maples overhung the rolling brick sidewalk, dappling the light from pseudo-gas lamp street lights. Expensive cars, all with The Club clamped to their steering wheels, lined both sides of the street. I could smell flowers, and the mournful wail of a saxophone followed John and me up the flight of steep granite steps to the massive front door. Inside, there was a vestibule and a second door of leaded, multicolored glass. Beyond it was a small, red-carpeted room with a narrow table against one wall and what looked like an elevator door on the other. Two polished brass mailboxes hung on the wall to our right. Ivory call buttons were recessed in a satiny walnut panel above them. He pushed the one marked SHAUGHNESSEY.

A woman's voice answered and John identified himself.

"Oh, thank God," she said. "Come on up. We're the flat on top."

The stained-glass door buzzed and we pushed through. There was indeed an elevator. Inside, however, there was barely enough room for the two of us. There were only two buttons, UP and DOWN. We wedged ourselves in and I managed to free my arm enough to push UP. The elevator started with a jerk and then, stuttering slowly, crept upward.

When we stopped, the door opened automatically into an expansive, expensively-decorated, two-story room that ran the depth of the building to a glass wall overlooking Storrow Drive, the Charles River, and the twinkling lights of Cambridge and the Harvard campus. A very pregnant Andrea Shaughnessey, the front of her ornately-decorated green silk kimono pushed out like she was hiding a watermelon, was standing by the end of one of two facing white couches. She smiled nervously and came across the room, shaking each of our hands as John made the introductions. She had waist-length, straight black hair, porcelain skin, perfect white teeth, and looked nothing like her father. "So you're Max Addams," she said, leading us into the room and gesturing us to seats on the couch across from the one she sat in. "You can't imagine how many times I've heard your name through the years. . . ." Her voice faltered and she quickly put her hand to her mouth, unsuccessfully muffling a sob as her eyes filled with tears. "Oh, you'll have to excuse me," she said, taking a tissue from a box on the cushion beside her. "I loved her so." She gently blew her nose.

I took a deep breath and looked at John. He had turned his head and was staring out the windows.

She balled the tissue and gestured to the coffee table in front of us. "There it is," she said. "Take the damn thing, please." Lying there on a copy of *Architectural Digest* was a plastic Ziploc sandwich bag. I picked it up. Inside was the wallet page with Red's driver's license. I handed it to John. He held it up, looked at it, and then stuck it in the inside pocket of his sportcoat.

"Stephanie was so afraid," Andrea said. "She wouldn't even come into the city. She stayed in an awful motel over in Somerville and made me take the T and different taxis just to see her. She looked awful. She kept saying, he was going to kill her like he did that other man." She put her hand to her mouth again. "And now he has."

"Who?"

"I don't remember." She was valiantly fighting back the tears. "She just said he shot him. Right in the head. In your lodge."

"No," I said. "I meant, who wanted to kill her?"

Andrea shook her head. "She wouldn't say. Only that," she pointed at John, "that fingerprint is his." She sniffed. "After she gave me that baggy, I didn't even tell Roger I had it. I've been petrified to leave the flat."

"Roger?"

"My husband." She smiled sadly. "If he knew . . . he's so afraid we'll lose this baby too, but I feel fine." She put her hand on the mountain under the kimono. "He's kicking right now." She began to tear up again. "Stephanie and I often talked about our babies playing together. Someday."

John and I let her cry. When she pulled another tissue from the box, I said, "No one knows about the fingerprint? That you have it?"

She shook her head slowly while she blew her nose. "I didn't say anything to the police even. And they've been here every day."

"They've been here more than once?" John asked.

She nodded. "Three times. Twice today."

He looked at me. "Doesn't sound like they think it was a suicide, either."

"There were two of them," she said. "Two detectives named," she looked at the window trying to remember, "O'Keefe and Bolick, I think. They asked me all kinds of questions about her friends, her business, who she dated. Did I know she was pregnant."

"Pregnant?" John and I said it together.

"Yes." She looked at us.

"But how . . . ?" I said. "I mean, I thought because of the cancer she couldn't . . ."

"Roger says it can happen. He's an obstetrician. In fact, he says it's not that unusual with the type of specific and localized chemotherapy Steph had."

"How pregnant was she?" John asked.

She closed her eyes and sighed. "Just," she said. "A few days. Maybe a week. Roger said it was something that only a careful autopsy could find." She looked at us, her eyes full again. "Stephanie never knew." She was going to cry again.

I stood. "Thank you," I said to her and looked at John. He stood also and we went to the elevator door. She got up slowly, wiped her eyes, and followed.

"What are you going to do with the fingerprint?" she asked.

"Where is the nearest police station?" I pushed the button by the door.

"There's a precinct station on Berkeley," she said.

"Two blocks south of Boylston. Ask for O'Keefe or Bolick."

"I know where it is," John said. The elevator door trundled open.

We thanked her again, squeezed into the elevator and the door closed in front of us. It was quiet. "You have to push down," I said.

"As soon as I find my hand, I will."

The ride down seemed slower than the ride up. We stood almost nose to nose. We didn't look at each other and neither of us said anything.

The door opened and we pushed through the stained glass door, by the mailboxes and out onto the granite stoop. At the bottom, we stopped on the bricks under the trees. An empty, light blue Ford Taurus was double parked directly in front of us. Its emergency flashers were blinking. John pointed to the right and said, "I think Berkeley Street's that way."

A familiar voice from behind us said, "My car's right in front of you. Get in!" We turned. It was Darren Foley. He stepped out of the bushes at the right of the granite stairs. He was holding a very large, very mean-looking revolver pointed right at us. He wore his tan sheriff's windbreaker with the Loon County seal on the sleeve. He shoved the barrel hard into my bruised belly. It hurt. "I said, get into the car. You behind the wheel, Max." He pointed the gun quickly at John. "You, in the passenger seat." He shoved the revolver at me again. "Now!"

We got in the car. It was only a two-door and Darren roughly pushed John forward in his seat as he climbed into the back. "Close the door," he said to John and scooted to the middle of the seat.

"A two-door?" I said. "Trying to save the township money, Darren?"

"Shut up and listen," he said, laying the barrel of the

gun on John's headrest and putting the muzzle in John's short hair. "Now. In a second I'm goin' to give you the keys, Max, and you're goin' to start the car and turn on the headlights and you're goin' to drive where I tell you. You're goin' to drive at the speed limit and observe all traffic signs. If you do anythin' stupid—" he tapped John's head with the gun "—I've got two options. One, I can put a nice little hole in your friend's fuzzy head. Or two, should what you do attract the attention of the police, I can produce the two warrants for your arrest and extradition back to Vermont that I have right here in my pocket." He patted his jacket with his other hand. "Are we understood?"

I nodded to his reflection in the mirror.

"I said," he cracked John on the head with the gun butt, "are we understood?"

John leaned his head forward, grimaced, and nodded.

"Now, whoever's got the fingerprint, give it to me."

John reached in his pocket and tossed the baggy over the seat to Darren.

"Alright," he said as he handed me the keys, "drive."

I started the car, turned on the headlights and put it in drive.

"Turn right at the next corner," he said. "And use your blinker!"

I did. It was a one-way street. At the next corner, the light turned red. I stopped and a BMW pulled up on my side. The woman passenger was wearing a fur coat. She looked over at us, her eyes widened, and she looked away. I was positive she saw the gun. She seemed to say something to the guy driving and he leaned and looked and quickly looked away. "Three blocks ahead," Darren said, "is the entrance ramp to Storrow Drive. Take it. And once we're on the highway, stay in the right-hand lane and keep it at fifty-five."

I nodded and the light changed. With a squeal of rubber, the BMW roared away. I started looking for the ramp.

When we were in the traffic flow on Storrow Drive, Darren seemed to relax. He kept the gun at John's head but sat back in the seat. He rolled his window down halfway and the sudden rush of cool air felt chilly. I was sweating. I looked at him in the mirror. "Who did you kill at the lodge?" I asked him. "Whose body was that in the fire?"

"Bull," he said.

"Why?"

"Had to. He was a hothead." Darren laughed. "And he knew. He knew that fingerprint was mine. Hell, he helped me kill Red."

"Why did you kill Red? What the hell did he ever do to you?"

"Poor Red," Darren said with a sigh. "I really hated doin' that, but he found out."

"Found out what?"

Darren frowned hard. "I could be real upset by all these questions, Max."

"What are you going to do with us, Darren?" I asked.

"Kill you, I suppose. What would you do?"

John and I looked at each other.

The frown faded into a smile. "But, hell, why shouldn't you know? Who the hell you gonna tell?" He settled back a little farther in the seat. "Red was doin' a lot of back and forth drivin' from the mill to the clear-cut and he saw some documents Claremont had for me. Red wasn't as dumb as he looked. It didn't take much for him to figure out who really owns that land on Morning Mountain." He shook his head. "If he hadn't called you on the two-way radio that day, Max, I would never have known he knew. But he did. And I heard him on my radio. What choice did I have? If he'd told you, then you would have blown the whistle. I couldn't have that. Neither could Claremont."

"Claremont?"

He laughed. "Good old Claremont. Why, if it wasn't for good old Claremont killin' his wife, we'd all still be up in Loon right now watchin' the paint peel." He saw the look of astonishment on my face and laughed again. "Sure, Max. Claremont gassed the old lady. Tried to make it look like a suicide." He shook his head. "Couldn't fool me, though. Old fool was an amateur. Anybody coulda seen he done it. And they woulda, if I hadn't helped him make the job, shall we say, a little more convincin'."

"You were blackmailing Claremont?"

"Call it what you like." He smiled. "As I like to say, it was then that we entered into a profitable business relationship."

"Claremont paid you?"

"Money!?" He laughed. "You mean, like cash? Hell, Max. What do you think I am? Claremont was paying me with Collari land. Ten, fifteen acres a month. Sometimes more. Hell, I'm the second largest landowner in Loon County."

"He was giving you Collari land? And Collari didn't know?"

"Old man Collari don't know shit 'bout what Claremont does. Hell, when they needed them logs this spring 'cause Canada dried up, they had to pay me for the loggin' rights to Morning Mountain." He frowned and pointed the revolver at me. " 'Til you screwed it up."

Its siren screaming and lights flashing, an ambulance approached from behind us, roared by, and darted off the next exit ramp. We were all quiet for another mile or two. Finally, John said, "Did you set fire to the lodge?"

He nodded. "Couldn't let Bull just lie there, now could I?"

"And Stephanie?" John said.

"Sure hated to do that," he said. "But she wouldn't give me the fingerprint. Besides, she saw me shoot Bull. What was I gonna do? She got away from me at the lodge. Jumped in Bull's truck and took off. I let her go. Knew I'd find her. And I did. Didn't take much to figure out she come down here when I found Bull's truck at the airport. Amateurs on the run always run home." He smiled. "I knew she was friends with Collari's kid." He shrugged. "So I come down here myself and watched that fancy house. Sure enough, the pregnant lady led me right to her."

"Why didn't you just take the fingerprint from Collari's daughter?" John asked. "Why wait until we got here?"

Darren just scowled at John and didn't say anything. He seemed more inclined to talk to me, so I asked, "Okay, how did you know we were going to get the fingerprint tonight?"

"Tapped your phone, Max. Had the phone company do it for me when I had 'em install your new service." He laughed. "Had myself a listenin' station up on the clear-cut. Originally did it 'cause I figured the Stephanie woman would call you. Then I found her by myself."

"You heard my call to Max?" John asked.

He ignored John and looked at me in the mirror. "Followed you and that mayor bimbo to the airport, Max. Took the plane right after yours." He smiled and sat forward. "And here we are." He pointed. "Turn off at this exit."

I turned on the blinker and we exited onto a street that ran under the elevated highway. Through a row of gentrified old brick buildings on the right I could catch an occasional glimpse of water. The almost vacant street was all flashing yellow signal lights for several intersections ahead and we didn't slow down.

John and I had exchanged several glances since leaving Beacon Street and I had gone over all the escape options I could think of. Creating an accident had seemed like a possibility until I remembered the cocked gun at John's head. Jumping out of the car when we slowed down made sense, at least for me. What about John? I really wanted to just grab the gun, but every time I mentally timed my moves, all I could see I would get for my heroism was a bullet in the face. Intellectually, I knew we were in trouble. Darren had killed three people and was going to kill us. But, I'd known Darren for so long, we'd fished together, for Chrissakes, I found it hard to take the threat he represented seriously. The fear I should have felt just wasn't there.

"C'mon, Darren," I said. "Surely there's a way we can straighten this out. . . ."

"Shut up, Max," he said. "Turn at that sign."

The sign read, OLD IRONSIDES, THE USS CONSTITUTION. GUIDED TOURS, MUSEUM AND SHOPS. BUSES KEEP RIGHT. Suspended under that, a small sign said, CLOSED.

I turned at the sign and we entered a large, dark, empty parking area littered with paper, styrofoam cups, and a maze of yellow sawhorses obviously used to route the immense volume of daytime traffic. Straight ahead our headlights illuminated a low building that housed several touristy businesses. A sign along the low roof read, SQUARE-RIGGER BAR/RESTAURANT & GUNBOAT GIFTS. I could hear the roar of the traffic on the highway that arched away toward the north above us to the right. On our left, bathed in spotlights, her rigging outlined with blinking lights, loomed Old Ironsides.

"Go around the bar," he said.

I wound through the sawhorses and down the side of

the building, around two overflowing dumpsters, to the back.

"Drive out there." He pointed straight ahead. I now realized we were on a giant, paved pier that ran along the side of Old Ironsides and jutted out into Boston Harbor. Ahead of us I could see lights dancing in the choppy water. A jet silently climbed up and out of Logan Airport three miles away and the sparsely-lit shadow of an oil freighter sat near the far shore.

I don't know how or why, but suddenly I knew that when we stopped, Darren was going to shoot us. He wouldn't say anything, he'd just pull the trigger. First John. And then, with a flip of his wrist, he'd turn the gun on me.

I kept driving. The speedometer read twenty-five.

We were about one hundred feet from the end of the pier, when Darren growled, "Stop here."

I floored it.

The inexpensive car took a split second to kick into passing gear and then it leapt forward, throwing all of us back into our seats. It wasn't exactly a drag racer, but Detroit had built enough muscle into the little six cylinder engine that by the time Darren yelled, "I said, Stop! Goddammit! Stop!" we were already doing fifty and closing fast on the low, railroad-tie guardrail at the end of the pier.

John looked at me and I could see he already had his hand on his door handle. I looked at Darren in the rearview mirror just in time to see him raise the revolver and then everything happened at once; I grabbed John's head and threw both of us to the seat, the revolver exploded twice, glass showered around us, and the light blue Ford Taurus plowed through the railroad ties doing seventy-five miles per hour.

The impact as we blew through the guardrail threw Darren over the front seat and hard into the windshield.

The gun clanged against the dash and disappeared into the darkness at my feet. Darren clawed at my head and I elbowed him in the face and, for a long five seconds, the three of us wrestled against the dash as the car, its engine screaming in high-pitched r.p.m.s, soared high out over Boston Harbor.

We hit the water hard upside-down and backwards and Darren, who was dangling half in and half out of the front seat, was thrown back into the back seat. The car rolled upright, tilted, and instantly began to sink grill first as thousands of gallons of cold, black water flooded in the open back window. I heard Darren's gurgling scream as the weight of the water rammed him to the floor behind my seat, surged forward, and sucked around my legs. "The doors!" John yelled. I found my door handle, yanked, and the water rushing in from the back did the rest. I was flushed violently out into the inky blackness fifteen feet under the surface of Boston Harbor. My ears pounding, I kicked away from the sinking car and fought my way to the surface. Sputtering and coughing, John popped up four feet away. We circled in the dark, treading water. The Ford was gone. There was no sign of Darren.

"He's trapped," John yelled.

"Tough shit," I said, spitting out a mouthful of foul-tasting water. Then I turned and, as a bell buoy clanged somewhere on the dark, oily water behind us, I began side-stroking slowly toward the blinking lights on Old Ironsides.

John swam up beside me. "The fingerprint," he said.

"It's been in water before," I answered.

CHAPTER ❦ TWENTY

I think I can say without contradiction that the Fourth of July in northern Vermont is by far the most popular and most festive of all the holidays. Certainly the glorious weather has a lot to do with it, but by comparison, Christmas and Thanksgiving are just dour, frozen days that tax our good humor and empty our wallets.

Independence Day is truly something else. More than just cookouts and fireworks, in Loon it's a day of band concerts, softball games, foot races, and, best of all, the biggest, gaudiest, rip-snortin', damn parade in all of New England. By ten o'clock the night before the parade all the good spots along Main Street have been staked out with webbed, folding aluminum lawn chairs and by nine on the morning of the Fourth, people from as far away as Burlington and Boston are packed sunburn to sunburn with the locals, five deep along both sides of the parade route. At ten sharp, it begins and for three solid hours they parade by; marching bands from twenty surrounding towns, motorcycle cops, clowns, herds of horses and riders, convertible after convertible with waving politicians, flat-bed floats, boy and girl scouts, nurses, WACS, WAVES, DARs, wheelchairs, old-fashioned bicycles, Vietnam Vets, WW I vets,

WW II vets, Odd Fellows, Kiwanians, the two-hundred-man-and-one-woman Loon Loggers' Association, the governor, senators, Loon town council, that year's Miss Loon Lovely and her court of thirteen, giant living puppets, flags, the Future Farmers of America, State Police, a three-story-high inflated Loon Lager bottle, and, to the delight of every child, an invasion-size force of tanks, armored personnel carriers, machine guns, jeeps, cannons, supply trucks, and soldiers in full battle gear from ten different National Guard armories across the state.

All of them toss lollipops into the crowd.

Except for the conspicuous absence of Sheriff Darren Foley and Claremont Taylor, this year was no different and when it was over Stormy, Rayleen, Ruth, and I hosted a barbecue, catered by Skip and Lo Ming, on the lodge lawn overlooking Sweet Lake.

It was a great time. People fished, children chased, and everyone ate too much. By eight o'clock the sun started setting out across the lake and guests began saying their goodbyes. By nine, it was dark and everyone was gone except the four of us. I'd built a stone firepit by the water for the occasion and now, with three logs crackling in it and the Loons calling out on the lake, we pulled up some lawn chairs close to the fire, put our feet on the stones and, with the high-pitched drone of the crickets punctuated by the baritone of frogs, we watched the sparks spiral into the dark sky and join the stars.

"Didn't think I'd ever be able to enjoy a fire outdoors again," Stormy said, scratching Spotter who lay between her boots.

"When're they deliverin' the new logs, Max?" Rayleen asked.

"Tomorrow," I said. The rebuilding of Whitefork Lodge was already underway. The old foundation had been saved and Ruth had found the original Wellesly

Hinton blueprints in the cellar of City Hall. On top of that, just before he closed the mill in Loon, Alphonse Collari ordered more than enough seasoned, thirty-six-inch diameter, spruce logs from a mill he had in Colorado to build one and a half lodges. Delivery was promised for the fifth and I already had a local architect working on plans to use the extra to build a small cabin on the low hill down by the Cobble, which Stormy thought we could rent for twice as much as a room in the lodge.

"Where you gonna have 'em dumped?" he asked.

"Right here where we're sitting probably," I said. Already most of the lawn and areas on both sides of the workshop were stacked with rough-sawn planks, twelve-by-twelve beams, sheet rock, nail kegs, and two-by-fours.

"Think they'll finish putting down the floor tomorrow?"

"I think so," I said. "Whitey and the crew are due to start framing on Friday." It was ironic. With the pulp mill gone and the lodge going up, I had become one of the area's largest employers.

Ruth reached over and put her hand on mine. "I'm really bushed, Max," she said. "Would you mind if I went to bed?"

"Of course not," I said.

Stormy stood up and stretched. "Think we oughta be goin' too, Max." She grabbed Rayleen by the collar, lifting him from his seat. "Ain't that right, you old buzzard?"

"Hey," he whined. "I got me half a Loon here."

She took the bottle from his hand, put it to her mouth, and drained it. "There," she said. "Now, let's go." Spotter got to his feet and blinked at the heat from the fire.

Ruth and I stood. I put my arm around her waist and

we walked with them up to Rayleen's International. The old pickup's bed was loaded with boxes of leftovers and garbage bags of trash from the party. He tossed his empty into the pile.

"I'll be here, bright 'n' early, Max," Rayleen said. The Harley was back together and running and now he was building the cabinets for Stormy's new kitchen. "Glue should be dry on them butcher-block countertops by tomorrow." He opened the truck door. "I'll put that snot-nosed Richards kid to sandin' soon as he shows up." Rayleen had hired deputy Mark Richards's younger brother Bill as a helper. Bill was home for the summer from Dartmouth.

"Goodnight, you guys," Stormy said. "See you at the office, Ruth." Until the lodge was finished, Ruth had Stormy working in her office preparing for September's primary.

Ruth leaned her head on my shoulder and smiled. "If I ever wake up," she yawned.

They climbed into the truck, Rayleen started it up, and Ruth and Spotter and I stood back as he turned around. As soon as their taillights disappeared into the trees, we slowly walked toward the big motor home parked on the hill where the new guest cabin would be.

"I almost hate to admit it," she said, as we climbed the aluminum steps and I opened the aluminum door. "But I'm learning to like living in this damn thing."

The motor home had been Stormy's idea and once the hearings and the trials were over, she talked Robertson Motors into loaning me their forty-five-foot Winnebago until the lodge was rebuilt. I protested and lost and she had them park it out on the hill by the Cobble. It was like a yacht inside. A tacky yacht, with wall to wall carpets and fake wood grain on everything, including the toilet seat. It had a massive bedroom, a "lounge area" with a color TV, and its own satellite dish on the

roof. The kitchen was a gimmick-lover's dream come
true, with more electronic gadgets than you'd find at an
inventor's convention. But the king-size bed was comfortable, the closet space was adequate for the two of
us, and the bath/jacuzzi/hot tub, fun after a long day of
fishing while everyone else worked.

Ruth began undressing as soon as I closed the door
and had her clothes off by the time she hit the bed.
"Goodnight, sweet Max," she said, pulling the covers to
her chin. "It was a nice day."

I kissed her sunburned forehead, clicked out the light,
and went back out to the fire. I toed new flames into the
logs, sat in my chair, and lit a cigarette. Spotter came up
and lay in the grass beside me and I reached down and
stroked his head. A shooting star streaked diagonally
across the sky above the lake.

The fire, the murders, the Ford careening out over
Boston Harbor seemed so far away now. Like they'd
happened in another lifetime.

After Darren had tried to kill us, John and I had
flagged down a passing car and gone directly to the police who, over the course of several days, hauled the
Ford and a very dead Darren from the Harbor, found
the fingerprint, interviewed Andrea Shaughnessey, and
contacted the Vermont State Police. For our part, John
and I stayed in Boston almost two weeks, attending
hearings and being questioned relentlessly by police
from two states. Ruth joined me for a few days and John
took a leave of absence from work. Everything took
longer than I thought it should, but by the middle of
May, the ripples from Boston rolled into Loon and
Claremont was indicted for the murder of his wife. He's
still awaiting trial and plans on defending himself.

My daughter and her husband tried to get me to
come to New York City and spend some time with them.
I declined the invitation and a week later they showed

up at the motor home. Ruth agrees with me that David's a pain in the ass, but she loved Sabrina. As usual, they brought a gift; a beautifully made, Seth Thomas eight-day schoolroom clock. Except that I have to wind it every week, I think it's something, like the Tuscan Grill, that'll be around a while.

Darren Foley hadn't been exaggerating when he'd boasted he was the second largest landowner in Loon. The investigation into Claremont showed that he'd given the sheriff just shy of seven thousand acres and the titles to three of the old brick buildings on Main Street. The inquiry also uncovered Darren's plan to subdivide Morning Mountain for vacation homes once the trees were gone.

Whether it was because of our feelings for Stephanie or the fact that I had exposed Claremont, Alphonse Collari became extremely solicitous of my friendship. He not only found the kind of logs needed to rebuild Whitefork, but has promised financial support to Ruth's reelection campaign. I don't really see much of him, however. He spends most of his time now in Boston with his new grandson, Sean Alphonse Shaughnessey.

I didn't need an injunction to stop the clear-cutting or close the mill, which, Ruth says, is being eyed by WalMart as the site for a new store and shopping mall. Loon Lager, which has been looking for larger quarters for their brewery, also has expressed interest in the space. Already the town is split on which they'd prefer and Stormy and Ruth survey almost daily as they attempt to construct the platform for Ruth's second term.

John called the other day from Dillingham, Alaska, where he's fly-fishing his way through several million years of the North American Plate. He tried to get me to join him, but Ruth said no. She thinks I should call some of the guests I had to cancel and tell them that, even though the lodge won't be available until next season, the river still is. Just bring their own tents or campers.

Wally Murray's the only one who really came out on top in this whole thing. The publicity surrounding the various trials and investigations kept him in the limelight for weeks. As a result, he's been made senior partner in his firm with a hefty increase in salary and perks. I see his sleek new Eldorado in town every now and then. And he waves.

According to *Northeast Business* magazine Tear-Pruf is in final negotiations with the *Carhartt* Company and the other day at the Starlight bar, Rayleen introduced me to their New England sales representative. He's a guy about my age named Jon Sturdevant.

Stephanie was buried beside her father and mother in a little cemetery overlooking the ocean in Duxbury, Massachusetts. Alphonse, Andrea, Stormy, John, and I attended together.

As we stood there in the gentle sea breeze, watching the casket sink from sight into the sandy ground, I couldn't help but think that we were burying two people, not one.

I hope she knew.

When a hotshot advertising agency asks Max Addams to shoot a beer commercial at Whitefork Lodge, Max is hesitant to turn the lodge over to a bunch of city folk. But when they start throwing around a bundle of money that the lodge desperately needs for remodeling, Max can't resist. The crew arrives and goes to work—but before long the irritating and arrogant producer turns up dead. With a slew of suspects ranging from the cast and crew themselves to the members of the disgruntled Loon community, it's up to Max to keep the lodge out of the spotlight—and more bodies from turning up.

DYING TO FLY-FISH

Book 2 in the Max Addams Fly-Fishing Mystery Series

by David Leitz

**Coming in September
from St. Martin's/Dead Letter!**

Author's Note

The following names are pseudonyms: Donald McGowan, John DeMarco, and Grant East.

E BW 1959

BOB

~~EDISON~~

BOB ED   ED BL WISE

EDBON

ED BON 1959

ED

EB WISE 1959

WISE ONES